THE JACK

M.K. HARKINS

THE IMMORTAL SERIES BOOK TWO

DEDICATION

Nancy Bailey

May 6th, 1953 - March 29th, 2013

There have only been a few people that I can say I loved on the spot. My children and you. I don't know if I ever told you this, but when you came to interview for the teaching job I decided that I would do anything to hire you. Pay you whatever you wanted, give you any hours you needed. The job was yours. You asked for little and gave so much. It's been five years and I still miss you every day. Some people are special like that. I saw the beauty, the light in you immediately. Thank you for all the pats on the back, words of encouragement, optimistic attitude...and laughter. You made everything better 😊

PLAYLIST

"The Luckiest"—Ben Folds

"In my blood"—Shawn Mendes

"I found"- Amber Run

"Anna (go to him)"—The Beatles

"Again"—Noah Cyrus

"Years & Years"—Eyes Shut

"Coaster"—Khalid

"Born to be Yours"—Imagine Dragons

"Soulmate"—Natasha Bedingfield

"How Long Will I Love You" - Jon Boden, Sam Sweeney & Ben Coleman

PRELUDE

THREE GROUPS LIVED in harmony for tens of thousands of years, unbeknownst to humankind: the Readers, the Jacks, and the Seers. All three acted as peacemakers. The Seers predicted events, the Readers had the ability to monitor the intentions and thoughts of others, and the Jacks would temporarily inhabit other bodies to change their minds if the person planned to harm another.

The Readers and the Seers were able to keep their original bodies for eternity without ever aging. The Jacks, however, didn't have this ability. They had to switch their form every forty years in order to retain their immortality like the others. Over time, they became jealous and bitter. They no longer wanted to help the other groups, choosing instead to turn their backs and use their power for control and evil purposes.

Afraid the Seers would predict their true intentions, the Jacks wiped them out in the Great War two thousand years earlier. Before the Seers died, they warned the Readers and let them know either the Readers or the Jacks would be saved by The Lost One.

For two thousand years, both groups searched relentlessly, convinced The Lost One was their key to survival.

The Seers' visions were true. Ann, The Lost One, was found, joined the Readers, and destroyed the Jacks in an explosion that wiped out Samara, their underground home.

But did all the Jacks die that day?

CHAPTER 1

Gray are the waves of discontent,
Washing away
The color of emotion.
My soul is black.

Two years later
Cannon Beach, Oregon

Archer

I SHOULD BE *dead.*

Pain shot through me like an ice pick thrust into my heart. I lowered my head and squeezed my eyes shut. God, the rejection was as physical as it could get.

Why didn't I stay in Samara and get blown to bits with the other Jacks?

"Are you okay?" A girl's voice cut through layers of fog that had wrapped its cold fingers around my brain.

How long had I been sitting on the bench this time, staring

at the ocean? Correction. Staring at Ann, not even aware someone was sitting right next to me.

I shot the girl beside me a quick glance. Pretty. Eighteen or so. A blonde-haired, blue-eyed beauty. Most guys would sit up and take notice. The only girl I could see, or would ever want to, was a hundred yards away. With her husband, who happened to be my cousin and former best friend.

I hated him almost as much as I loved her.

"Beautiful family," the girl observed.

Whatever. I pushed down the searing pain and took a deep breath to keep my pounding heart steady. "I like to people-watch. It can be entertaining," I told her as I turned away from Ann and stared at the ocean. The intruder needed to leave before I snapped.

"Do you know them?" The girl tipped her head toward my obsession.

The words slipped out before I could filter. "I knew a girl like her a long time ago. I loved her deeply." I should have stopped talking but kept going. "But I made mistakes, and I couldn't fix them." What was wrong with me? I'd barely spoken to anyone in two years, and now I was giving this stranger my life story. I shifted my glance toward her. Two clear blue, innocent eyes stared back.

Just a normal girl sitting with me on the bench.

"That's too bad." She frowned.

I settled my eyes back on Ann. Her light brown hair danced with the melody of the wind. She laughed as she dipped her son's toes into the lapping waves.

"Did you ever try to make things right?" the girl asked.

"I sacrificed my happiness for hers." And handed her right

over to Devon. "Painful, but worth it." My thoughts drifted back to the night of the explosion. "I saved her life, but she also saved mine."

The girl placed her hand over her heart. "Oh, that's so romantic."

I stifled an eye roll. It wasn't romantic. I'd lost Ann forever. Misery rippled through me like the waves crashing to the shore. A mortal would never understand. They were all the same. So simplistic.

"Will you see her again?"

"No," I said while staring directly at Ann.

"Hey," the girl whispered.

I forced my gaze away from Ann to the stranger's ice-blue eyes. Such an unusual color. "Yeah?"

"I understand what it's like. You know, being alone."

I almost laughed. I wanted to ask, *Oh, you do? You know what it's like to be living with people for thousands of years yet feel completely alone? To form friendships knowing there would be a day you'd have to make a choice that may betray them? To trust your mother only to find out she was an imposter? To finally fall in love, have it change everything, then lose her at the last moment?*

Getting closer to Ann would never be an option. I stayed partially hidden by an ancient boulder and some beach scrub. Devon would either kill me on the spot or put me in the Colorado Compound. Of those two choices, I'd go with death. The Colorado Compound was built thousands of years ago as a warning to all the Readers: If you committed murder, you had a ticket there for all eternity. An eight-by-ten box without windows or human interaction. Mere scraps of food thrown in a few times a day. Dark, musty, cold. A living hell. I shivered remembering my last visit. Torment and the lack of hope were the only visible signs of life in the inmates' eyes. They'd be better off dead.

I'd killed my friend Markus and betrayed the Readers, so I had a one-way ticket with my name on it.

But if I killed Markus, why couldn't I remember?

The bench I sat on felt like cold marble. Atarah. She posed as my mom for over two thousand years. Pure Jack evil. I wondered what part she played in the murder of Markus. I shook off the possibilities. Didn't matter. I'd never know. The Readers would never believe me anyway, and the truth died with Atarah when Samara had exploded, leaving the home I once loved in bits of rubble and ash.

It was enough for me to see Ann and know she was okay. I didn't need anyone or anything else. I deserved loneliness and accepted it.

"Are you okay?" the girl asked for the second time.

No. "I usually sit here alone." *Take the hint and leave.*

"Oh." Her voice dropped. "It's just that, well—"

The ground beneath us shook. "What was that?" I scanned the beach, but all I could see was the short grass blowing in the breeze. "An earthquake?" Ann and her family were the only people in sight. They continued to splash around in the shallow waves like nothing had happened. The houses behind me stood solid, no damage. Could be my imagination. But something was off. Where were all the seagulls?

The girl looked down, then closed her eyes. "No, no, no," she said, and then gasped.

The ground continued to shake. "It's just a little earthquake." I pointed behind us. "Look, the houses all look fine. No damage."

She lifted her head slowly, and we locked eyes. Arctic eyes. Blue like a glacier. A chill ran down my spine.

"What's going on?" I asked. Something shimmered in her eyes. What the hell?

She blinked. "The epicenter is ninety miles offshore. That means you have fourteen minutes to warn Ann and her family to get to higher ground before the wave hits." She turned away.

What the hell?

I touched her elbow to get her attention. "What are you talking about? How did—" I dropped my hands. A buzzing sensation started at my fingertips and worked up my arms. "Who are you?" I shouted and stood to shake out the feeling.

"I'm, I'm...no one. Forget you saw me."

"The hell I will. How do you know about Ann? Is this a trap?" I yelled at the girl.

Her eyes bulged, and she shook her head.

"Tell me right now," I demanded.

"I can't."

"Are you a Reader?" I moved in front of the bench to block her escape.

"No. No. I'm not one of them."

I narrowed my eyes. "But you know about them. The Readers."

She pressed her lips together and, after a moment, said, "I've never heard of them."

"Liar!"

She jerked back. "Now you have twelve minutes. Do you want to spend it arguing with me, or will you save them?" She pointed at Ann and her family.

"I can't... They can't find out. I mean, they wouldn't be happy to see me."

Understatement of the year.

"It's your choice." Before I could react, she darted from the bench. I turned to grab her arm, but she pulled away and sprinted in the opposite direction.

Damn, she was fast. I'd never catch her and still have time get back to Ann. Now what? Save Ann and risk the Colorado Compound or death? I bent over and held my head in my hands.

Think!

The fear and anxiety of exposing myself to the Readers left immediately. I took a deep breath and looked at my cell for the time. Eleven minutes until the tsunami hit, if the girl was telling the truth. For some undefinable reason, I believed her.

I jogged the short distance between the bench and Ann. Devon's back was to me as he held their child while pointing to something in the distance.

The splashing of my feet as they met the water alerted Ann. She dropped the sand dollar she held into the water. Recognition flitted across her face. She stifled a smile and covered her mouth. "You're alive," she whispered. Her glance shifted to Devon. "Archer, it isn't safe for you here. Part of Devon knows you saved me from the explosion, but he's still angry about your betrayal."

"There's a tsunami coming," I blurted.

Her face paled. "The shaking? I didn't imagine it?"

"No. Some girl warned me. I don't know who she is. Maybe a Seer? I didn't want to..." I looked over at Devon. "Ann, please, get your family to higher ground. You only have ten minutes."

Just then, Devon turned and faced me. His mouth dropped open, his shoulders sagged, and he took a deep breath. Then his eyes closed, and he shook his head. Exactly what I expected from him. Anger. His face reddened, and he pointed at me. "What the hell do you think you're doing?" he yelled as he stormed through the shallow water.

"Wait, Devon," Ann said as she stood between us. "There's a tsunami coming. Archer came to warn us."

Devon sneered. "He's a Jack, not a Seer." He clutched their child closer. The boy looked exactly like his father. Dark brown, curly hair and a cautious expression in his eyes.

Like I'd harm Ann's child. *He thinks I'm insane.*

"I met a girl on the beach. She's—I don't know. There's something different about her. After the earthquake, she told me to warn Ann. How would she know her name?" Time ticked away, along with the possibility of escaping the tsunami.

Devon's eyes darted to Ann's. He lifted a brow.

Ann motioned frantically to Devon. "Let's go, now. We can't take any chances. The ground shook, but I thought I'd imagined it."

My job here was done. Time to get the hell out. I turned to leave.

"Not so fast." Devon held up a hand, his eyes darting from the shore to the beach house and back to me. "You're the last person I want to ask for help, but Lucy's at the house alone, babysitting the neighbor's twins. Adam's gone to the store, and she'll never make it out in time."

I stormed away from the water's edge. Why was he so sure I'd help? He didn't have time to stop me or fight when every second counted.

He knows I'd never been able to say no to his sister Lucy.

She'd always been like the sister I never had.

Eight minutes.

I changed course and charged into their beach house interrupting Lucy making airplane noises as she flew a spoon toward a child's mouth.

Out of breath, I shouted, "Lucy!"

She dropped the spoon and clutched her chest. "Archer. I knew it. I knew you were alive." Her face brightened for half a second before the realization struck. "What are you doing here? It's not safe. Devon." Her eyes flashed panic before shifting toward the door.

"Tsunami," I choked out. "We have to leave. Now."

"Wh-what?" She paled and stood in front of the young, brown-haired children in their high chairs. "What are you trying to pull? I'm not going anywhere with you."

Didn't blame her. "No time to argue—"

The door burst open. Ann entered gripping her son with Devon close behind. "Why aren't the twins in the car yet?" Ann's frantic gaze darted around the room.

I moved to pick up one of the wide-eyed children. Lucy stood in front of them with her hands up. "Not so fast." Her eyes darted to Devon. "What's going on?"

"No time for questions." Devon narrowed his eyes. "How many more minutes?"

"According to the Seer, about seven."

"Seer?" Lucy shouted. "What? That's impossible!"

"Move." Devon grabbed her arm. "We'll take both cars. Ann, call Adam and warn him. Lucy, you'll have to let Archer drive while you get the kids secured. No time." He threw me the keys. "You better not be lying. If anything happens to them, I'll hunt you down." He glared at me. "And this time, I'll find you."

I nodded and reached for the closest child. Lucy paused for a second then moved to let me by. I grabbed the little boy as gently as possible and ran out the door to the waiting car. Lucy dove into the back seat and reached out and plucked the child from my arms.

"Go south down 101. We don't have time to evacuate to Portland." She pointed to the right with a shaking hand.

Gravel shot behind the back wheels as I peeled out from the driveway. A look in the rearview mirror showed Devon's Jeep close behind. Lucy turned her back as she furiously latched the children into their car seats. "Buckle up, Lucy." I floored it, careful to look for anyone else entering the road. The streets were empty.

Was the girl on the beach a fake? Maybe a convoluted plan for me to expose myself?

"If you get to the overlook at Silver Point, we should be safe. It sits high on a cliff."

"Okay. Hang on." I increased the car's speed.

"Archer?"

"Yeah?" I glanced back.

"It'll be okay, right?"

I shifted my eyes back to the road. Lucy's red hair and typical fierce expression always made me think of her as fearless. But not today.

"Right." I lied because I wasn't sure. My entire world was morphing into the Twilight Zone.

What was I doing here? I should be back at my hideout doing what I'd done for the last two years, staring at the walls, trying to figure out what had happened, why I was even alive, why Markus was dead, and why Ann belonged to my former best friend.

My own special hell.

"Archer, look out!" Lucy shouted.

I slammed on the brakes and veered to miss a car pulling out onto the highway. The wailing of the emergency sirens cut through the air.

"Oh, God. There really is a tsunami coming. All these people. Will they have time to evacuate?" Lucy's voice wavered.

Not a chance. But I kept my opinion to myself. "How many miles to the overlook?" I asked to distract her.

"Maybe five?"

"Okay." I kept my focus on the side streets. With the sirens blaring, people would try to flee in droves. A few minutes later, I caught sight of our destination, a small parking area off the side of the road. I pulled up to the guardrail and looked out over the one-hundred-eighty-degree view. Devon's Jeep squealed to a stop next to us. I got out and walked to the edge of the sheer four-hundred-foot cliff. Hopefully, we'd be safe.

"Do you see it?" Devon asked.

I put my hand up to shield my eyes from the sun. Sure enough, about a mile out, a large swell at an unnatural height crested on its way to the shore.

Lucy approached. "Does this mean what I think it does?"

"That a Seer made it through the Great War?" I responded.

"Yeah. And everything we thought we knew about the world has just been shattered."

CHAPTER 2

Sadie

THE STEERING WHEEL slipped in my sweaty hands, almost plunging my speeding car over the mountain cliff as I maneuvered the winding road to reach my cottage. I regained control as I rounded the last bend and peeled into the driveway, slamming to a stop inches before I hit the garage door.

That was close. I pulled my T-shirt away from my sticky body as I cut through the garden, hurrying to the door, but my foot snagged on the garden gnome, and I landed in the dirt, flat on my face. The same dirt I'd just mixed with a lovely, fragrant manure earlier today.

I flipped over onto my back. Ugh. "Gnomie, you did that on purpose." He stared back. Of course he did. Two thousand years mostly on my own. Not trusting anyone does that to a person. Conversing with inanimate objects was a new low. I needed to talk to my roommate, Eve. She was the best listener and the only one on the planet to know my secret...well, until today.

I wouldn't let myself think about the day she'd—I blinked back the moisture in my eyes. Why did I allow the friendship when I knew what would eventually happen? She'd die, and I'd be alone again. I'd stopped making friends a thousand years ago, but Eve was quiet and unassuming, and I needed companionship. She had nestled into my heart without me even realizing it.

I tried to clear my mind and hoped a new vision would pop in. Nothing. Ever since the Seers disappeared from the earth, my powers had diminished, my visions now sporadic, almost always appearing minutes before the event happened. Geez, I hoped all those people along the beachfront would be okay.

Safety and comfort spread through me, calming my mind. *No one will die today.*

I shot up to a sitting position. "Really? No one?"

Silence.

Sometimes I didn't know if the voices were real or wishful thinking on my part.

I flopped back onto the dirt and stared up at the sky. I loved my cottage on the hill. It had everything I needed. A peek-a-boo view of the ocean, garden beds for my vegetables, and even a white picket fence. On the smallish side, with three bedrooms and one bath, an open concept kitchen and living area. Vaulted ceilings gave it the airy feel I treasured. Large French doors led to the back patio that sat under huge cedar trees. Summer days included shade and a nice breeze. Most people would call the interior farmhouse chic. I called it cozy, or home.

Would I have to leave now that Archer and the Readers knew about me? Or was this the event my mom told me about, the one that would catapult everything into motion?

The smell of dirt was a favorite, but the stink of manure stung my nose. I got up and brushed off. A shower and a long talk with Eve would help clear my head.

I stepped into the front hallway. "Eve, I'm home. Did you feel the earthquake? Don't worry, we're high enough to miss the tsunami." I peeled off my shorts and T-shirt and threw them into the hamper as I headed toward the shower. "I found him, Eve. And guess what? I talked to him! I'll tell you all about it when I get out of the shower. I'm a mess." I grabbed some clean clothes from the laundry basket in the hall.

The last pieces of clothing dropped to the floor right before I entered the tub. I let the warm flow of water coming from my rain showerhead soothe my building panic. What had I done? My plan was toast. I was only supposed to talk to Archer, get him to think I was a normal girl, not reveal myself.

Stupid. Stupid.

Two thousand years I'd stayed hidden, ever since the Great War between the Jacks and the Seers. Every person I'd loved or cared about—gone in a matter of hours. Memories of my family floated in and tightened around my heart like a vise. My eternity with them stolen by those jealous, murderous Jacks.

I finished my shower and changed into clean clothes. After opening the bathroom door, I called out, "I'll meet you in the living room. I've so much to tell you." Once down the hall, I flopped onto the sofa, covering my face with my hands. I didn't want Eve to see the guilt on my face. "Oh, dear Lord, he was beautiful up close. How could someone so evil look like that? Ugh. He looks like an angel." *More like an angel of death.* "How is that fair? I mean, most Jacks were able to choose their bodies, but to be born like that? It's not right."

I flipped over on the couch to look at her. "And when he touched me, a zap traveled through my body, and I melted. I mean, like, I went all warm, and my breath left me." I turned away again. "What's wrong with me?"

I liked how Eve listened intently, her head cocked and her soft eyes holding my gaze. But right now, I wanted her to tell me why I had these feelings of doubt.

I sat up. "He must have done some hypnosis thing on me. That must be it. The plan to talk him up, get him to trust me, was a total fail." I squeezed my eyes shut. "But I opened my stupid mouth and warned him about the tsunami."

I got up and shuffled into the kitchen to get a bottle of water. I spent most of my two years living here painting daisies on the white cabinets, the kitchen table, and some light switches. Last spring, I continued the theme and painted a daisy border on the hardwood floors. "I only told him so he could save Ann's family. That's why." I nodded. "I didn't do it for him."

My stomach sank. *Did I?* A confirmed Jack, but his tortured eyes drew me in. Could he fake that? Jacks didn't have souls. They only served themselves, liked to create havoc and ruin lives just for fun. But...but Archer. He seemed to be suffering, and I felt it right to my core.

"Do you think he could have real feelings because he's only half Jack?" I twisted open the cap and took a long swallow of water. "He has to be more Reader than Jack, because he doesn't have to jump bodies like the other Jacks." Who was I trying to convince? "It doesn't matter. I still have to go through with—"

A knock on the door startled me, and I jumped back, my

heart hammering as I peeked out the window.

Thank goodness. I flung open the door. "Donna, great to see you."

"Oh, dear. Oh, dear." My petite, white-haired neighbor rushed in through the door. "I was worried about you. You left, and then the earthquake hit. Is Eve home?"

"Yes, she's in the living room." I smiled. Donna, nearing eighty, made it her business to check on us when in town.

She twisted her hands and sat on the stool in front of the island. "The television reporter said the tsunami caused property damage along the shore."

"That's awful," I said and tried to look surprised.

"But with the early warning system, they believe most people got out in time. Just one girl is missing, a sweet college student." She tapped her head. "What was her name? Oh, that's right. Becca. Her mom said she's probably visiting at a friend's house, though."

That was a relief.

"Should we drive down and help?" Her soft brown eyes questioned.

I patted her shoulder. "We'd just be in the way. I attended the emergency preparedness classes the city council held last month. They have teams in place for this type of thing."

"Okay, honey, if you say so." Her eyes brightened. "I almost forgot. I baked you an apple pie." She looked down at her empty hands. "But with all the excitement, I forgot to bring it!"

"No worries. I'll stop by later and pick it up." I gave her shoulder a little rub. Donna possessed a great memory. But it couldn't last forever. A sad, little twinge hit my chest.

"But I remembered to bring the caviar Eve loves so much."

She dug around in her shoulder purse. "Here it is!" She placed the jar in my hands.

"You spoil us, you know that?"

"Just making up for lost time." Her smile warmed my heart.

"I was glad to see you moved back into your cottage yesterday. You're here a little early this year though, aren't you?" Donna split her time between Arizona and Oregon. When I noticed the activity around her cottage, I'd thought about asking if she needed help. But she didn't. Four rugged-looking men helped unload her belongings. Probably three too many.

"Yes, I'm early. I was excited to get back! I love the stormy weather in April." She paused and asked in a nonchalant voice, "Did you see my helpers? I came over to introduce them to you, but you didn't answer the door." Her attempt to distract me by moving the flower vase from one end of the counter to the other gave her away.

Matchmaker. Sweet, but it would never happen.

"I'm sorry. I was taking a shower."

"It's okay. They're coming to my welcome-home barbeque next week. Can you make it? Thursday at seven?"

"Sure." Ugh. Why couldn't I be one of those people who easily lied on the spot? I wanted to tell her I'd never love again. I'd been in love with a mortal once, but the pain of watching him get sick and die was too high a price. I did my acting thing, pretending to be normal, even flirting a little. But it would go no farther. I'd rather sit in the garden and chat with Gnomie. He was safer.

She stood and clapped her hands together. "Good, it's settled. I've asked the mayor and his son, Ian, to come as well." Her eyes turned mischievous. "Have you seen him yet?"

Yes, and I'd considered breaking my self-imposed solitude. Well, for about thirty seconds. Another man too darn good-looking for his own good. I hadn't talked to him, but with those looks, he most likely hadn't developed a decent personality or a solid character yet. The frustrating thing about most mortals was their limited time on earth. If they had a talent, they'd put all their energy into it while ignoring the rest. His talent probably included looking in the mirror.

"I haven't met him, but I've seen him around."

"We must fix that! He's a charming young man."

"If you like him, I'm sure he's great." Now, how to politely get her to leave? "Eve and I were about to take a nap." A nap? That was the best I could come up with? I needed to attend a school for liars.

"Oh, you poor thing. You must be exhausted from today. Near death can do that to a girl." She patted my arm.

I smiled to reassure her. "I wasn't close to death." Donna always exaggerated things. I rarely minded and would've loved to sit and talk with her for hours, but I needed to form a new plan with Eve about Archer and the Readers. "I didn't sleep well last night."

"Okay, sweetie." She took a step out the door and raised her voice an octave. "Eve, I hope you love the caviar. I found it at a new shop in Sedona."

A quick hug and she departed on the two-minute path to her house. After flopping back down on the sofa, I rubbed my hands over my face and said to Eve, "We have to go to Plan B, but I don't have a Plan B." I blew out a frustrated breath. "I don't want to move again." Two years at the beach had ruined me for any other type of living. I loved our adorable cottage, and our neighbor, although slightly overprotective, was sweet.

The ocean... Oh, the hours I spent watching Archer were the best. The smell of seaweed and wildflowers thick in the air, the calming sound of the waves as they crashed to the shore, the beauty of the vista. All of it. I loved every bit.

A memory of living underground surfaced, and my stomach sank.

"Mom, why do we have to live underground? I hate it!"

"Sadie, we're trying to stay hidden to delay the battle with the Jacks for as long as possible."

"Can't we battle the Jacks now? You said the vision showed you I killed the last Jack."

"Oh, Sadie. We need to talk."

The pain of that day still clenched every muscle until black dots formed in my eyes. My mom told me I'd be the only Seer to survive. She also let me know about a traitor living within the Reader Compound, and that person would end up betraying them. So I'd stayed clear from the Readers all these years, observing from a distance.

The Jacks all died two years ago. I'd thought the vision was wrong. How could I kill the last Jack if they were all gone? Then I found out Archer still lived.

"Okay. Let's talk about Plan B. I can still get Archer to trust me, right? His precious Ann and her family are safe because of me. There must be a way to get him to tell me if any other Jacks are still alive. I have to be sure." I'd shadowed him for two years, and he never met or talked to anyone. All he did was go from his beach bungalow to the ocean and stare at the waves. All day. Every day. "What do you think?"

Meow. Eve jumped up on the chair and stared at the jar of caviar.

Poor kitty. A quick skip into the kitchen, and I opened the lid. "Sorry, Eve. This day has been crazy." She licked me with her sandpaper tongue, and I scratched behind her ear. She purred, and I gave her a kiss on top of her furry head. "Plan B it is."

CHAPTER 3

Archer

THE SHEER CLIFF plunged four hundred feet to meet the crashing ocean waves. All I'd have to do was hop over a rusted two-foot barricade and walk off the edge. The never-ending hell that had tormented me for the past two years would finally end. But something felt unfinished.

"Don't even think about it." Devon's low voice broke through my contemplation.

"Did you read my thoughts?" I'd perfected blocking the Readers. Hadn't I? A glance back at Lucy and Ann standing by the cars, each holding a twin in their arms, confirmed they couldn't overhear our conversation. I turned back to Devon.

"Didn't have to. You've never been good at hiding your emotions." His eyes shifted toward Ann.

"I guess the better question is why the hell would you care?"

He knew I loved Ann, that I'd continue to risk my life for her a thousand times, but he must hate me as much as I did him. Forgiveness was not an option for what I'd done.

"The Seer contacted you. There must be something big going on if she stayed hidden for two thousand years and picked now to appear." He scratched his jaw.

I hadn't considered that. "Maybe she's just a psychic?"

"A psychic who gave the exact time for a tsunami?" He raised a brow. "Modern-day psychics can only guess on vibrations and physical cues from the people around them." His eyes focused on mine. "No. Whoever you talked to had powers. And I'd guess she wasn't a descendant. She must be an immortal Seer who survived the Great War."

"Do you think there might be others?" I wondered if that would be a good or bad thing. Even considering the possibility made my gut twist.

"Others?" Ann asked. She'd approached from behind with a child on her hip while holding her son Henry's hand. The wind made her light brown hair shimmer in the sunlight. The freckles sprinkled across her nose and cheeks were just how I remembered. I loved every one of them. My heart sped up, and it took everything in me not to step closer. Getting near her was dangerous. I wanted more.

"Seers," Devon told her.

"Oh." She bit her lip. "Do you think there's anything to worry about?"

"Nah. The Readers and the Seers have always been aligned. It's this one," he said, tilting his head toward me, "who has something to worry about."

"Ah." Her eyes squinted. The wind picked up a little, and she turned to keep the hair from her face. "We must talk about...well, everything. Why are you here, anyway?"

Damn. I knew that question would come up. I shot a glance at Devon, and his expression turned dark.

"You aren't the only ones who enjoy the beach." *Don't look at her lips.*

Devon's eyebrow hiked up. "This beach?"

"Call it nostalgia." I'd been coming along with the Readers to Cannon Beach for centuries, long before Ann showed up. Maybe he'd buy it.

He looked at me long and hard. "Let's say, for argument's sake, that's why you're here. What are your plans now? Are you willing to help us find the Seer?"

I'd have to be around Ann. These few minutes with her tied me up in knots. So close, but I couldn't touch her soft skin, or move the strands of hair whipping against her face. Wasn't love supposed to be a good emotion? The closer to her I was, the more excruciating the pain. Like a million needles poking into every square inch of my skin. If only I could figure out how to stay away.

Defeated, I answered, "Yeah. I'll help you find her and then head out."

Devon cocked his head. "That's fair." His eyes narrowed. "We don't have to worry about you in the interim?"

My jaw clenched. But I didn't blame him for asking. "I risked everything to give you the warning. If I had any bad intent, I would've, you know, let you drown with the wave."

"What a relief!" Lucy joined our group. "The radio reports said the wave only came as high as the first floor of the waterfront beach houses. It sounds like everyone survived. Thank goodness."

Ann's searching eyes seemed to look right into my soul. "We would've been the only casualties. Thank you, Archer." Her glance shifted from Devon to her son, Henry.

I shrugged and crossed my arms over my chest. I tried to swallow, but my mouth had gone dry.

A car screeched into the parking area, sliding and kicking up dust in every direction. The driver's door flew open, and a dark-haired man leaped out and ran toward us. I tightened my fists, ready to take him on, until I noticed the relief on Lucy's face.

"Adam!" she yelled and opened her arms.

"Lucy, oh thank God. I was so worried." He embraced her then sobbed, mumbling something into her neck.

I shook my head. I didn't recognize Adam at first glance. His dark hair was longer and had more waves. He'd always been high-strung, but I didn't remember him as the type to fall apart. Adam and Lucy? Even though women thought his black hair and blue eyes were attractive, we always laughed at his attempts to win Lucy over. I thought she'd put him in his self-important, arrogant place a century ago.

A glance at Devon confirmed it. He rolled his eyes and shrugged.

This felt familiar, like how it was before my world turned to hell. Devon and I would always communicate without speaking. No. I pushed my fingers through my hair. We could never go back to those days. I'd killed any chance of that.

Ann ignored their display and turned back toward me. "This is the second time now, you know, saving my life and all." A sad smile tilted her lips.

Devon still glared.

"Just passing on information." I tugged at my collar, but it still choked me like a noose around my neck. Why were my clothes so tight?

Without warning, pain shot through my right cheek, landing me on the gravel and asphalt. Before I could take a breath, another blow, this time to the left side of my face.

What the hell?

"Bastard!" Adam yelled while he leaned over and continued to pummel me. I put up my hands in defense, opting not to throw any return punches.

Because he was right.

Devon tugged Adam's arm, pulling him away. "Okay, you've made your point."

Adam tried to wrestle his arm free. "What's he doing here?" His murderous glare was aimed right at me. He turned his scowl back to Devon. "You, of all people? Why haven't you tossed him over that cliff like he deserves?" He motioned to the area I'd just considered jumping from. How ironic.

Devon kept a hold of Adam's arm. "Yeah. I've had days where that's all I've thought about. Finding Archer"—he took a deep breath—"and giving him everything he's due. I still might, but there are too many questions. Too many things don't add up."

"He's a traitor, a Jack! What else do you need to know?" Adam's face turned beet red as he glanced at everyone else in the group. "Wait a minute. Why are you all standing around with this guy like nothing happened?"

"This guy is the reason we aren't a couple miles offshore, floating away with the tsunami." Devon released his arm. "He risked everything to warn us."

I grabbed the tail of my shirt and wiped the blood trickling down my face. Ann took a step toward me, stopped, then stepped back. I held in a smile. Ann had an instinct to help. I propped up on my elbow. "I'm going to stand up, Adam. Are you through?"

"For now." He glowered.

I rose to my feet and brushed off the gravel and dirt clinging to my clothes.

Lucy placed her hand on Adam's arm. "Devon's right. He came to warn us after the Seer approached him, knowing it could've landed him in The Compound."

"He *should* be in The Compound!" Adam froze, then whipped around. "Wait. What did you say? A Seer?"

Lucy nodded. "Yeah. She might've survived the Great War. She's the one who told Archer about the tsunami."

Adam huffed and paced, shooting me a glance every few steps. He probably worried I'd run off and he wouldn't have the pleasure of killing me. "This is so messed up." He stopped and stared out at the ocean. "There was some terrorist attack in one of the southern states. The news reports came in about the same time as the tsunami."

Lucy gasped. "Oh my God. A terrorist attack? Does that mean...do you think more Jacks survived?"

Adam approached Lucy and took her by the shoulders. "No. No. Don't worry." He took her in his arms. "It's probably just leftover negativity from the Jacks."

"But...but there've been no reports for almost a year. This shouldn't have happened." A tear rolled down Lucy's cheek.

My heart tightened, then began to hammer and thud at an irregular pace. It wasn't the first time I'd been ashamed of the

Jack blood coursing through my veins. I'd always denied it, even to myself. Remembering the day my dad told me who I really was made my stomach clench. Half Reader, half Jack. I'd always wondered why he treated me differently. Always so cold. He spat the words out like garbage in his mouth. *"Your mom left you. She wanted nothing to do with you."* Abandonment followed me from that day forward. An emptiness, a void. I didn't fit into either world.

Centuries passed, and Mom contacted me. She said my dad lied because he was ashamed. As an Elder, a top council member, he didn't want a potential scandal. My own father worried more about his standing in the Reader community than his only son. A dirty secret he wanted to stay buried. But she wanted and loved me. Relief consumed my entire soul. Finally, someone who not only knew about me, but also accepted me.

Well, that's what I thought happened.

Except my mom wasn't really my mom. She was an imposter who ruined my life, and everything that followed was a blur.

"What type of terrorist attack?" I directed my question to Adam.

He paused and shifted his gaze to Devon. He gave him a slight nod. "They deactivated the chlorination system and added hydrogen cyanide to the reservoir in a small town called Harmony. Over two hundred people died."

Adam might as well have punched me in the stomach again. My body froze. *Hydrogen cyanide.* "The Jacks were working with that chemical before they died."

Lucy covered her mouth and whispered, "Oh no."

I had another bomb to drop. "And I don't know how to tell

you this, but they also worked on cloning more Jacks."

Everyone stood still and stared at me, the horror of my words sinking in.

"But...but...they all died in the explosion," Ann stuttered out.

"They did." I rubbed my face. "And no, before you ask, I had nothing to do with this. The Jacks haven't contacted me either. They tolerated me only because of my mom—I mean, Atarah. I hated all of them, and the feeling was mutual." The truth churned like poison in my gut. "This could still be a leftover from the negativity they put out into the world. It doesn't mean one of them is alive." The words felt false on my tongue. Something wasn't right.

"Archer is right," Ann spoke to Lucy. "Atarah made sure all the Jacks came to Samara to witness—um, to make sure they were all in the building. I read her mind, and she accounted for every single one. They were all there."

Lucy nodded, but clung to Adam with shaking hands.

The building panic in my brain gave way a little. Atarah thought the wedding ceremony between me and Ann wouldn't be valid unless witnessed by every Jack. She'd made sure they were all in attendance. "There was no way one of the Jacks could've escaped. After I dragged Ann out, I engaged the lockdown system and bolted the last door." I shook my head. "No one got out."

"Okay, that's good." Lucy sighed and straightened. "What about the clones? Do you think it's possible they were successful? How far were they in the process?"

Did they have enough time? "Sorry. They didn't let me near their top-secret activities. I guess that should've been my first red flag." Duped and betrayed. Hatred sizzled through every cell. If the Jacks weren't already dead, I'd happily kill each one. "But I heard they'd only be able to produce three clones every two years."

Devon groaned. "We passed the two-year anniversary."

The realization struck. Even though we stood outside in the fresh ocean air, my lungs couldn't seem to get enough oxygen. Lucy clutched her chest, and Ann leaned into Devon.

"Let's not panic yet." Devon put his arm around Ann and gave Henry's back a rub. "We'll let the FBI and police do their jobs. Once they have a suspect, we'll head out and read their thoughts. That'll settle it once and for all."

Adam looked my way. "Now what? What do we do with him?"

Sweat broke out on the back of my neck, but at least I got my breathing under control. If any Jacks, or Jack clones, were still alive, they'd target Ann first.

Devon held his usual stance—hands on hips with a scowl. "We'll need to keep him close to locate the Seer. Then he should come with us to help read the terrorists."

"Damn it, Devon." Adam looked at me like I wielded a knife and might start killing on the spot.

"We have children to consider. Lucy and I need to take care of the twins until we're able to connect with their parents. And you have Henry. What if he goes all Jack on us and kills everyone in their sleep?"

Couldn't blame him, although he was being hyper-crazy right now. "Adam, you can keep an eye on me during the day, and I'm fine with handcuffs at night if it will help all of you sleep better."

Ann tilted her head, and her eyes softened.

God, I loved her. The pain intensified, and I tried to keep my expression neutral. Didn't want to give everyone more to worry about. Two years to get myself under control and the hard-fought armor cracked within seconds of seeing her.

She might have loved me if it weren't for Devon.

But Devon had been my best friend for centuries, almost since the beginning. I'd spent most waking hours since Ann arrived in our lives in a tug-of-war between hatred and love. Both equally excruciating.

I needed to get away from them, but I wanted them close. It was dysfunctional at best.

Adam clapped his hands together. "Okay, everyone. Looks like we have a plan. We'll go back to the beach house and grab our belongings and connect with the twin's parents. After that, we'll head to Portland and rent two rooms at the Heathman Hotel. Sound okay to everyone?"

For an emotional crier, Adam did a good job taking charge. Maybe too good? Was he good enough for Lucy?

What was I thinking? Lucy was like a little sister, but I'd given up any right to look out for her anymore. *Old habits die hard.* At least while I was around, I'd be able to keep an eye on Adam. Which shouldn't be too difficult since he had the same plan in reverse.

I shared the car ride back to the house with Adam. He'd made it clear he didn't want me around, but they needed my help, so he was sticking close.

"You had us all fooled," he said quietly, right before we turned into the driveway.

I figured he'd say this eventually. "I know you won't believe this, but I wasn't trying to fool anyone. Well, not at first, anyway. After Ann arrived, things got a little cloudy."

His voice turned sarcastic. "Oh, you're using the I-don't-remember-anything excuse."

"I guess I am." Didn't have the energy to defend or argue.

Adam pulled up close to the beach house. A few inches of murky water came to the second step of the stairway leading to the front door. He turned in his seat. "Lucy loved you and was crushed by what you did. If you so much as touch a hair on her head, make her cry, or even look at her sideways, I'll kill you myself."

The problem with that scenario was he'd be doing me a favor. I just didn't have the guts to carry it out.

Yet.

CHAPTER 4

Sadie

I PLOPPED DOWN on my living room sofa with Eve in my arms. "Ugh. They've gone to Portland. Now what?" I scratched her jaw, and she purred, making the motor sound I loved. "According to the note they left on their kitchen table, they'll be downtown at the Heathman. Hmm... I guess I could check things out."

Guilt about breaking into Ann and Devon's beach house bothered me, but it had paid off. Besides, it wasn't a break-in since they'd left the back door unlocked. I'd call it more of a walking and entering.

After packing an overnight bag, I tossed it in the back of my car and returned to get Eve. "How about you stay with Donna for a few days? You know how much she loves you." Eve purred and rubbed her cheek against my arm. "It's settled then." I scooped her up and headed for the door. "Wait. Your food. Sorry about that." I grabbed her food and headed out the door.

Once outside, I breathed in the familiar scent of salt air. "I'll just go for a day or two, don't worry." I wasn't about to leave her all alone, even for a few days. My steps slowed. I'd never separated from Eve before. A stray that showed up at my door a couple of years ago, we'd been a package deal ever since. I lifted her higher and kissed her wet nose. "I'll miss you."

I blinked back tears. Great. I'd fallen in love with the cat. Like most pets, in ten years or so, there'd be another goodbye. I was hopeless.

As I raised my hand to knock on Donna's door, it flung open. "Perfect timing!" Her face brightened.

"It is?"

"Yes. I have someone I want you to meet." Her eyes held a mischievous glint as she guided me into her living room. I loved her cottage. It was always cozy and smelled like a mixture of vanilla, chocolate, and cinnamon. But all I wanted to do now was escape.

"Ian, can you come here for a moment?" She lowered her voice and added, "He's building some shelves for me in the spare bedroom. He's such a doll."

"Yes, Donna. I—" He walked into the room and oh, wow. He was even better looking up close, like, movie star gorgeous. Tall, with a mop of thick, chestnut waves on his head, brown eyes rimmed with dark lashes, and were those dimples? My heart stumbled and sped up. First the cat and now this mortal. I didn't do love. Well, okay, maybe a little with my cat. But to get shocked silent over a random hot guy? What was wrong with me?

His eyes locked onto mine. I clutched Eve, attempting to protect myself from the chemical reaction taking place. A thrill swept through my body, and I willed myself to get a grip. And then he smiled, and all bets were off. Dear Lord, he was pretty.

"Hey." His gorgeous eyes, soft-looking hair, two-day stubble, and dimples were aimed straight at me.

My eyes shifted away for a moment, and I hugged Eve tighter. "Hi." Thank goodness I choked at least one word out, even though I was looking at my shoes when I said it.

"I was just telling Ian about you," Donna gushed.

"Oh?" I sputtered. Two words down. Maybe next I could put them together and make a short sentence.

"Yes! I told him all about your writing."

His head tilted. "You're an author?"

I swallowed. "Yes. I write...words." Gah! My brain. Where did it go?

The corner of his mouth quirked up, and his eyes did that crinkly thing that made my mouth go dry. He was possibly the most handsome man on the planet. Well, maybe he was tied with Archer. Ugh. Why were there hot guys everywhere all of a sudden?

Donna stood next to me and rubbed my arm. "She writes historical non-fiction. She has awards and everything."

Wait. How did she know about that? "Um..." I raised an eyebrow at Donna.

"Sorry if I spilled a secret. I Googled you right after you moved in." She turned to Ian. "She wrote a book about World War II, and it won The National Book Award."

Ian leaned against the doorframe and crossed his arms. "Cool. That's one of my favorite subjects. Maybe we could get together and exchange information?"

Danger! Danger!

Donna tittered next to me. Since when did eighty-year-olds giggle?

"Sure. Maybe sometime." Like, never. I looked down and saw I was almost suffocating poor Eve. "I almost forgot. Donna, can you watch Eve until tomorrow? I have to go to Portland on business."

Before I finished the sentence, she scooped Eve out of my arms and cradled her. "I've been waiting for you to ask. I'll get Eve all to myself." Was Donna purring into Eve's ear? Eve nuzzled Donna's neck. I guess I wouldn't have to worry about a lack of attention.

"Alrighty then. If you're sure." I laughed and turned to leave. "Nice to meet you, Ian." I waved over my shoulder as I made my escape out the door. What little was left of my brain cells fled at an alarming rate.

"Wait," he said. "I'll walk out with you." He waved at Donna and followed me out the door.

That was enough to throw me off-balance. I tripped over the doormat, and my arms did that windmill thing. Before I could right myself, Ian tugged on my T-shirt, spun me around and my feet were off the ground. Held in his arms, my only coherent thought was how good he smelled. I closed my eyes and took in a deep breath. "You smell so good, like dirt." My eyes popped open. "I didn't mean...I meant to say outdoors."

The vibrations of his laugh seemed to echo through my body, ending around my chest. Warmth and safety wrapped around my heart for a moment before I shoved it away. Ian seemed familiar and yet, I'd just met him. Why was that?

"I was helping my dad out in his garden today." His smile seemed genuine.

Wait. *Quit looking at the hot guy.*

"Okay, time for me to go. Can you put me down now?"

The smile intensified, and his voice got deeper. "I don't know. Can I trust you to get to your house safely?"

I pointed to my cottage right across the driveway. "It's right there. I can manage."

He put me down. "I'll walk with you. Anything could happen." A wink and a grin followed.

I stifled an eye roll, but I had to admit a few more minutes with this guy intrigued me. I hadn't felt this way around a mortal in, well, forever. Now, if I could manage to walk and talk for the next few minutes that would be fantastic. "Come on." I faked a groan and started the trek to my car.

He walked beside me on the gravel path. "I really am interested in your writing. World history has always been my favorite subject."

I shrugged. "It pays the bills." I also didn't want to take full credit since I had an unfair advantage over the other historians. I'd lived the history.

He cocked his head. "You won an award?"

"Yeah. It was rigged." I laughed.

His eyebrows shot up. "Rigged?"

"I'm kidding." Sort of. "Here we are." I reached over and opened my car door. "Thanks for escorting me to my car." I motioned to the path we'd just traveled. "See? I can walk without falling on my face."

"Impressive." He chuckled.

My cheeks heated as I slid into the driver's seat. I shut the door and rolled down the window. "See you around."

"You weren't kidding when you mentioned you planned to

leave soon. Something important in Portland?" His hand rested against the car door.

"Yeah. Business stuff." Could I be any vaguer? I turned the ignition and a weird grating noise vibrated from the engine. It didn't start. Great. I tried again.

"That doesn't sound good."

"You think?" Frustration turned me snarky. I needed to get to Portland before the Readers went back into hiding.

He shrugged. "Sorry. I know a little about cars if you want to pop the hood."

He looked like *that*, could discuss history, *and* fix my car?

"Okay." Lovely. I was back to one-word sentences.

He waited for a moment. "You want me to do it for you?"

I blinked slowly, trying to clear my mind. "What?"

"See that lever right there?" He pointed to the hood release and had the decency to hide his smile.

Oh crap! He probably thought I was an idiot. I reached over and pulled the lever. The heat in my cheeks went from warm to burning. "My car's been dependable, so, well...I forgot." *Good one.*

"No worries. Let me see what's going on here." He tugged on the hood and propped it on the metal thingy that held it up. Right about now, I regretted skipping any auto mechanics education.

"Okay, try starting it again," he instructed.

I turned the key in the ignition with the same result. Now what? If I didn't get to Portland, I might lose Archer and the Readers for years, maybe even centuries. My palms began to sweat. Ian knocked around the engine area, making a bunch of clanging sounds.

He walked around to my door. "I think it's the distributor cap. I have a cousin who has an auto repair shop in Astoria. Do you want me to help you get this towed?"

"No!" I shouted. "I mean, no," I added in a quieter voice. "I have to get to Portland today. I can't wait around to have this repaired."

"Gotcha. I'll drive you then." He tilted his head toward a gray Toyota truck. "I'm off for the rest of the day."

"No. I can take the bus or even an Uber. There's no reason for you to go out of your way."

"I've been meaning to go anyway. I've had my bag packed for days and I've been putting it off. I'm supposed to meet someone."

A girlfriend? I hated myself for wondering. I didn't even know him, and the whole mortal thing was wrong and very bad. A recipe for disaster.

Remember what happened last time you let a mortal close. I squeezed my eyes closed for a moment and let the pain wash through me. *Stop it. Don't go there.* I shoved thoughts of the past aside and focused on the situation at hand.

He leaned against my car. "Besides, you'll never find transportation with all the emergency workers coming back and forth from Portland."

That was true. "Okay. That'd be great. Can you drop me off downtown at the Heathman Hotel? Do you know where it is?"

"Yeah. Right on Southwest Broadway. I plan to stay there myself until I wrap up my visit."

I raised an eyebrow. A coincidence?

He grinned. "No, I won't be following you around. My dad

has an account with them. We stay at the Heathman every time we're in the city."

Hmm. He wasn't technically a stranger. I'd seen him at a distance around town with his father many times over the past two years. Donna seemed to love him, and I was more than able to defend myself. I patted the side of my backpack, the pepper spray and stun gun placed strategically in their usual spots.

"I'd love a ride. Thank you. And don't worry about giving me a ride home. I'm not sure how long I'll need to stay."

"Sounds good. I'll grab your bag." He reached into the back seat.

"No! I'll get it." It came out a little forceful, but he laughed and threw up his hands.

"Sure. I should have known better than to touch a girl's things." He smiled again.

Geez. This guy oozed charm. Maybe too charming? Ugh. I was on Paranoia Level Four.

I buckled myself into Ian's truck, and we headed out on Highway 101 to Portland.

"We have about forty-five minutes for you to tell me everything you know about World War II," Ian said as he merged onto Highway 26.

"You enjoy boredom? Is that it?"

"You're calling me boring?" He flashed a lopsided grin with, yes, the dimple on his right cheek on display. Every woman on the planet was in danger from that smile.

"Not even close." The words slipped out before I thought to filter myself.

"I wasn't kidding. I love the entire World War II era. It

fascinates me."

"Which part?"

"The mentality, how so many societies were swayed by evil."

He didn't know about the Jacks and their role in the war, how they only cared about destruction and power.

"Okay. I can give you some facts most people don't know. First, have you heard about the Polish doctors who saved eight thousand Jews?"

His eyes narrowed. "No. Are you making that up?"

"Nope. Two doctors in Poland discovered the Nazis wouldn't deport anyone to a concentration camp who tested positive for typhus, in fear it would spread to their armies. The two injected Jews and non-Jews in their city with a vaccine containing dead epidemic typhus that would test positive but have no adverse effects." I remembered those doctors well. They'd risked everything to save innocent lives.

"Wow. That's fascinating. You got more?"

I checked his expression to make sure he wasn't just being polite. He kept his eyes on the road, but a crease formed between his brows.

"Sure. One more. You've heard people refer to carrots as good for eyesight, right?"

"Yeah."

"Well, that's true to a certain extent. The information was spread around by the British because they wanted to prevent the Germans from finding out they carried radar aboard aircraft. They started a rumor their pilots had excellent night vision from eating lots of carrots."

Ian tipped his head back and laughed. "You're a wealth of information. How about you give me two facts a day for the next month and I'll..." His nose scrunched up while his mind apparently ran through options. "I'll weed your garden."

I almost laughed out loud at his attempt to get to know me better. I would have said yes to a date because he intrigued me. Sure, he was outrageously attractive, but he seemed genuinely nice. He'd be easy to fall for, but I knew how to protect myself and would make sure he stayed in the friend zone. If I started to get too close, I could always back away. I was an expert at it. I'd worked hard to make sure I wasn't a social recluse, most recently hanging with Donna and Miss Gianni, who worked as the town librarian. I needed to interact with people, so I kept practicing the skill of normal conversation. But any relationship needed to stay at a comfortable distance. That was the easy part. It wasn't easy, though, to forget what soul-crushing loneliness felt like.

"That won't work. I love gardening." I pictured the two garden beds placed close to my front door. Potatoes, carrots, corn, and tomatoes were my favorite. The vibrancy of the colors, and mostly, "The smell of dirt is the best."

"So when you told me I smelled like dirt, that was a compliment?" He pressed his lips together, and his eyes crinkled.

Busted.

"I like all sorts of smells." Pathetic save, but at least it was something.

He glanced over at me and must have seen my flaming cheeks. "You want to know my favorite smell?"

"Hmm?" Relief that he changed the subject settled over me.

"The salty tang of the ocean. I even like the smell of seaweed."

"That's just wrong. The seaweed part, that is."

"I'm studying marine biology, so it's sink or swim. No pun intended."

I studied him for a moment. His looks were off-the-charts, so I'd assumed there wouldn't be much more to him. Instead, he was intelligent, charming, funny, and appeared to be down-to-earth. Maybe we could hang out a little? But we'd need to be acquaintance-type friends. The type of friendship where your heart doesn't go splat when they disappear from your life.

We drove in companionable silence for a long stretch along the scenic highway.

"How long have you lived in Cannon Beach?" I asked.

"About two years. I think a few months after you came. Once I arrived, I kept hearing about the beautiful girl in the cottage on the hill." His eyes darted toward me again. "I'm sorry I haven't met you until now. Ever since my dad started his job as mayor, I've been trying to finish my studies in Portland. I've been busy, to say the least."

"No worries. I'm usually tied up with my writing. I don't get out much."

He put his left hand over his heart. "Well then, I'm honored I can be the one to get you out of the house. When you get back, maybe we can go see some sights? The Oregon Coast has some of the best hiking trails in the world."

He didn't look at me, but he swallowed hard and gripped the steering wheel tight. He couldn't be nervous. A guy like him?

Not sure how I wanted to respond, I searched around for a distraction. "Oh, look. There's the hotel. That went by fast."

He pulled up to the valet. "Too fast," he muttered.

I smiled to myself as I reached back for my backpack.

"Thanks so much for the ride. I appreciate it."

He smiled and nodded. "Sure thing."

I hopped out of the truck, turned, and ran right into a wall of muscle.

"Excuse me." I took a step back and adjusted my clothes. "I'm a klutz ninety percent of the time."

"Is that right?" an amused male voice said.

My eyes drifted up from his snug T-shirt to a deceptively angelic face. "Archer."

CHAPTER 5

Archer

"I'D THINK, WITH thousands of years of practice, you'd have the walking thing down by now," I said while watching for her reaction. Seeing her again, right in front of our hotel, threw me a little.

"What?" came her breathless reply.

"You know what I'm talking about." I raised a brow. She looked a little different from the first time I saw her at the beach. Or maybe with all the distractions, I hadn't noticed her blue eyes had specks of purple. I'd also thought her hair was a basic blonde, but now I noticed streaks of silver and gold throughout. Unique.

Her eyes widened, then her shoulders slumped. She exhaled and said under her breath, "Busted."

"What did you expect? That you'd predict a tsunami almost

within seconds and we wouldn't figure out who you were?"

She shrugged. "I made a lucky guess?"

I almost laughed at her hopeful expression. I crossed my arms and waited.

Her eyes shifted to a car pulling away from the curb. "Okay, okay. I kinda knew you'd figure it out. I didn't come to talk to you, just Ann and Devon."

There it was. Again. Distrust. I hated this new existence even though I'd brought it on myself.

"They're around." I lowered my voice. "Something big is going down, and I need to discuss it with you."

"Me?" Her head cocked to the side.

"I thought you might help."

"Why should I help you?" she blurted.

"Not me, more like mankind."

She placed her hands on her hips. "Exaggerate much? You think I'll help you with a line like that? Do I have idiot written across my forehead?" A scowl spread across her face.

Great. A firecracker. Why couldn't she be sweet and sedate like she pretended to be at the beach?

"Listen. You were on that bench for a reason. Did you know about the tsunami? Were you sent to save Ann and her family?"

She moved her hands from her hips and crossed them over her chest.

"We think there might be some Jacks still alive," I added.

That got her attention. She paled and stuttered, "Wh— what? No. No, you're lying. You're the last one." She slapped a hand over her mouth. "Ugh! That slipped."

My stomach twisted in an unfamiliar knot, and I pressed my lips together to prevent a laugh from escaping. Who was this girl? I remembered the Seers as a serious group, as if they carried the weight of the world on their shoulders. This girl, with her flushed cheeks, clumsiness, and flustered behavior didn't match up with my distant memories.

Maybe a different angle would work. "We've already established you know who I am, but I'm at a disadvantage. I don't know your name."

She bit her lip and seemed to consider my request, tapping a foot against the pavement. Her unusual eyes bored into mine. Sweat broke out across my forehead. I ignored it and matched her stare.

"Hey." Lucy's voice came from behind. My eyes stayed locked on the Seer before I glanced her way.

"Just trying to get my Seer friend here to give me her name." I motioned to the blonde.

She narrowed her eyes at me, then turned to Lucy and smiled. "I'm Sadie, and you must be Lucy."

Lucy whispered, "Are you...I mean, were you the one who warned Archer on the beach?"

Sadie matched her quiet voice. "Yeah, but don't get your hopes up. It doesn't happen often."

Lucy's smiled faltered. "Why not?"

"Yeah, how come?" I asked.

She sighed, and her brow furrowed.

Lucy touched her arm. "Ann and Devon are in the library doing research. Let's go talk with them. That's why you're here, isn't it?"

"Yes," she said slowly, drawing out the word while shooting

me a glare.

Lucy smiled warmly. "It's okay, Sadie. I don't know how much you found out about our past, but Archer seems to be trying to help."

Sadie snorted. "I know he tried to kill all of you. Is that what you mean?"

Oh hell. Well, at least that explained her hostility.

"It's a long, complicated story. Let's go talk in private." Lucy motioned toward the revolving door leading inside.

Sadie walked with us into the impressive wood-paneled lobby. The space sparkled with crystal chandeliers hanging from towering ceilings. Before she could hesitate, Lucy tucked her arm in Sadie's while guiding her to the elevators. We ascended in silence to the library located on the top floor.

Lucy kept her hold on Sadie as we exited the elevator. We walked down the long hallway and entered through the big double doors. I'd been to this room a few times, but it never failed to fill me with a sense of awe. Twenty-foot ceilings and thousands of books stacked in rows of mahogany shelves. The smell took me back to Samara, the musty odor of old books and leather. Skylights gave the room an airy glow.

Devon and Ann huddled over a computer in the back corner of the empty room. Good. We wouldn't have to worry about anyone overhearing our little meeting. This should be interesting.

Devon looked up from the computer with one eyebrow raised when he saw our guest. "Hey," he said to Sadie, then turned his questioning glance to Lucy.

Lucy stepped forward, still clutching Sadie like she feared she'd run off. "This is the girl from the beach who warned us about the tsunami."

"The Seer?" Ann's eyes widened.

"That's me." Sadie raised a hand and smiled awkwardly. "Sadie."

Ann grinned and approached Sadie. "I'm thrilled to meet you. Thank you so much for the warning. I thought you were all... I mean, I thought you were—"

Sadie broke free from Lucy's iron grip and turned to Ann. "Dead? No worries. I've had years to adjust to life after the Great War."

"Aw, Sadie. No one adjusts." Ann held only compassion in her eyes.

Sadie nodded, took a deep breath, and a tear escaped her right eye. "You're right. It's been hell."

Whoa. Where did that come from? Watching her made me feel, I don't know, empathy maybe? Emotions that were better kept numb and dormant wormed through, making my skin crawl. Warmth, and another emotion I couldn't place, created a tug-of-war within me. I needed to get back to the safer territory of cold and uncaring.

"I know." Ann put her arms around Sadie and patted her back. "Two thousand years is a long time to be alone." She paused. "You are alone, right? You're the only one?"

Sadie wiped the tear from her face. "I think so, unless they're hiding, like me."

"Interesting..." Devon scrubbed his chin.

"Why is Archer with you guys, anyway? He stalks you for two years, and now you're working together?" Sadie glanced my way.

Damn. How did she know?

"I wasn't stalking anyone. I like the beach." I lied.

"Yeah. Tell that to someone who believes you." Unfortunately, Sadie had returned to hostile.

"You've been stalking us?" Devon's eyebrows shot up, but he didn't look as angry as I would've thought.

"No, I've been at the beach the entire time. Even when you weren't. Ask my little Seer stalker friend here." I glared at Sadie. I left out the fact they rarely visited Samara, choosing to spend most of their time at the beach house.

"Yeah. It must be a coincidence they've spent only three weeks away the entire time." Sadie narrowed her unusual eyes in my direction. "And also—" She halted and bit her lip. "Never mind."

Ugh. This girl is full of secrets.

Lucy chimed in. "He warned us about the tsunami when he didn't have to. He could have just left us."

Sadie shook her head. "Who knows his motivation though? He's a Jack. The Jacks, they killed...they killed my family and all the Seers! They're evil—you all know that!" Sadie's face flushed red, and her knuckles turned white from fisting her hands.

"I'm half Jack, half Reader. I wasn't involved in the Great War." Not that it would make a difference judging from the disgust and most likely hatred pouring from her.

Lucy turned toward Sadie. "It's true. Did you know Archer saved us from the Jacks? When it all went down, he was the one who handcuffed Atarah to make sure she didn't interfere with Ann's plan to detonate the bomb, destroying Samara. If he hadn't done that, the Jacks would still be alive, and who knows what would have become of us." She smiled softly. "Archer chose the Readers when it mattered."

Lucy still believed in me. The realization almost floored me.

My throat tightened, and I swallowed to rid myself of the sensation. As it was, I had a hard time keeping my composure. Trying to fight off my relief and to breathe at a normal pace took all my concentration. *Don't break down. Don't break down.*

Sadie cocked her head, and those eyes of hers stared into mine again. What was she looking for? I wanted to break away, but couldn't. Something about her seemed so familiar.

She's quite beautiful.

But hostile, and bitter. Maybe even vengeful. Her eyes narrowed, and she continued to study me. If I didn't know better, I'd have thought she was trying to read my thoughts.

"I can't read minds, but I watch body language."

My eyes widened.

"You looked a little unnerved, so I made an educated guess." A small smile curved her lips.

Lucy clapped her hands together. "This is fun. Tell me more. What else do you see?"

I rolled my eyes. "Nothing. She's playing psychic like one of those reality shows. They're all fakes."

Sadie's chin raised. "Oh yeah?"

I nodded.

"Well, Lucy..." Sadie shot me a you-asked-for-it glance. "When you told me about Archer coming through for the Readers, did you notice his expression?"

"He didn't have one," she answered.

"Yes, he did." A sly grin appeared. "He looked stoic, I'll give him that. What you said meant a lot to him. His breathing increased by forty-five percent, his eyes blinked at twice his usual rate, and he swallowed three extra times."

Damn. "This is bullshit. Are we going to sit around and play games or form a plan to get to the terrorists?"

Sadie's body stilled. "Terrorists?"

That should shut her up, or at least get her off the topic.

"Yeah." Lucy cringed. "There's a possibility the Jacks made some clones before they died."

Sadie's expression...*hmm.* Instead of fear, she almost seemed relieved. Why would she want more Jacks around?

She regrouped and said, "Oh, that's horrible. Are you sure?"

Devon answered. "No, not yet. There was an incident in a small town in Arizona. Poisoning of a well, something a Jack would do. We plan to travel there to see if we can read them." He pointed to the computer screen. "The news reports say they have two people of interest in their county jail." He turned to Sadie. "Would you be willing to come with us? It should only take about four days."

"Why? I can't read minds."

"Just in case you get another vision. It'd be helpful if we run into trouble."

"I only have about one vision every five years. Without the energy of the other Seers, I've lost most of my ability."

"Really? Oh hell," Ann said, but then perked up. "How about you come with us anyway and tell us about your history and what you've been doing to stay hidden. If there are other Seers out there, the information could prove helpful."

"Maybe. I don't know. I should get back to my cat." Sadie winced right after saying it.

I almost laughed out loud, but suppressed it.

She pointed. "Don't you dare say it."

"What?" I tried to keep my expression bland.

"I see those little laugh lines around your eyes, and no, I haven't turned into a Cat Lady. She's a stray that showed up a few years ago and stayed. I left her with a neighbor for the day." She chewed on her lip. "Give me a second and I'll call Donna to see if she can watch Eve for a few more days." She moved to the other side of the library with her cell phone propped against her ear.

"She's a little...odd, don't you think?" I asked Lucy.

Lucy covered her mouth and giggled. "I like her. I think she sees a little too much for your comfort." She winked.

"No, not that." Well, it was one of the things that made me uncomfortable. I wondered if I'd ever be able to stop lying. "It's her eyes. Have you noticed the odd color and how they seem to shimmer?"

"Shimmer?" Lucy asked.

"Yeah. Like the sunlight is playing with her irises, even when we're inside."

"Um. No. Maybe you need to get your eyes checked." She chuckled.

"Ann, Devon, have you seen it?"

"Sorry." Ann shrugged.

"Nope," Devon answered.

Sadie returned. "It's all set. I can go. Are we flying?"

Devon paused from tapping away on the computer. "Nope. We only travel in modes we can control. I've rented two cars. We should be there in two days. Archer and Sadie will take one car, and the rest of us will take the other."

Sadie and I shouted, "No!"

CHAPTER 6

Sadie

COULD I DO it? When the time came, would I be able to kill Archer?

My mom had prepared me, told me I would be the one to kill the last Jack. God forgive me, but relief swept through me hearing there might be more Jacks. What was wrong with me?

Those vulnerable eyes and handsome face.

I'd have to, though. The Seer's visions were never wrong. My stomach dropped like it always did whenever I thought about it. That I'd take a life never left my mind. It'd always been in the distant future, something to avoid. Now the reality loomed like a boulder on my chest. What was the alternative? Ignore the vision and let the Jacks destroy the planet? Nope. I owed it to my parents and the Seer race to end the Jacks for good.

"What are you thinking about?" Archer finally asked.

We'd been driving in silence for over nine hours, both

stubbornly ignoring each other.

"Oh, you know, about how I was enjoying the silence."

A small smile played on his lips. "After living alone all these years, I'd think you'd welcome the company."

"Depends on the company," I shot back.

"Touché." He laughed. "How about this." He paused and rubbed his chin. "We call a truce until we get this all figured out. We're both here for the same reason."

"Are we? You'd be okay with wiping out any remaining Jacks? You're half Jack, you know." I watched for a change in his expression.

He blew out a long breath. "You don't have to remind me. Believe me, that's all I've been thinking about for too long." Shaking his head, he put on the blinker and exited the freeway. "At least you belonged to a group. I've never had that."

"Nope. Nada. Not going to fall for it." He would not manipulate me into feeling bad for him. Well, perhaps a little. I crossed my arms, determined not to show it. I took comfort from the fact I was part of something great. The ability to keep my immortality and some of my Seer abilities were never taken for granted. But what was it like for Archer? He probably never felt at home in either group. He lived a lie, fell in love with Ann, lost her, then found out his mom had duped him for hundreds of years. But still no excuse for what he'd done.

He chuckled and seemed to shake it off as he turned onto a side street. "God, you're feisty. I thought the Seers were all calm-like and Zen. What happened to you?"

Did he just wink at me? Ugh!

"Did you know your face turns five shades of red when you're angry? And you do this scrunching thing with your nose." He motioned to my nose and laughed.

"It's not funny! You're a Jack, an enemy of the Seers. The blood running through your veins is the same as the monsters who killed everyone I loved. I've been alone for two thousand years, and you want me to feel bad because you didn't fit in?" A surge of pain accompanied the words.

Archer turned into the hotel parking lot and parked under a tree. "You're right. I shouldn't joke about it." He rubbed his face and pushed back his wavy, blonde hair. "This must've brought back a lot of horrible memories for you."

I turned away and looked out the window.

"Can you look at me for a minute?" he said, his voice low and quiet.

I turned, and we locked eyes for a moment before he spoke again. "You have my word, I won't hurt anyone. I've learned my lessons the hard way and don't plan to repeat them."

I couldn't make him the same promise. As I continued to look into his eyes, I wondered if I'd be able to do it—end his life. But there might be more Jacks in Arizona. Maybe it'd be someone else I'd have to kill. Someone who didn't have clear, green eyes that crinkled when he smiled. Or someone who didn't show pain and vulnerability in every unguarded expression.

Stop it. He's a Jack, my enemy.

Just as the thought flitted through my mind, Archer glanced at my lips and then back to my eyes.

He wouldn't dare.

He cleared his throat. "Devon rented a room here for us. We should get going."

"You're joking." My hands fisted by my sides.

His eyes narrowed. "Why would I be joking?"

I let out a frustrated groan. "I relented and said yes to the car ride with you after Ann convinced me the group needed to *talk strategy*"—I said using air quotes—"during the car ride. But there is no way I'm sharing a hotel room with you. Who are you people? Why would anyone think I'd be okay with this?" I wanted to smack the grin off his face.

"Um. The other car is a few minutes behind us. Devon rented two rooms. One for you girls and Henry, the other for us." He pursed his lips together, but a snicker escaped anyway.

"Oh."

"Yeah."

"Maybe I jumped to conclusions a little."

"And your face is doing that angry, red thing again." He continued to grin.

That only increased my temper. "Just so you know, I've never punched anyone in my entire life, but I'm considering changing that soon."

His head tipped back, and he let out a loud laugh. "I don't know why I enjoy making you angry." He opened the car door and motioned. "Come on, Spitfire, we'll get to your room and you can punch the pillows instead."

"It wouldn't be as satisfying." I crossed my arms.

He paused and moved toward me slightly. Looking at my lips again, he said, "No, that wouldn't satisfy me either."

Everything went still. Even the air seemed to be sucked out of the car. My heart beat so fast and loud, I worried he could hear it. I hated him. Right? But why was every cell on fire, and why did his lips look so—ugh—kissable?

"Oh, good. You haven't killed each other." Lucy giggled as

she pulled open my door. "Come on, we'll bunk together, and I heard there's a hot tub around somewhere." She stretched her arms over her head. "I can't wait to soak these tired muscles."

"Okay." I grabbed my bag and darted out of the car at record speed, leaving a deep chuckle behind me.

Lucy linked her arm in mine and we walked toward the hotel lobby. "What was that all about? The tension in your car was like two boxers right before the starting bell. Did you two fight the entire time?"

No. But I considered kissing him. My enemy. What is wrong with me?

"We didn't talk until right before we parked. Then Archer said some stupid things, and I thought about punching him. Maybe you picked up on that?" I shrugged.

Lucy laughed. "I can tell we'll be great friends. I've wanted to punch Archer a few times myself. Although..."

We entered the lobby of the hotel. Devon and Adam stood at the front desk, collecting the key cards.

"Although?" I asked.

"There's something that just doesn't add up with Archer and the Jacks. I haven't figured it out yet. But I will." Her brow creased as she tried to puzzle it out.

"Figured what out?" Ann asked from behind Lucy.

"Geez!" Lucy jumped back and clutched her chest. "Don't do that. You about gave me a heart attack."

"Sorry." Ann laughed and scanned the room. "So, spill it."

"It's time we got to know Sadie a little better. Let's hit the hot tub on the second floor. It's the perfect place for some girl talk, and we can compare notes." Lucy motioned to the elevators at the far end of the lobby.

"I didn't pack a swimsuit." But a hot soak did sound relaxing.

"No worries. I packed an extra."

I took in Lucy's curvy body and sighed. "I don't think so." My girls would take a swim of their own in her oversized bikini top.

"Don't worry. We'll find you something." Before I could object, Lucy grabbed hold of my arm and tugged me across the lobby. I stopped in my tracks halfway. "You have to quit doing that."

"Doing what?" Lucy's eyebrow raised.

"What you always do." Ann laughed. "I thought it was just me. She must really like you because I'm usually the only one with the honor of being dragged around by Lucy."

Lucy's cheeks flushed. "Oh no! I'm so sorry. My feet get ahead of my brain sometimes."

"I'm exactly the opposite. My feet go before my brain, and I usually end up tripping or flat on my face."

"See? We're the perfect match! I'll keep hold of your arm, and you'll never fall when I'm around."

"Okay." I held out my arm. "Lead me to the hot tub."

"We'll need to drop off our luggage first. Then we'll head out."

Fifteen minutes later, we were in a warm, bubbling heaven. "This is nice, but if anyone walks in, they'll think we're naked." Lucy only packed strapless suits so the one I borrowed needed to be clipped in the back to keep it from falling down. I yanked it up again.

"The windows are steamed up. No one will see us."

"Let's get down to business." Ann rubbed her hands together. "What's up with your theory about Archer and the Jacks?"

The steam made Lucy's cheeks flush, and her red hair curled into ringlets. She swished her hands through the water and leaned forward. "We have to get Sadie caught up with everything first."

"Good idea." Ann tapped her cheek with her index finger. "Where should we begin?"

"I'll start." Lucy turned to me. "I assume you know the Seer vision about the Readers and the Jacks."

"Yes. The soul mate vision," I answered. "Whichever group had The Lost One would control the outcome of the battle between the Readers and the Jacks."

"Exactly. After the Great War, both groups went into hiding. The Jacks scattered, but the Readers stuck together and built our mountain home, Samara. The vision stated The Lost One would be the soul mate to one of us—Archer, Devon, Markus or *moi*." Lucy pointed to herself. "Whenever the Reader scouts would find another Reader, they'd be thrown at us to see if sparks flew." She moved a few feet to the right to get in front of the sprayer jets. "It was entertaining at first, but after a few thousand years, it got old. All our hopes would get raised, just to be disappointed. And then my pal Ann came along." She winked at Ann.

Ann smiled. "I was in big-time denial. I'd originally hoped it was Archer, because he wasn't as arrogant as Devon." She shrugged. "But we didn't have the chemistry."

Lucy added, "Yeah, talk about denial. Devon went out of his way to antagonize you."

Sounds familiar.

Ann sighed. "Oh, sweet memories."

Lucy giggled and splashed water at her. "At least he came to his senses when Markus made his move on you." Her expression clouded. "Poor Markus."

"What happened to Markus?" I asked.

"You don't know?" Lucy said.

I shook my head.

"Don't freak out, but Archer killed him." Lucy cringed.

Ice filled my veins. "What?" I squeaked out. "I knew he planned to help the Jacks wipe out the Readers, but he killed someone?"

"Here's what I think happened. You know about Archer's fake mom, right?"

"Atarah?"

"Yeah. She was some Jack leader. Her title was kept quiet, but it should have been princess or something similar. Anyway, the Jacks were doing lots of scientific stuff—like mind-altering things. They wanted to erase Ann's memory so she'd forget Devon, marry Archer, and live happily ever after." She rolled her eyes. "The Jacks thought the vision meant whoever had Ann would win the war. But they didn't realize the power of a true soul mate match. Readers can't read other Readers' minds. It's always been that way. But Devon was able to send Ann messages even after Archer kidnapped her."

I examined Ann to look for signs of anger or lingering trauma. Her warm smile remained, and even seemed peaceful, not at all what I'd expect.

Lucy continued, "This is where it gets weird. Okay, so we know the Jacks were doing all sorts of mind manipulations." She turned to Ann. "You described Archer acting like a different person at the Jack Compound in Montana, right?"

She nodded. "Yeah, he was. But I figured it was his true self—that he'd been faking with the Readers."

Lucy sat up straighter. "That's where things get fuzzy for everyone. I mean, he's this down-to-earth guy for thousands of years, but then suddenly goes off the rails?"

"What are you saying?" Ann's brow furrowed.

"I believe Atarah used mind control on him. She wasn't even his mom, so what was stopping her? She knew Archer was one of the four who would be a possible match for The Lost One, so I think she used his vulnerabilities to manipulate and control him from the start. And Markus was found dead with no witnesses, and the tapes of the murder are missing." Lucy shook her head.

Ann sighed. "I've always thought that was strange. Where could they have gone?"

"Archer could have destroyed them. But if someone else killed Markus, they might have hidden or tampered with the tapes." Lucy drummed her fingers against her lips. "The murder was set up to make Devon look guilty. All of us thought it was Archer. But what if it was Atarah all along?"

"Wow. Now that I think of it, it could be a possibility. But Archer admitted to killing Markus."

"Maybe Atarah planted the memory? Made him believe he did it?"

Silence descended as we contemplated the idea.

"I mean, it's possible. It's also possible we don't want to believe Archer is capable of murder." Ann shifted in her seat.

Lucy frowned. "We should investigate this. At least find out why the tapes are missing."

"Wow. You've worked all this out." Ann studied Lucy with a concentrated stare.

"It's been bothering me for years. Now that Archer's back, I'm remembering the way he was before. Sure, he seems defensive and a lot quieter, but now that he's not connected with any Jacks, his old self is coming back."

"What do you think, Sadie?" Ann quirked a brow.

"I wouldn't know. But he is kinda obnoxious. Has he always been?" The girls laughed and splashed water at me. Suddenly, realization struck. My heart warmed when I realized these people were my allies. They trusted me. The Readers and the Seers had always been aligned. I wouldn't be left on my own. They'd be my family now. Peace spread, comforting like a warm spring day, and my eyes welled with tears.

"Oh, I hope we haven't overwhelmed you with all this. I'm so sorry." Ann placed her hand on my arm.

"No, no. I'm beginning to understand I'm not alone. I won't have to say goodbye to you in ten or twenty years. Or whenever."

Lucy squeezed my arm. "We're soul sisters now."

The door opened, and a middle-aged man appeared, took one look at us, made an excuse, and backed out.

"He made a fast escape." Lucy laughed.

I lowered my voice. "He probably thought we were naked!"

"Oh! That's what it was." Ann gasped, and we all laughed together. She turned. "Can you come stay at Samara when we get back? You'd be a huge help, and I think you'd love it there."

My mind searched for all the reasons to say no, but only one mattered. "Can I bring my cat?"

"Of course! Your cat can chase the huge, disgusting rats."

Ann shivered.

Lucy smiled warmly at Ann. "We don't have rats; we have cute little mice. Ann has a tad bit of a phobia, but she's getting better." She patted Ann's arm.

The door to the sauna/hot tub room opened again. Lucy whispered while laughing, "Maybe he decided a bunch of naked women wasn't such a bad thing."

But instead, Archer stepped into the room. His eyes darted around the steamy area, down to the water where the three of us sat, and back up to lock on me. The heat made my cheeks flush, but his intense stare, I'm sure, notched it up by a couple more shades.

His eyes widened, and he moved his hands up to cover them. "Oh hell. I saw nothing. I promise."

Lucy chuckled. "You can relax, Archer. We have swimsuits on."

"Oh." Without removing his hands, he said, "I have somewhere I have to go. Yes. I have errands. Bye."

We broke out into peals of laughter after he left the room.

Lucy caught her breath and said, "Oh my gosh, Ann. Did you notice that?"

"I sure did." She smiled and nodded.

"What? What did I miss?" I looked back and forth between Lucy and Ann.

"Archer's obsession with Ann seems to be dwindling. He only looked at one of us before good sense kicked in when he thought we were naked."

Embarrassment hit, because I'd noticed, too. He'd only looked at me.

"And, he was blushing!" Lucy's eyes widened. "I can't believe it."

"I'm sure it was just the heat from the room." Yeah, that had to be it.

"Or the heat from a certain someone." Lucy leaned back. "This is such a huge relief. I worried Archer would pine away for Ann for eternity."

"No, the vision—" Darn. I almost said too much.

Lucy and Ann sat silent, waiting for me to finish.

"I meant the vision didn't have all the answers." Which was only a half-truth. I couldn't tell them Archer wouldn't be around much longer if he turned out to be the only living Jack.

CHAPTER 7

Archer

*S*ILENCE.

 I snuck a peek at Sadie's still form in the passenger seat. Arms crossed, she looked out the window as the desert landscape whizzed by. Another long, quiet day in the car. She already hated me, and now because of last night, she probably thought I was some perv. What was I supposed to do? I walked into the spa room to see her all flushed pink and gorgeous with her hair a little messy, and those eyes. God, her eyes. Her full lips, parted just a little, struck me dumb, and I stared at her like an idiot. I couldn't have moved if my life had depended on it. What was it about her? She wasn't anything like Ann. Ann was sweet and kind, while Sadie was feisty and combative.

 Maybe by blocking the feelings of attraction for Ann, I'd unwittingly transferred them to Sadie. My hands tightened around the steering wheel. Why was I so messed up? I'd spent the past two years thinking about—correction, *obsessing* about—Ann, and now I couldn't stop thinking about another woman. Not just any woman, a woman who hated me. Someone who would always blame at least part of me for what happened to her family. Damn Jacks. I wished their blood could be drained from my veins.

"I call uncle." Sadie breathed out a huge sigh.

The sound of her voice made my hands jerk on the wheel. "Uncle?"

"Yeah. You know what I'm talking about. Two long days of silence is like watching carrots grow."

"Carrots?"

"Ugh, you know what I mean. Tedious, monotonous, dull. This barren landscape isn't helping much either. We'll get to the police station in about an hour, right?"

I looked at my GPS. "About sixty-five minutes."

"Okay. So, look, surely we have enough safe topics to talk about for an hour to pass the time. Either that or I'll jump out of this car from sheer boredom."

"That's a tempting offer." I couldn't help myself.

"Ha ha." She rolled her eyes. "How about we talk about everything except the Jacks. That work for you?"

"Maybe." I was also sick of driving alone with my thoughts.

"Can you tell me about Samara? I heard it's built into a mountain."

Samara. *Home.* Warmth filled every inch of my body. I took a deep breath. "Samara was beautiful. It was almost like living outside most of the time. Thousands of tubes built into the ceilings brought in natural light everywhere. We constructed a waterfall and rainforest room, complete with wind and rain.

The Reader scouts furnished Samara with custom wood pieces, artwork, and handmade linens." I smiled to myself. "I never even felt the need to leave. But the Elders insisted we all go out on rotation, so we wouldn't become too separated from the world."

"That sounds fantastic. Did they build the replacement Samara the same?" She leaned toward me.

"No idea."

"I guess we'll see after we wrap up here."

"You're going?"

"Yeah. Ann and Lucy invited me."

"You mean you'll actually leave your—" I stopped before I broke out laughing.

Sadie narrowed her eyes. "My cat?"

A chuckle escaped my lips.

"Ugh! What is wrong with you? Eve is the best cat ever." She shook her head.

"I'm sorry, but I hate cats." They were flea-ridden and a general nuisance. "But maybe yours is different."

"You'll find out soon, because I'm bringing her with me." Her chin rose.

Fun times. "Great. Can't wait." I was pretty sure she detected the sarcasm.

"Okay, now we have two subjects we won't discuss. The Jacks and my cat." She crossed her arms.

"Deal."

Her eyes narrowed, but she changed the subject. "Now I have questions about your Reader abilities. Is that safe territory?"

I shrugged. "I guess."

"How far from the person do you need to be to read their thoughts?"

"For me, it's about twenty feet. Devon and Lucy can read from fifty feet. Ann from about ten feet."

"Why only ten for Ann?"

"She's a mixture of Reader, Jack, and Seer. That's what makes her so special. But on the downside, her abilities for each are limited. For instance, she only has visions sporadically, and we don't know if she can change form like the Jacks because she's never tried."

"No wonder I felt a connection. I guess she's like a distant cousin or something." Her eyes drifted back to the landscape.

"Maybe. It's a rare mix that took place in the early days, so no one knows."

She turned back toward me. "Yeah. I remember it was taboo to, um, cross-pollinate between groups."

"Cross-pollinate?" I snickered.

She blushed. "Archer, just stop before I really jump out of the car. This time out of embarrassment." She covered her face. "Sometimes I speak before my brain kicks in."

"Surprise, surprise," I said under my breath.

"I heard that!" She punched my arm.

A burst of warmth and sparks, and something else I couldn't define, started at the point of contact and spread down my arm. I slammed my foot on the brake and steered the car off the road with my left hand.

"What the hell was that, a stun gun?" I rubbed my arm.

She'd gone pale, and her eyes stared back at me like a frightened owl.

"Did you feel that? It was like a buzzing or something." I rubbed my arm.

"What?" Her eyes darted everywhere but on me. "It was just a little punch. No big deal."

She's lying.

"I guess I didn't realize my strength. Sorry about that." She pursed her lips.

Closed down. *Again.*

"Yeah. You pack a mean punch." If she wanted to play dumb, I'd go along. But I'd find out why. I'd never heard about the Seers having any extra powers besides their visions.

The rest of our trip passed without another word. I pulled the car into the parking lot. In the front of the courthouse sat a town square flanked with a bakery, hardware store, and other quaint little shops. By a newsstand in front of a small cafe, Devon, Ann, and Lucy sat at a wrought iron table under an umbrella. Sadie and I each grabbed a chair and joined them.

"Where's Adam?" I asked, then scanned the courtyard.

"Henry's taking his nap, so we're taking shifts." Lucy grinned. "He lost the coin toss."

I glanced at the building. Like a lot of small towns, the courthouse, police station, and jail were all housed together. Devon or Lucy should be able to pick up chatter from this distance. "Have you been able to read?" I asked Devon. His skills surpassed those of any Reader.

"Two policemen, one policewoman, a dispatcher, and the fingerprint technician." Devon held up a finger for each person he named.

"What are they thinking?" I asked.

"One guy, Stan, has the hots for a girl named Judy. He keeps imagining her naked."

Lucy slapped Devon's arm. "Quit joking. Can you hear the thoughts of the terrorists?"

Devon rubbed where she slapped. "I'm not joking, and no, not yet."

"Shouldn't you have heard something by now?" Lucy stared at Devon while she sipped her coffee.

If the Jack prisoners were in the building and we couldn't read them, something bad was going down. The Readers could always hear a mortal's thoughts, even during sleep.

"This isn't good, is it?" Sadie asked Devon as her foot tapped an impatient beat.

"We can't jump to conclusions yet. They might have transferred the prisoners." But Devon rubbed his right eyebrow, something he always did when he was nervous.

Lucy leaned forward and lowered her voice. "Jacks can't block."

I cleared my throat. "Atarah knew how to block and taught me. If we're dealing with clones, they might have figured out how to pass that skill along."

"How hard is it to block?" Lucy asked me.

"Once you have the skill, it's like breathing. It'll be hard to figure out if they're Jacks or terrorists until we can get closer."

Devon scanned our group. "Only one way to find out. Who wants to file a police report?"

"Oh, me!" Lucy jumped up from the table. "I'll tell them someone stole my dog."

Devon sighed. "I guess that's as good as any other excuse."

I stood. "I'll go with her."

"No. She needs to come across as alone and flustered." Devon turned back to Lucy. "You have fifteen minutes. Will your damsel-in-distress act get you close enough to the prisoners?"

"Yeah. I'll ask to use the restroom and get *lost* before I get back to reception." She looked at the small, gray building. "It hasn't failed me yet." She batted her eyelashes and laughed.

Ann stood and hugged Lucy. "Be careful."

Lucy pulled out half of her shirt from her pants and mussed up her red hair. After pinching her cheeks a few times, she conjured up some tears. With a few quick breaths, she marched toward the front door.

Sadie's mouth dropped open. "Wow. I want to be her."

"Yeah. She's a pro," I said, but I still worried.

Sadie's brow wrinkled. "What happens if the terrorists or the Jacks figure out what she's up to?"

I smiled to reassure her. "You don't have to worry about them. They're behind bars, remember?"

She nodded. "Okay." But the crease between her eyes remained.

Fourteen long minutes later, Lucy exited the building and casually walked toward our group. "I got nothing. Devon, you should go in next."

"What do you mean, nothing?" Devon frowned.

"I could read everyone in the station. The jail cells are back behind locked doors. Either they're blocking me, or they've been transferred."

Damn.

Devon tapped his fingers on the table's edge. "Did you see or hear anything unusual on your way to the bathroom?"

"No. Two of them thought about different ways to get me out of their hair." She sighed. "One of them planned to send me to the park a few blocks down the street, knowing I wouldn't find my beloved dog." She shook her head and scowled. "Jerk."

I stood. "I'll go."

Lucy rolled her eyes. "Not gonna happen. No one will believe your pretty-boy face did anything wrong."

Devon put his coffee on the table. "I don't know about that, but I have a plan."

Ann groaned. "You're going to get yourself arrested again?"

"No. But I'll get myself into one of the holding cells."

Her shoulders slumped. "How?"

"I'll tell them I've seen a spaceship land and plan to make myself a sacrifice. They'll most likely put me in a cell until the men in white coats come along."

"That's a great one." Lucy rubbed her hands together.

Sadie looked from one to the other, studying each face before she asked, "You've done this before?"

Devon smiled. "A few times. We try to get creative for each excursion."

Lucy opened her purse. "You happen to be carrying your fake ID?"

"Yes. Got it right here." Devon patted his back pocket.

She snapped it shut. "Good. My purse is a disaster. I have at least three or four of your IDs under candy bar wrappers and lipstick."

Ann approached Devon, put her arms around his waist, and rested her head on his chest for a moment. I braced for the inevitable stab-in-the-heart pain that always followed. After holding my breath for a few seconds, I realized it wasn't coming. Where was it? What was happening? The gnawing, almost constant agony that'd been heavy on my chest for over two years had diminished. Probably just distracted by all the events, but I let myself relax a little.

Devon disappeared through the large metal doors, and we all settled in for the wait.

"Will this be dangerous?" Sadie asked me.

I considered it for a moment. "Nah, just a bit inconvenient if they put him on a twenty-four-hour mental health watch."

"He'll walk out about ten minutes after the psychiatrist arrives," Ann assured Sadie. "He's great at convincing people to do what he wants."

Memories of all the times Devon and I had teamed up to get things done filtered in before I could shut them down. Instead of anger clenching my stomach, the comfort of our friendship slid back in. We were a team. Unbreakable, I thought. Now, I was like the loser kicked off the high school football team. An outcast. The familiar cold blanket of rejection wrapped its icy fingers around my chest, forcing out any remaining thoughts of belonging or friendship. I'd help them find out if the terrorists were Jacks, then go back into seclusion where I belonged.

I glanced at Lucy sitting across from me at the table. Head tilted, she seemed to study me. I smiled a little, and her face brightened. The warmth in her eyes told me everything. Lucy wanted to forgive me. Maybe she already had. But that didn't mean I deserved it.

Lucy glanced at Sadie and Ann before she whispered, "I think Atarah did some brainwashing or mind control on you. Maybe even advanced hypnosis, I don't know." Her gaze was intense. "I know you, Archer. Not just as a cousin, but a friend. None of this adds up. I want to get to the truth."

Sadie perked up. "What truth?"

"Oh, you know, about the Jacks and what's going on." Lucy smiled innocently.

That seemed to satisfy Sadie, and she continued her conversation with Ann.

Lucy sent me a conspiratorial wink, and I shook my head. It always amazed me how Lucy kept her child-like wonder and innocence regarding the world. She wanted to believe the best in everyone, not only the Readers, but also the mortals. Lucy always thought the Jacks were responsible for the negativity in the world, and when they were wiped out, the world cultures would go back to their natural inclination toward peace and become unified and harmonious. She was right; changes had started. But the Jacks were back and probably planned to undo all the progress that had been made.

"When we get back to Samara, the first thing I want to do is dig out the security tapes. The Elders put them in the storage room in the basement right after the move. We don't have access, but I don't care anymore. This has gone on long enough. I want to prove you didn't kill Markus."

What the hell? My heart rate spiked.

"How can you prove I didn't kill Markus when I remember doing it?" I rubbed the back of my neck, the memory making me sick.

"Do you remember killing him, or the aftermath?" Her eyebrow rose.

Restlessness and a dry mouth propelled me to the café for some water. I paid the attendant and took a large gulp. God, I didn't want to remember that night. Did I kill Markus? That part remained foggy. But I remembered the knife and the blood on the ground next to his dead body. I took another sip and hoped it would calm my racing heart. Where was I in the room? My breath caught when I realized my memories were more like pictures. Nothing moved.

Lucy gave me a glimmer of hope, but I still thought she was wrong. I remembered wishing Markus dead. It was bad enough trying to win over Ann with Devon always lurking. I must have killed him in a jealous rage.

I rubbed my temples. *But if that's true, I would've killed Devon before Markus.*

After another drink of water, I returned to the table. "Lucy, I appreciate it. I do. But it'd be a waste of time."

She grinned. "Time? Oh, Archer, you're funny. We have plenty of time. And besides, you set up the entire security system. You should be able to access all the different camera angles."

"Yeah, but if the prisoners turn out to be Jacks, we'll—" I stopped to watch two men in lab coats enter the courthouse. "That was fast."

Ann stood and paced next to our table, muttering, "Okay, Devon, work your magic."

Lucy got up and matched Ann's strides, hooking their arms together. "Remember the time Devon persuaded the Black Jack dealer in Vegas he'd won with only sixteen? He was so convincing; the guy didn't even check his own cards."

Ann smiled and shook her head. "This whole thing has me a little off-balance. If those terrorists are Jack clones, I wonder what else they could have put in their DNA." She stopped and asked me, "The Jacks weren't working on any superpower kind of stuff, were they?"

I wanted to laugh at the suggestion, but held back, because I realized it wasn't funny...and might even be true. "Who the hell knows?"

Sadie gasped, and I followed her gaze. Devon exited the courthouse. But something was wrong. Ann straightened, but Lucy held her arm.

"What did they do to him?" Ann's voice came out in a strangled whisper.

"He's so pale," Lucy said.

Devon approached and placed his hands on the table. He looked up and met my eyes. "It's bad. Worse than we thought."

CHAPTER 8

Sadie

DEVON DID NOT look good. For the short time I'd known him, he always appeared confident and in control. But not now. He kept rubbing his face and eyes like he wanted to banish whatever he saw inside the prison.

"What happened?" Archer asked him.

Devon sighed and sat at the table, placing his head in his hands. "There are two Jack clones in there."

Ann sat next to him and gently laid her hand on his. "Are you sure?"

Devon looked back up at Archer, seeming to study him. "Archer, I need to ask you a question."

A crease formed between Archer's eyebrows. "Yeah?"

"Do you remember Atarah or any of the Jacks taking samples from you, for instance, hair or skin?"

Archer's eyes narrowed. "No." His expression darkened. He

got up from the table and took a step back. "Oh, God, tell me this isn't what I think it is."

Devon nodded. "They have their 'terrorist' prisoners in the back, who also happen to be twins. Or I should say clones. They look exactly like you, have the same voice patterns, even dress like you. The weird thing is, I was within ten feet, but I couldn't read them."

"This is so, so bad." Lucy put her hand over her mouth and stared at Devon.

Archer isn't the last Jack.

An unnatural comfort swept through me. I nodded to Lucy. "That's horrible." Did the tone of my voice give me away? I hoped lightning wouldn't strike. Those clones could wreak havoc throughout the world given the opportunity. I asked the group, "Are we going to take them out right now? I noticed a gun store a few blocks away."

The air seemed to still as everyone froze and stared at me.

I blinked a few times. "What? We have to get rid of them, right?"

Archer bit his lip and turned away.

I glanced at each one. "Why are you all staring at me?"

Ann covered her mouth and coughed. "It's not that. We weren't expecting that reaction from you."

"Reaction?"

"The going in with guns blazing." Ann smiled.

I guess I need a little training for the hit woman role I'm destined to fulfill.

"Oh, that. Well, um, I guess I jumped the gun a little." I shrugged and waited for them to get the joke.

Lucy giggled and put her arm around me. "Oh, Sadie. That was so bad, it was funny. You, my dearest Seer, are a breath of fresh air."

Archer turned back toward our table. His face resumed its normal scowl while he ran his fingers through his hair. "Why?" he asked. "I mean, why me?"

Devon frowned and shook his head. "Don't you see it? You're the perfect mix. A Jack who can read minds and has immortality." He locked eyes with Archer. "Atarah found a way to control you. I'm sure she implanted them with instructions before she died. They won't have your recent memories, but I'm sure they were implanted with enough information to fake it if they planned to impersonate you at some point."

Archer's lips pressed together. "Even from the grave, Atarah causes problems. She won't get away with it again if I have anything to do with it." He looked down and muttered, "I hate every last one of them."

Devon nodded and took a deep breath. "Okay, let's get started. We need to get a plan formulated. When I was in there, I read the lead detective's thoughts. The FBI and Homeland Security decided the US Marshall office will handle the interrogation. They'll come tomorrow afternoon at two to interrogate them, so we need to move fast to figure out the best way to take them out."

Lucy tugged on Devon's sleeve. "Should we try to interrogate them before they die? Maybe they can tell us about the other clone and its location, or what their instructions were after this? Perhaps we can prevent the other clone from doing more damage."

Devon shook his head. "I've studied cloning for years. The Jack clones they created will most likely be mostly a blank slate. They'll have the basic skills, but beyond that, they'll only know what they've been told. They were most likely instructed to inflict damage wherever they could. That's why this was a relatively small event. Every day, they'll become more advanced and dangerous. It's more important we take them out now."

Lucy nodded. "Okay. You're right." She took a sip of coffee. "How about poison?"

"It can't be obvious. It has to look like either natural causes or human error." Devon scratched his jaw.

"They won't believe natural causes if they both die at the same time." Lucy huffed.

"True. Let's go with human error." Devon nodded.

"I know!" I couldn't believe my gardening obsession might be helpful. "Poisonous mushrooms. Death caps are often mistaken for generic, wild mushrooms. They're deadly. And guess what? They grow here in Arizona."

"How long does it take to work?" Lucy asked.

I tucked a piece of hair behind my ear. "About twelve hours. They'll think they have the flu at first. If the police don't rush them right to the hospital, the Jacks should be out of commission by this time tomorrow. Death might take a little longer." A lump in my throat formed, and my mouth went dry.

Don't think about it.

Ann sat up straighter. "Oooooh. Good idea." She asked Devon, "Do you know where they get prisoner meals?"

"Yeah. They have a small, commercial kitchen in the back, with only one door that leads to the jail cells. One of the cooks came out and announced lasagna would be tonight's dinner." Devon turned to Archer. "Do you still order lasagna from Italian restaurants? We need to make sure the clones eat large amounts of the death cap."

Archer groaned and shook his head. "This is just...creepy." He looked up at the sky, appearing like he wanted to escape. "Yes."

"Perfect. We can hide the mushrooms in the sauce."

Lucy shot a quick look at Archer. "Archer loves mushrooms, so we can add extra and know the clones won't pick them out."

"That's all good, but how are we supposed to get them in the sauce?" My brain drew a blank.

Devon glanced around the courtyard. "Ann?"

She nodded. "I can do it."

Devon took her hand. "You sure?"

"Positive."

Lucy let out a deep breath. "Good, we'll need to make sure only the two clones eat the mushrooms."

"The dinners will be in clearly marked individual servings with each prisoner's number so that shouldn't be a problem," Devon added. "Because they only have two prisoners it will be easy to avoid a mix-up."

"We'll dig up the mushrooms first," I offered. "We'll just need to sauté the mushrooms in a tomato sauce before we put them in the clone's dinner. Also, whoever breaks into the kitchen will need to leave some mushroom residue in the refrigerator. That's what will make it look like an accident when they do their investigation afterward."

"That's brilliant!" Lucy smiled and raised an eyebrow. "You have a devious mind, anyone ever tell you that?"

"Thanks, Lucy." I took her comment as a compliment. "I'd also like to be the one who puts the mushrooms into the lasagna." I'd fulfill the prophecy.

"You want to break in?" Archer stilled, and his intense gaze focused on me.

Devon shot Archer a look and then studied me for a moment.. "Ann will need help once she's in the kitchen. Sadie should be the one to deliver the meals because the clones won't know who she is. Ann can hang back and try to get a read on the Jacks."

Lucy leaned toward me. "She's a supercharged Reader/Jack/Seer. She can do it all."

Archer had already told me, so I just nodded.

"I heard that." Ann elbowed Lucy. "She didn't mention that some of my abilities are limited because I'm only a third of each. But Lucy is right. Because I have all three races, I'm the only one who can read the Jacks."

"Yep." Lucy nodded and smiled at Ann. "That skill will sure come in handy today."

"Ugh. I can only imagine the ugly thoughts coming from them. The Jacks are an evil...." Ann straightened. "Oh, sorry, Archer."

He shrugged. "I doubt you hate them more than I do."

I studied him. Was he lying? I looked for the telltale signs. Shifting eyes. Tugging on a collar. Wiping the back of his neck. Fidgeting. Nope, nothing. Just those hurt and vulnerable eyes. Could that be faked?

"I doubt that." Adam joined our group and plopped Henry in the seat next to Ann. "He slept like a champ, but I think he's hungry."

Ann grabbed her diaper bag. "I have just the thing." She pulled out a bottle, and Henry smiled and gurgled his baby sounds of delight.

My stomach dropped, and, for the first time in two thousand years, the loss and absence of having children in my life squeezed at my heart. Before the Great War, children were an integral part of our daily lives. All the joy and laughter were sucked from us on that horrible day. The Seer children were killed, and the Readers were no longer able to conceive. Until Henry. The negativity of the Jacks needed to be erased from the world before more Reader children could thrive on the planet again.

But now the Jacks were back. And if instructions were left behind on cloning, there was the possibility of them multiplying if we didn't stop them.

"How about we get started on the plan?"

Adam perked up. "What? There's a plan?"

Lucy rubbed his arm. "I'll get you caught up later." She smiled at Adam, and they locked eyes.

His expression softened, and he moved a lock of her unruly red hair over to the side, his eyes never leaving her. Wow, Lucy was lucky to have someone devoted to her. My stomach sank again. Geez, what was wrong with me? First, I was missing children, now love.

Get a grip.

I could live just fine without either. I'll kill the last Jack like the visions foretold, then I'd go back to my cottage on the bluff.

Alone.

"Hey, what are you thinking about?" Archer's voice was low as he tipped his head in my direction.

"Nothing," I lied.

"You looked, I don't know, kinda lost."

I glared at him.

"Okay, now you look pissed. Never mind." He laughed.

My blood boiled, and my cheeks took most of the heat. "What do you know about anything? You're just a...a...a Jack," I spat out before my mind caught up with the words.

Archer's face fell, and he looked away.

"Damn straight," Adam muttered under his breath.

Now I felt like a jerk.

Devon rapped his knuckles on the table. "Okay, everyone. Let's get back to the plan." I liked how Devon kept the group on task. I also appreciated the change of subject.

Lucy turned to me. "Sadie, do you think you'll be able to find the mushrooms we need in the next few hours?"

"Sure. We passed through a large forest about five miles north. The death cap mushroom likes shade, so some of those big oak trees would be a good spot to look."

"Good plan." Ann winked and turned back to the group. "I can take Sadie mushroom hunting. Then we can go back to the hotel and sauté those suckers."

"Ann, I'll take Henry while you and Sadie go on your errands." Devon picked up Henry from his booster seat.

"What about me?" Lucy asked Devon.

"Stay here with Adam and monitor any unusual activity around the courthouse. Call me if you notice anything off."

"Okay. Looks like coffee and a crossword puzzle are in my future." Lucy slouched in her chair.

"And Archer, stay hidden in the hotel until we leave. We

don't want the police to think one of their prisoners has escaped."

Archer sighed and rose from the table. "You're right. I'm lucky there hasn't been a lot of activity today."

Devon cast a glance at the entrance to the police station. "They're probably focusing all their manpower making sure those two don't escape. This is a big deal for a small town. The US Marshalls will come tomorrow to take over. We need to move fast."

Ann looped her arm through mine. "Let's go, Sadie. Our first mission is to find those death cap mushrooms."

Forty minutes later, I considered my options, which included giving up. My hands and legs were scratched and bleeding because of all the bending and digging while trying to locate the mushrooms. I stood, stretched my arms over my head, and breathed in the air, thick with the smell of vegetation. I also questioned my decision to wear shorts and a T-shirt today. Full protective gear would have been a better choice. But then again, I hadn't planned to kill off two Jack clones either.

"Hey, I found something." Ann wiped her forehead while pointing with her free hand.

I grabbed the small plastic bag and approached to get a better look. Sure enough, the mushrooms were a greenish yellow color with a white stalk. The size looked right—about four inches. I picked up a stick and moved one mushroom to the side. Yep—there it was. The telltale sign of the death cap under the dome: a pinkish brown color to the gills. "We have a winner here," I said and scooped up five into the bag. "We only need one mushroom for each, but, to make certain, we'll double the dose and add one extra, so we can leave the residue in the restaurant."

"Yay." Ann bounced on her heels. "We even have a few minutes to spare. Come on." She waved me toward a fallen tree. "We can rest for a minute on this log before we head back."

"Sounds good." I wiped the moisture from my forehead and didn't argue, even though I was eager to get this task over and done with.

Ann dug around in her backpack and produced two bottles of water.

"You're a saint." I took the cool, plastic bottle and twisted the top open.

Ann turned her face up to the filtered sunlight. "It's peaceful here."

Once I let myself relax a little, I had to admit, the quiet calmed me.

I'm here to kill two Jacks.

I stood. The serenity vanished. Poof! Probably fleeing through the woods never to be felt again.

Ann patted the log next to her. "Sit back down."

After taking a deep breath and rubbing my sweaty palms against my shorts, I avoided the looming panic attack. I'd only experienced a few, but when they came, there was no stopping them. I sat back down on the log. "Sorry. You're probably thinking I'm crazy. One minute I'm roaring to go kill the Jacks, and the next, I'm scared to death." I grasped my shaking hands in my lap.

Ann put her hand on my back. "It's true we have to take lives today. But please remember, we'll be saving thousands, if not millions, by doing so."

I nodded. "I know. My mind knows it, but the reality gets a

little tricky when I think too much about it." I smoothed my T-shirt and pressed my lips together, but the question blurted out anyway. "You think Atarah is behind everything? That she framed Archer? It seems like a stretch."

Ann smiled softly. "Yeah, it does." She met my eyes. "Sadie?"

"Yes?" My heart beat faster.

"If I tell you some things, will you keep them secret?"

"Of course." Whatever she told me would stay sealed. "I'm great at keeping secrets."

She studied me for a few seconds. "I believe you," she said, then took a deep breath. "The Elders don't want us digging around about the past. Lucy and I plan to search every square inch back at Samara anyway to get to the truth."

"Really?"

Ann gazed out into the forest. "We'd all like to forget. But now that Archer's back, it's more important to get to the truth and find out how much Atarah had to do with Archer's behavior."

"Could you get in trouble?"

"Yes, but we'll just make sure we don't get caught."

"You'd risk that for Archer, a Jack?"

"Part Jack. And yes, if he is innocent, we need to clear his name. Those Jacks worked on mind control for hundreds of years. We think they used Archer as their guinea pig."

I bit my lip. "I hadn't even thought of that possibility."

"When Archer kidnapped me, I believed I was witnessing his true side. But after thinking about it, I realize how weird and different he was acting."

"How so?"

"He seemed robotic, kinda out of it. I thought it might be the stress, but after seeing him again, I'm convinced Atarah was the one pulling the strings. Remember, he spent thousands of years with the Readers. Then he met Atarah, and everything changed."

"Is it possible he changed his mind?"

"I spent three months with Archer and Devon. You can't fake that kind of friendship or camaraderie." Her lips pressed together, and she hesitated. "No. We spent countless hours talking about everything. Our hopes and dreams and future plans for the Reader Compound. After the shock of it all—the betrayal, the plans for the wedding and, ultimately, the explosion that saved the Readers, but took my parents—I remembered some of the details. It clouded my memory for the first year. Then I questioned everything. Archer's behavior, that night, the explosion."

"I'm so sorry about your parents." It was my turn to comfort her.

She put her hand on her chest and rubbed a little. "Thanks. I'm healing, but sometimes it still hurts."

"Have you talked to Devon about your doubts about Archer?"

"A little. It's a hard subject to bring up for obvious reasons." She chuckled. "He kidnapped me and tried to force me to marry him. It looks bad for Archer, but I have this feeling..."

"Can you prove any of this?"

She leaned forward. "I might. If we could gain access to the old digital files, they may prove Archer didn't kill Markus. Then we'll have our answer to at least a small part of what happened."

"Can't you just ask Archer's dad? He's an Elder, right?"

"Archer's dad has always been ultra conservative. He's always about following the rules and never deviating. Archer never measured up in his father's eyes, so their relationship has always been strained and sometimes awkward. It's probably why Atarah coerced him so easily." She brushed some hair off her face. "His dad would never give permission, so we'll need to keep this top secret."

That makes sense.

"What do we do?" I asked.

"We get business taken care of here first." She held up the bag of mushrooms. "Then we get back to Samara and start searching. I want to see what happened the day Markus died."

"Think you'll find anything?"

Her smile started slow, but reached across her face. "Oh yeah. By the time we're done, we'll know exactly what happened."

CHAPTER 9

Archer

"I'LL KEEP AN eye on Sadie," I told Devon. I leaned over the small hotel kitchenette counter and watched Devon pour a can of chopped tomatoes into a pan and place it on a small burner.

"Oh, I bet you will." He tried to cover his smirk with a cough.

"It's not like *that*. She seems, I don't know, almost naïve, but she puts on a brave front." I shifted on the stool.

He met my eyes. "Yeah. Trusting. We're all guilty of that."

His words might have well been a punch to my gut. "About—"

"No." He put his hand up. "We have plenty of time to hash that out when we get back to Samara. For right now, I want to focus on taking these Jacks out, so they can't inflict more damage."

The door burst open, and Ann, followed by a giggling Sadie, stumbled into the room.

"Success!" Sadie held up a clear bag of large mushrooms. "Ann found them." She waved the bag around. "She saved me from a certain death of thorn bushes versus Seer."

"Uh, you girls weren't ingesting any of those by any chance?" I asked, only partly joking. But they were acting strange.

"No." Ann shook her head and joined in with Sadie's giggles. "I learned today, when Sadie gets nervous, she laughs, and it's contagious."

They broke into another round. Ann grabbed Sadie's arm. "Oh, we have to stop and get you cleaned up."

Cleaned up? My eyes shifted down to her legs. In two strides, I took Sadie by the sleeve of her T-shirt. "You're coming with me."

Her eyes widened, and she tried to pull away. "What do you think you're doing? Let go of me!"

"What do you think I'm doing? You have open wounds, and you were out in the forest with poisonous mushrooms. The exposure is not enough to kill you, but you could get sick."

She paled, and her mouth formed an O. "Oops." She glanced at Ann and tried to stifle another giggle.

"Come on." I pulled her toward the bathroom.

"Quit pulling my T-shirt." She tried to keep her feet planted, but I yanked hard. "Wait a minute. I'm not going into the bathroom with you. Nope. That's not gonna happen."

We were at the door. "Either you come in on your own, or I'll pick you up."

Her eyes narrowed. "You wouldn't."

Without giving her time to think about it, I scooped her into my arms and walked through the door. With my foot, I shut the door before I plopped her down. That electric buzzing sensation zapped through me, almost knocking me to my knees. I shook out my arms and studied her expression to see if she'd felt it. Blank. It must just be me.

She raised an eyebrow. "Am I too heavy for you or something?" she asked, but her voice wavered.

I walked past her and turned on the shower. "Okay, get in."

"Not with you in here." Her chin rose.

"I won't look. If you're worried about it, just get in with your clothes on. I have to make sure your wounds are clean before I apply the ointment." I took a deep breath to keep my patience.

She scowled and didn't move.

"I assume you have other clothes?" I'd never been a patient person, and she was pushing me to the edge.

"Yes. But I can do it myself."

That's it.

I checked the water to make sure it was the right temperature. I prepared myself by gritting my teeth and scooped her up again.

Oh hell. My entire body feels like it's on fire.

She squirmed. I glared, waiting for permission.

"You don't scare me." Her words sounded strong, but she could hardly catch her breath. She reached over and scratched at one of the red welts on her legs.

"Well?" I cocked my head, not believing I'd met someone more stubborn than me.

She groaned. "Fine. But make it quick."

Not willing to wait for her to change her mind, I jumped in. The water beat down on both of us, soaking our hair and clothes from head to toe as we locked eyes—a power struggle she would lose. I set her down and backed her up against the shower wall, our faces only millimeters apart. The water seemed to intensify the warm currents running through my body. Now that I was touching her for longer than a few seconds, I realized the sensation was good. Maybe even the best I'd ever felt.

Why her? Why now?

Did she feel it? I let my hands run up and down her arms. She turned like she would pull away, but instead closed her eyes and shivered. I wrapped an arm around her and pressed closer. Her head tilted upward, and her lips parted. "Sadie," I whispered and leaned toward her. I wanted to be near her, to protect her. "I'll never hurt—"

Bang. Bang. Bang.

"What's going on in there?" Lucy shouted through the door.

We both jumped back away from each other. That was close. What was I thinking?

Sadie yelled back, "Archer's gone all alpha on me and thinks he is the only one who can clean my scratches." She crossed her arms and glared at me. She tried to appear nonchalant, but the rapid pulse in her neck gave her away.

"That's because he's the only one with the ointment. Archer, you did bring it, right?" Lucy called through the door.

"Yep." I reached out of the bathtub stall and grabbed the tube from my shaving kit. Sadie backed farther away. "The Readers developed this about a hundred years ago. It basically kills any bacteria or poison on contact. You may get a little sick because the spores had time to work into your blood, but this should take care of any major symptoms."

"Oh. Well. I can do it myself." Her pretty face flushed.

"No, you can't. It was formulated only for the Readers to touch with their hands. If a non-Reader touches it, it will burn right through their fingers. It was formulated to discourage the Jacks from developing chemical warfare.. If we're already protected by the ointment, the Jacks wouldn't bother with the poisons."

"It will burn me?"

"No. It will only affect your fingers. The Reader scientists didn't want the Jacks to use it. They altered the chemical structure so only someone with Reader DNA could apply it." I glanced down at her legs. The blood was gone. I turned off the water and hopped out of the shower. "Sit here." I motioned to the edge of the toilet.

She stayed put with her arms crossed.

"Are you always this stubborn?"

"Yes." She huffed and got out.

"Sit." I pointed.

She rolled her eyes and complied. After removing the cap of the ointment, I squeezed a little out on my fingers. "See, doesn't hurt." I gently dried her leg with a towel and dabbed a little on her largest scratch. "That okay?"

She smiled. "It tingles."

"About the tingling," I started. As soon as the words left my mouth, she straightened and looked away. "Is that normal with you? You felt that, right?"

She shook her head vigorously. "I felt nothing. Nope. Nothing. I don't know what you're talking about. Why would I feel anything? That would be ridiculous. I mean, who feels stuff? I can't imagine what you mean." She halted and pressed her lips together. She turned her head away and whispered, "Ugh. So stupid."

"Hey, you guys about done? We have a meeting in five," Lucy shouted through the door.

"Almost," I yelled back, and then glared at Sadie. "If you sit still, I can finish this up."

A deep sigh and an "okay" followed.

I rubbed a fine coat of the ointment over the rest of her legs. It seemed to help reduce the zapping sensation when I touched her. Maybe I needed to carry this for my own protection.

"Thank you. It feels better."

Our eyes connected again. That shimmering was back. She looked away and stood up. "Okay, well, I have mushrooms to sauté."

"Why do your eyes shimmer like that?" I didn't think she'd tell me, but I asked anyway.

She stilled. "Shimmer?"

"Yeah. It's almost like looking into a river, all swirly."

"The Seers eyes shimmer sometimes, but only other Seers are supposed to see it. All this craziness and stress probably has something to do with it."

"Why only Seers?"

"Uh. It's so we can identify each other. I didn't think it worked anymore. It's kinda weird you can see it. I wonder if it's because you're multiracial."

I shrugged. "No idea."

"Maybe it only happens when I get stressed." She grabbed a

towel and wrung the excess water out of her hair.

"Perhaps." Was she lying?

Sadie motioned to the exit. "We better go before Lucy breaks down the door. And now, because of you, I have to change my clothes and shoes."

"I save your life and that's the thanks I get?" I tried not to laugh. "And you're forgetting that in my rush to, you know, save your life, I also got wet."

"How did it go from getting sick from mushroom spores to dying?" She put her hands on her hips and tilted her head.

"Okay, so you might have just *felt* like dying. But still." I chuckled.

More knocking. Ugh, Lucy again. "She's worried about you in here alone with me." I raised my eyebrows up and down a few times.

"Ha ha. She knows I can take care of myself."

"Can you?"

"What is that supposed to mean?"

"Well." I thought for a second about another excuse, but nothing came. "You seem trusting."

"And that's a bad thing?"

"It can be if you trust the wrong people. You want to see the best in everyone."

"Do you fall into that category? Untrustworthy?" She seemed to stop breathing while she waited for my answer.

"No. When this is all said and done, it will probably be me saving you from someone you shouldn't have trusted."

"Cocky much?"

I laughed. "Perhaps. But it's the truth."

She groaned. "Let's go see about this meeting. I don't want your head to explode before we get this done."

Two hours later, I was ready to crawl up the hotel walls. Devon, Lucy, and Adam were in the same shape. The air seemed energy charged, thick with anticipation. This had to work.

"Ann and Sadie will be all right," Lucy said for the hundredth time as she paced the room. "They'll be in and out of there in no time at all."

Adam grabbed her hand as she made a pass by the dining room table. "Here. Sit down. They aren't late. You'll wear yourself out."

Lucy nodded and let out a deep breath. "I have a bad feeling about those Jacks." She blinked back tears. "I thought we were rid of them. Our world was finally learning how to interact in a peaceful way. If this doesn't work, who knows what they'll do next." She flopped down on the chair next to Adam and put her head on his shoulder. He whispered something I couldn't hear and rubbed her back.

Adam stood. "I'm going out to get sandwiches. The usual?"

We all nodded. Not hungry at all, but it was important to keep our energy up.

Even though I'd never liked Adam much, I was happy Lucy had someone so devoted to her. A flutter of sadness whirled around inside my chest. The darkness of loss started to suffocate me like it always did whenever I thought of Ann. *Wait.* This time it was only a flutter instead of a piercing pain, and the darkness wasn't black, but a light gray. My eyes shifted to Devon. He sat across from Adam and was staring at a blank wall, his fingers tapping an impatient rhythm.

My head cleared. Devon really loved Ann. It wasn't a competition. It wasn't just to win. He didn't take Ann away from me to be spiteful. They were meant to be together. Why had it taken me so long to figure it out?

"The Jacks' brainwashing lasts for about two years." Devon said.

My eyes just about bugged out of my head.

"I'm not reading you, but I've been watching you since Portland. It's wearing off, isn't it?"

I nodded. "Yeah."

He let out a deep breath. "That confirms it then."

"What do you mean?"

"That Atarah and the Jacks used their brain control methods to compel you to carry out their mission. Now that it's wearing off, you seem more like yourself."

"I don't know." I rubbed my temples. "I always felt in control. My feelings were real."

"That's how the process was designed. After you died...I mean, left Samara, our scouting team reported back about the Jack experiments on mortals. In every case, they believed what they were told. To test them, the Jacks instructed them to commit murder."

Murder. My throat constricted, and my stomach clenched. Markus. I loved him like a brother, and yet I—My thoughts stopped. I couldn't bear to remember what I'd done. "I'd love to think I wasn't responsible for killing Markus, but there's no way to know. Atarah died. Even though her little science project has hatched, she wouldn't have given the clones the information about what really happened."

"I think—"

The hotel door swung open and hit the rubber stopper on the wall. Ann entered first, wild-eyed, pale, and out of breath.

"Where's Henry?" Her eyes darted around the room.

"He's sleeping in the bedroom," I told her.

Sadie came in next, looking just as stricken. "We have to go now. Right now."

"Why?" Devon and I both asked at the same time.

Lucy jumped out of her chair and grabbed the keys and some snacks.

"No!" Ann shouted. "We don't have time. It's a trap. They're coming."

"Trap?" Devon grabbed Ann by the shoulders. "Who's coming?"

She squeezed her eyes closed. "More Jacks. They poisoned the well to draw us out. They also said something about a phone signal, but I couldn't figure it out. We have to get out of here now."

Devon swore under his breath. "I'll grab Henry. Ann, get to the car and start it up." He said to the group, "We only have seconds. If the Jacks have pinpointed us, they won't waste time."

Lucy held up the keys. "I'm ready."

Before I could even move, Devon shouted, "Go! Go!"

Lucy grabbed Devon's arm. "What about Adam? Is he in danger?"

"I don't know. We'll swing by the sandwich shop and get him. Now move." Devon ran into the bedroom, and Ann grabbed the diaper bag by the door.

Sadie tapped my arm. "I have the keys."

We all left at a dead run down the long corridor to the exit stairwell, taking the two flights to the ground floor. Once in the lobby, we tried to look natural as we exited through the revolving doors. My heart raced, and I barely felt Sadie's iron grip on my arm as we broke out into another run toward our cars in the overflow lot about a block away.

Sadie's hands shook as she handed me the keys. "I don't think I can drive, can you?"

"Yes." I pulled her close. "Don't worry. It'll be okay." Her entire body trembled, and I wanted to comfort her, but it would have to wait.

Ann buckled Henry into his car seat, while Devon gave instructions. "Let's hit Highway 60 East, hook onto Route 180 North, and double back on Highway 40. If they have any Jack scouts posted, they'll most likely be checking 93, but keep your eyes open."

"Oh no." Sadie stood stock still and stared at the hotel.

"What is it?" I asked. Her eyes were frantic.

"Everyone get behind the cars! There's a bomb in the hotel!"

I grabbed Sadie as the last words came from her mouth. We crouched behind the car. Ann and Devon jumped into the Jeep to shield Henry's body.

I kept my eyes on the hotel when red and blue lights flashed, almost blinding me. A vibration and a loud grumbling started. For a second, it was eerily silent, then the explosion blasted out the windows to both our rooms on the second floor. Muffled wailing of car alarms started all around us in the parking lot. A huge plume of smoke and fire rose from the hotel windows. Shards of glass, wood, metal, and what looked like fabric rained to the ground. The taste of chemical fumes burned my tongue, but we were far enough from the blast zone. We were safe. For now.

Devon jumped out of the car. "What the hell?"

Ann stood with her hand over her mouth. "We're okay."

Devon wrapped her in a tight hug.

"I hope no one was hurt or..." Ann looked back at the hotel.

"Were those our rooms?" Lucy choked out. "What about Adam? We didn't leave him a note. If he took the elevator, we could have missed him. He might have been in the room waiting for us." She cried into her hands. "If Adam dies, I don't think—"

Devon tried to calm her. "It was too quick. There wasn't enough time to get the sandwiches and get back." His eyes shifted around the parking lot. "We have to get out of sight in case they're still around."

"Okay." Lucy stood a little straighter and wiped her tears. "You're right. He'll be okay. He has to be okay."

Just as she finished her sentence, Adam came around the corner, and stood in front of the hotel, staring at the remnants of the explosion with his back to us.

He must think we're all dead.

Lucy started toward him. I grabbed her arm. "It's too dangerous. We'll pick him up on our way out."

Adam grabbed his cell from his back pocket and put it to his ear.

"He's calling now." She rummaged through her purse. "Where is my phone? Where is it? I need to talk to Adam."

Devon tugged on her arm. "Let's go pick him up instead. We have to get out of here." He practically pushed her into his car and nodded at me. "Follow behind. You remember where the gun is?"

"The usual?"

"Yep."

"Got it."

The shrill sound of emergency sirens, most likely fire and police, increased in volume as they drew closer.

Sadie and I jumped into the car, and I started the motor. Devon screeched out of his parking space. Adam turned toward the sound of the Jeep, and his mouth dropped open.

"Oh, poor Adam," Sadie said. "It's like he's looking at ghosts."

Devon's car careened around a few cars in the lot and sped the one block to Adam. I heard him yell, "Get in. Now!" Adam dove into the back seat of Devon's car before it came to a stop. The Jeep screeched out onto the street toward Highway 60.

We followed at a safe distance for about a mile. After a few turns, my heart slowed, and my vision and hearing seemed to return to normal.

I glanced over at Sadie. "So, what did you do today?"

CHAPTER 10

Sadie

"Very." I took a breath. "Funny." When I inhaled, what felt like a scorching fire burned from my throat into my lungs. "I can't...I can't breathe right." I put my head between my knees.

Archer pulled the car over to the side of the road. "You're hyperventilating." He reached into the back seat and dumped toiletry items out of a paper bag. "Here, breathe into this."

Spots formed before my eyes. I breathed in once. "It doesn't." I tried again. "Work." I needed fresh air. I fumbled with the door handle and got it open. I needed out.

Please don't faint. I bent over and placed my hands on my knees.

"Give it a chance." The words were muffled like I was in a tunnel. He placed the bag over my mouth and nose. I tried to calm myself while Archer's hand rubbed my back.

Slowly, the breaths went back to normal, and the black

spots disappeared. "I'm okay now."

He scanned me up and down. "Are you sure? You don't look so good."

The jerk! "Am I supposed to look good after someone tried to kill us? Is that in the Reader or Jack handbook? Because it's not in the Seer guide." My fear turned to anger.

Archer held his hands up. "I thought you needed a few more minutes."

Ugh. He was right. My shoulders slumped. "I'm sorry. I'm just freaked out."

"Don't blame you. We haven't talked about what went down today. How bad was it?"

I put my hands on my hips. "Well, it started out with my legs getting all scratched up while trying to dig up poisonous mushrooms. Then, for my efforts, I got shoved into a shower and had some super-secret ointment put on my body."

"No, I meant at the jail." His lips pressed together.

"Are you laughing at me?" If he was, I'd kick him.

"Me? No, no." His face went blank.

My eyes narrowed as I studied him, not sure if I believed him. "We're sitting ducks out here on the side of the road."

"That's true. You want to get back in?" He tilted his head and smiled.

"Not really."

"How about we stop and get lunch? When I scouted the area yesterday, I found a greasy spoon restaurant about a mile off the road. It's tucked away, so we should be safe."

French fries and a milkshake.

"I guess so." I stomped over to the car and flopped myself into the passenger seat. Archer got behind the wheel, started the car back up, and pulled out onto the highway.

Twenty minutes later, six French fries were crammed into my mouth. Archer had discovered the perfect spot. A themed 1950s diner with a jukebox and a waitress by the name of Betsy. The white lace curtains with ketchup stains added to the ambiance.

"Are you ready to tell me what happened at the jail?"

Really? Now he asks. "You didth that on purposth." Bits of French fries sprayed from my mouth.

He pursed his lips and shook his head.

I grabbed my chocolate milkshake and took a sip. Since it was midafternoon, we were the only customers, so we could speak freely. "Okay, here's how it went down." I ate one more fry. "Did you know Ann could put thoughts into people's minds, and they believe it's their own?"

"Yep. Comes in handy."

"She had one of the cooks take out the garbage, so we snuck into the kitchen when he wasn't looking. Then she planted the thought that both cooks and the dishwasher had to go to the bathroom." I smiled remembering. "You should have seen them shoving at each other to get out the door first. Anyway, we had those mushrooms placed into the lasagna for the clones within a few minutes. Then we scattered the residue into the walk-in pantry."

"That was it?"

"No!" I put down my milkshake. "I thought it would be. But when the cooks came back, Ann did another mind thing on them. The head cook asked me to deliver the lunches to the prisoners."

Archer nodded. "Smart. Were you nervous?"

"Yes. I was shaking like a leaf. Ann warned me they might read my mind, so I needed to keep it blank or focus hard on something, so they'd only get the surface thoughts."

"I can't read your mind, so they shouldn't be able to."

I shrugged. "Ann wasn't sure if they mutated any of the DNA, so it was just a precaution."

"What did you focus on?"

"Something they'd believe." I tried to hold back my smile.

He quirked an eyebrow. "And?"

"I thought about how handsome they were."

Archer threw his head back and laughed. "You didn't."

"I did."

He shook his head. "You're something else."

I shivered, remembering. "They were creepy."

"Thanks a lot." He frowned.

"No, Archer, not like that. They look like you, sure, but they didn't have your soul. Does that make sense?"

He rubbed his chin. "Yeah, I guess."

"I sensed something evil. It's like they've got your genetics, but not the essence of who you are." I thought for a moment. "I think they're soulless."

He shot me a glance before he looked out the window. "I worried that might happen. They were manufactured and given specific instructions. I just hope the ones remaining don't evolve. It could get worse."

My stomach tightened. "That's comforting."

He turned his attention back to me. "I don't want you to be scared, but I needed to warn you just in case we run into more of them. They might not be this easy to kill next time, if, in fact, they're dead. Were you able to see them eat the dinner?"

"No, they were too busy staring at me. Like I said, it was creepy. But I don't think they suspected anything."

He took a bite of his cheeseburger and swallowed. "Tell me again what Ann found out."

"She picked up enough to know that the poisoning of the well was to shake the Readers out of hiding. They want them dead. That's their goal, or maybe what was implanted into their memory card or whatever you call it. When I returned from delivering the food, Ann gave the head cook the thought of serving the meal to the prisoners. She gave the other cook and dishwasher the same memory and a few more so they wouldn't remember either of us in the kitchen."

He leaned forward placing his elbows on the table. "And...anything else?"

"Ann also said something about a phone and a connection in Oregon. But she wasn't able to pinpoint the city or location." I sighed.

"There's a Jack spy in Oregon orchestrating this?" He frowned.

"Appears so."

He rubbed the back of his neck and looked out the window again.

I sat up straighter and studied his profile. His face was almost perfect. High cheekbones, a strong jaw, a straight-edged nose with the slightest bump at the bridge, giving it more character. And from a side angle, I could analyze his thick, dark eyelashes that curved up almost to his eyebrows. It wasn't fair; only women should have eyelashes like that. No doubt, he was a beautiful man. I stifled a chuckle knowing Archer wouldn't appreciate my labeling him beautiful.

Still gazing out the window, he said, "I hope it worked and those Jacks are dead. Then we'll need to track down the last one."

My heart squeezed. How many more Jacks would I need to kill? Would my life ever be normal again?

After a few minutes, he asked, "What's going on with you? I thought your visions only came every five years or so. This makes two in a short amount of time."

"Yeah, I was thinking about that. I wonder if it has something to do with the clones? Maybe the stress of everything is putting my spidey senses on high alert or something."

He nodded. "Makes sense. The Seers could always forecast evil. That's why the Jacks kill—I mean, well, that's why they wanted them gone."

"You don't have to sugarcoat it. I've had many years to adjust," I lied.

His expression softened. "I remember your parents."

"You do?" My heart kicked up a beat.

"My dad is an Elder. Did you know that?" His eyebrow arched.

"Ann mentioned it." Of course, I knew.

"Anyway, I snuck into one of the important meetings with the Seers and the Jacks." He shook his head. "My dad found out and became furious."

"What made him so angry? Was he worried about your safety?"

"Honestly, I think he feared the Readers would find out I was half Jack. He made me keep it a secret, like I was damaged goods." He chuckled, but I thought it was probably to cover the pain.

"That couldn't have felt good." A sudden urge to touch him, so he knew he wasn't alone, almost overcame me. What was wrong with me?

Jacks are the enemy. Archer is a Jack.

Well, only part Jack. Stop it, stop it, stop it. I would not fall into a trap of feeling sorry for Archer. He might be trying to trick me. The Jacks were sneaky.

But Lucy and Ann think he might be innocent.

"Did you know you sometimes talk about what you're feeling? It's quite entertaining." Archer snickered.

Ugh! "What did I say?"

"This time you told yourself to stop it. The rest was a little mumbled."

Thank goodness. "Oh, that. I was missing my cat." My cat? That was the best I could come up with? "I mean, I told Donna I'd only be a few days, and I wondered how Eve was doing."

"Okaaay."

"And I'm not a Cat Lady." Maybe I was a little, but I wouldn't give him the satisfaction.

"I'm sure you're not. The criteria is to have at least three to be a Cat Lady. You're just obsessed with your only cat." He smiled and winked at me.

My stomach dipped, and were those butterflies? And I'd broken out into a sweat, and my heart thumped an extra beat. Just a wink did this? I mean, in the shower, this type of reaction made sense; he was right up against me. Of course, there'd be a physical response. But now? He hadn't even touched me. Did that mean...?

"You look like you're going to throw up. Are you okay?" His teasing expression turned serious. A crease formed between his eyebrows, and his full lips turned down.

Quit looking at his lips!

"I'm better. But it's been a long week. I'll be glad to get home and sleep in my own bed before I head to Samara. I'm a little tired."

"We'll meet up in Portland and take different cars to Samara in case anyone is watching. Because we're already car buddies, Devon asked me to stay behind and pick you up when you're ready."

"Goodie."

"I'll ignore your sarcasm. Will five days be enough to get everything in order? You might be in Samara for a long time."

"How long is a long time?"

"Months, maybe even years."

"Years! Um, no. That will not happen. I'm not staying underground in some compound for years. I need the ocean, fresh air, room to breathe."

He smiled, and his eyes crinkled. "Just wait and see."

Another two long days later, and we pulled up to my cottage. Ahhh, so good to be home. I glanced at Donna's house. Eve. My arms ached to pick her up and cuddle. I'd tell her about all my adventures and she'd rub her wet nose against my face.

"Who's that?" Archer asked.

"Who?"

"Right there sitting on your porch swing. Who's that guy?"

I followed his finger pointing in the direction of the intruder. But it wasn't an intruder at all.

"Oh, that's only Ian."

"Only?"

"Yeah. He's good, you know, being the mayor's son and all."

Archer put his head in his hands and didn't move.

"What's the matter?"

"Did it occur to you he could be a Jack? He might be the spy in Oregon they talked about."

"Ian?"

"Yes, Ian." He glared at him through the car window.

"He's been around for two years. You think he's some evil Jack, going to college, doing handiwork for sweet, retired people like Donna? What's his motivation? If you haven't noticed, this is a small town, and not much happens. Your logic makes little sense."

He turned his green eyes my way and the muscles of his jaw clenched as he studied me.

"What?" Impatience simmered below the surface.

"How long have you lived here?"

"Two years. But that means nothing. I just came to watch you." Oh. My brain cells came alive and figured out what he was getting at. "You think he's here because of you?"

"And the light bulb goes on." He turned to eyeball Ian a little more.

"If that's true, why wouldn't he have made his move already? I mean, they tried to blow us up in Arizona. Why wouldn't he take you out here?"

He shook his head. "I don't know. Maybe I'm just paranoid." He opened the car door and got out.

"Hey. What are you doing? You're just supposed to drop me off and be on your way."

"I'm not leaving until I'm sure you're safe. Come on. Introduce me to the mayor's son." And he winked again. *Grrr*.

I left my things in the rental car and tried to beat Archer to the front door. "Hey, Ian. This is a nice surprise."

The history book on his lap fell to the ground when he jumped up. "Sorry, I was so absorbed in reading, I didn't hear you pull up."

Archer slung his arm around my shoulder. "Hi, Ian. I'm Archer." He reached out his other hand to shake Ian's.

I tried to pull away, but he just held on tighter. Ian's eyes widened as he got the wrong impression. "Oh, so sorry to interrupt. I came to finish the job with Donna and check on your cat. And then I thought I'd just hang here." He cleared his throat. "Again, sorry."

Poor guy, he looked like he wanted to sink into a hole and disappear. I gave Archer a push and got free. "No need to apologize. You can sit here any time you'd like, especially if you're here checking on Eve. I'm sure my *friend*, Archer, would agree." I shot him a death glare.

"Whatever you say, honey." He gave me an innocent smile.

"Anyway, Archer is going now." I gave him a nudge with my elbow. "I'll see you whenever."

"Five days. Sooner if you need me." He became serious and his green eyes bored into mine. He was actually worried. Hmm.

Before I forgot, I ran back to his car and grabbed my overnight bag. Archer came from behind me and whispered, "I don't trust him. He's too good-looking to be mortal."

"What?" I yelled in my best whisper voice. "You don't trust him because he's hot? That's crazy."

"Remember, the Jacks try to get the best looking, most physically fit humans to hijack."

I shifted my bag to my other shoulder. "Aren't you forgetting something?"

"What?"

"Motivation. If he planned to do either of us harm, don't you think he would have done so, I don't know, maybe like, two years ago?"

"Just watch yourself. Remember what I told you about trust."

"Yeah, and you're a Boy Scout."

He winced.

What was it about Archer that brought out my snarky side? "I didn't mean that. I think—"

"I know what you think." He turned his back, got in the car, and drove off.

That went well.

"I hope I wasn't the cause for that." Ian moved right next to me.

I jumped back a little. "You startled me!"

Archer's warnings made me paranoid, but Ian's baritone laugh set me right at ease. "No. It's just the way Archer is. He's annoying."

A smile lit his face. "I could see that." He reached for my bag. "Here, let me take this."

I held on tighter.

"That's right. I almost forgot. You don't like anyone touching your things." He pulled his hand back. "It's a habit. My bad."

"No worries." I started toward my front door. "I have breakable items in there, so, you know."

Ian followed me up the steps. "I don't want to make this awkward or anything." He crossed his arms and shifted. "But I really want to take you out."

What? "Like on a date?"

He chuckled. "That's usually how it goes."

"Why?" I blurted.

He cocked his head. "Do you have a mirror?"

"Yeesss." Of course I owned a mirror. Didn't everyone? I narrowed my eyes while I tried to figure him out.

"Do you ever look in it?" His eyes seemed to dance as he pressed his lips together.

"Oh." He thought I was pretty?

"But that's not the only reason," he said. "I enjoyed getting to know you during our trip to Portland and wanted to follow up on my promise to take you on a hike along the coast."

I'd almost forgotten. Hesitation took hold. Archer was right. Ian was incredibly handsome. Maybe too good-looking? Could he be a Jack? I looked into his eyes and searched for deception. Nothing. His cheeks were a little flushed, almost like he was embarrassed because of my hesitation.

"Sounds like fun," came out of my mouth before I could

overanalyze it any more. I'd taken care of myself for centuries. I wouldn't live in fear. I needed a little normal in my life. I'd just pack my pepper spray and a stun gun. No problem. "When?"

"Tomorrow around eleven?"

That should give me plenty of time to catch up on my sleep. The fresh ocean air was just what I needed. "Sure, that'll work."

"Good. And don't worry about lunch. I've got that covered."

Did he just say he'd bring the food? "Impressive," I muttered. I stood and smiled at him like he was a piece of chocolate.

I'm pathetic. Wave a chicken leg at me and I'm all yours.

"Yoo-hoo! Look who I have here," Donna called from the front porch of her cottage. She held my sweet kitty in the crook of her arm.

"Eve!" I needed a cuddle, and quick.

Ian chuckled. "I guess that is my cue. See you tomorrow?"

I threw a "yep" over my shoulder as I fast-walked to Donna's house. I gently scooped Eve from Donna's arms and held her close, petting her nose to tail. "She feels so soft." I took a sniff. "And she smells like lavender." I took a closer look. "Her fur even looks whiter."

Donna laughed. "That's because I gave her a bath."

"Say what?"

"I thought she could use a little pick-me-up."

"I can barely get her to drink water." Dozens of times coaxing and pleading, even bribing would not get that cat in a bathtub. "How'd you do it?"

"Caviar. I put some in the water. By the time she'd chased it around the tub, she was nice and clean."

"You are a miracle worker. Thanks again for watching her." I snuggled her closer. "I missed her so much."

"I wouldn't have guessed it with the five calls a day." She chuckled.

"Geez. Sorry. I didn't realize I'd checked in that often." *Well, that's embarrassing.*

"Oh, honey. It was no problem at all. Eve is your companion, so you aren't all alone. I know what that's like." She rubbed my arm.

Do not cry. Do not cry.

I blinked a few times and took a few even breaths. When people were nice, it was the only time I'd break down. Not this time though. "Thanks. I appreciate it more than you'll ever know." When I looked at Donna's sweet and gentle face, my heart felt heavy. She reminded me of my grandmother, and I'd give anything to have her back. I needed to leave before I became a blubbering mess.

"Anytime." She reached over and gave Eve's head a soft scratch. "We had a grand ole time, didn't we sweetie? I left a few times, but never more than an hour."

"I hope you did something fun."

"I've been on street watch. Did you know, after most natural disasters, there are people who loot houses because the owners have left? Isn't that terrible?"

My stomach sank. "Yes, it's awful. But they put you on street watch? Isn't that dangerous?"

She laughed. "Oh, honey, they don't let us old folks in on the action. We get walkie-talkies and just report suspicious activity. They also said our presence on the street will act as a deterrent." Her eyes brightened. "This is the biggest thing to hit this town in decades! The city council called up everyone in town to help the merchants and residents along the waterfront. It's quite rewarding."

"It sounds like they have it organized well. Just remember to be careful." If anything happened to Donna... *Don't go there.*

"I will." Eve purred and rubbed against Donna's hand.

"Wow. She lets no one get close to her. You must be a cat whisperer or something."

"We have a special little bond. Don't we?" She whispered. "It's the caviar."

I laughed. "Nah, you're special, and that's why she likes you so much."

Donna's cheeks turned a little pink, and her eyes misted over. Maybe she was lonely just like me. "Have fun on your hike tomorrow." She gave a little wave and walked inside her house.

How did she know? Ugh. Small towns. Ian must have told her. I squeezed Eve close. "You'll never guess what I've been doing while I've been gone. Lots of adventures. I'll shower and put on *Gilmore Girls* again, and then tell you all about it."

Eve purred and licked my nose with her sandpaper tongue. "And I think Donna slipped caviar into your cat food." I'd seen her put a tin can into her bag of kibble.

After my shower and selecting my coziest pair of—yes—cat pajamas, I gathered up some popcorn for me and caviar for Eve. "This is my favorite episode. Rory goes to Yale."

Eve curled up on my lap as I filled her in on the five days I'd been gone. I yawned and rested my head on the sofa.

Knock. Knock. Knock.

Where was that coming from? Where was I? The dim light from the TV illuminated the room. My heart beat hummingbird fast while I tried to get my bearings. I was home. *Breathe.* Eve was asleep on the couch. *Relax.* A sliver of light filtered in through a crack between the curtains. *Oh no!* The exhaustion from the last week had caught up to me. I ran to the door and swung it open. "I'm so sorry, Ian. I overslept."

He looked me up and down. "I can see that. Those are the sexiest pajamas I've ever seen."

"Uh oh." I squeezed my eyes tight. After a few seconds of denial, I peeked down and decided a giant sinkhole would not be unwelcome.

"Really. I think they're cool. But you'll need warmer clothes for our hike. It's windy on the beach today."

"Okay. I'll be right back." I wondered if a person could die from embarrassment. Like, a heart attack or a stroke? "Come on in. You can hang with Eve." I didn't want Ian to have to wait too long, so I raced into my room and threw on some yoga pants and a sweatshirt. I darted back into the living room. "Ta da! Less than five minutes is a record for me."

He quit petting Eve and his mouth dropped open. "Wow. You did all that in five minutes? I think it's a record for everyone on the planet."

"I have many talents. This is just one of thousands." I laughed.

"You'll have to tell me all about it in the car. You ready?"

"I just need to grab my backpack." Including the pepper spray and stun gun I wouldn't need to use. But I liked to be prepared for anything.

"There's a cool overlook about five miles south. Are you hungry yet?"

I woke up famished. "Perhaps I could eat."

He laughed. "Okay, then picnic first, hike second."

"I'm agreeable to that plan."

We pulled over to a spectacular overlook in Arch Cape. Beautiful, and not a soul around. "Why aren't there any people here? This place is gorgeous."

"It's a town secret. Most locals know, if you jump the guardrail, there are quiet places for lunch and even better views."

"How far?" My energy was sapped, and I didn't want to be trudging around for miles.

"Ten-minute walk, tops." He smirked.

"I know you're thinking I'm a hiking baby, but I'm not. I'm a tired baby." Ugh. That sounded worse.

He broke out in laughter. "Come on, I don't want you to faint from hunger."

"Just ignore what comes out of my mouth today. I don't trust myself." I'd be kicking myself for weeks, maybe even months, for opening the door while wearing cat pajamas. Could this date start out any worse?

"Over here," he beckoned.

"Oh, it's lovely. It has a fabulous view, and I don't even have to worry about falling off the cliff." I loved being up so high to take advantage of the endless, ocean panorama. The sun beat down on the water, reflecting a sparkling sea with what appeared to be a million diamonds. A cloudless blue sky sent warmth that weaved into my soul. I needed this today. My body relaxed, and I leaned on a rusted iron fence that separated adventurous hikers from the sheer drop.

Ian put a checkered blanket on the ground about ten feet away. "Sit here, it has a better view." He rummaged through his backpack for the lunch. I hoped he brought a lot of food because this would be my breakfast and lunch. My stomach growled to confirm the thought.

I moved over and sat on the blanket. "The view is better over—" Within a second, my right wrist was handcuffed to the fence. "Wha—"

"It had to be done." Ian looked away, so I couldn't see his expression.

My backpack with my pepper spray and stun gun sat ten feet away. They turned out to be a false sense of security. Tears threatened, and I blinked furiously. I wouldn't die crying.

What a fool I've been. I should have listened to Archer.

CHAPTER 11

Archer

M Y GUT SCREAMED *don't leave her,* but my brain told me she was right. If Ian wanted to do either of us harm, he would've made his move by now.

But I didn't like the way he looked at her. Was that a good enough reason for me to sit on her front porch and tell him to stay away? I imagined the stormy look in Sadie's eyes if I showed up early and interfered with any socializing. She scared me a little, which, for some weird reason, I enjoyed. I liked the fire in her eyes, the way her cheeks turned red, and how her hands fisted when she was angry. It made me daydream about all the ways I could calm her down. Or make her angrier, because there was nothing more attractive than a woman with passion, and she had it flowing out of her like molten lava.

A vibration next to my leg snapped me out of my

ruminations. I grabbed the phone and put the speaker on. "Have you found anything?"

"Is the line clear?" Devon spoke in a low voice.

"Prepaid. Bought from Target. I assume you read my text."

"Yeah. Wanted to make sure. Okay, so, as you know, Ann read one clone. He was thinking about the instructions from Oregon, but it faded into what he wanted for lunch, so she couldn't get a good read. Ann also believes Oregon is where they were 'born' if you can call it that. They had images in their head of Portland and Cannon Beach."

"Here? Have they been stalking us?"

"Well, this gets kinda weird and confusing. They also have images of you in their head, but it's hard to know which *you* it is. You or one of them."

"That'll probably be impossible to distinguish."

"Ann remembers something specific that might help. She noticed a red mark under either your or their right ear."

Something cold crept up my spine. I touched the side of my neck. "I had a red mark in that area from cutting myself shaving on the day of the tsunami."

"Damn. It was you then."

"I wonder why they took pictures of me. Or who took the pictures? Does Ann know?"

"She doesn't, but it's obvious they wanted to make sure you looked the same. Their master plan must be to frame you. We ruined it because the authorities have their dead bodies, but you might not be so lucky the next time."

"The mushrooms worked? I haven't been able to check the news yet."

"Dead as they come. Tell Sadie thanks for the great idea."

"I just dropped her off. When I go back to pick her up, I'll pass along the message." I turned the last corner to my bungalow.

"Do you think she'll be okay on her own? It's getting dangerous."

"Don't know. Talking her into a roommate for a couple of days didn't fly. She thinks she can take care of herself. Who knows? She's scary when she's angry." I laughed to myself.

Devon paused for a moment. "I don't know. We almost got blown to bits back in Arizona. Is there anyone who lives close in case of an emergency?"

"Just an old woman and Sadie's cat."

"That's not comforting. Can you—"

"I'm a step ahead. I'm going back to my place to pack, and I'll head back up to her cottage to observe from a safe distance."

"We need her safe. She saved all of us, you know."

Anger clenched my gut. "Is that it? You want her around just because she might have another vision and save you? It almost sounds like you want to use her. She isn't just a Seer. She's a real person. She may be a little hot-tempered and maybe a klutz, but she's also kind and funny and—"

"No, no, no," he said in a rush. "I didn't mean it like that. Ann and Lucy already love her. They would be devastated if something happened. It's true, we might need her help, but it's more than that."

My temper cooled a little. "The only problem I can see is, she seems to be very loyal to the few people she interacts with and is way too trusting."

"That's a problem. Especially now. We don't know the Oregon connection yet. You'll need to keep a close eye on her until we get to the safety of Samara. We can plan our strategy for tracking any other clones from there."

"Sounds good. Also, can you have Adam do some research on a guy named Ian Roberts? He's the mayor's son here in Cannon Beach. I've seen him around the past two years from time to time, but I'm wondering about everyone now. Maybe I'm just paranoid, but I'd like to be sure."

"I'll get him right on it. I'll call you back on your second phone. You purchased five, right?"

"Just because I've been gone for a few years doesn't mean I forgot protocol." Irritation stirred in my gut.

"Sorry. I just..."

"You just?" He said nothing. "You just what?"

He blew out a deep breath. "I wanted to make sure you're safe, as well."

What? "Why?"

He chuckled. "I'm starting to believe what Ann has been questioning all these years. If that's the case, then I'll owe you an apology. We'll find out what really happened, Archer."

I stilled, and my throat tightened. "I appreciate it. But if it doesn't go as planned and you aren't able to find proof, then I'll take off before my dad, the great and moral Elder, puts me in jail."

"I won't let that happen. I've put some thought into this. You've helped us every step of the way. If the Elders are still out for blood, I'll not only warn you, I'll help you escape."

"You'd do that?"

"Sure. Even if everything turned out to be true, you saved

Ann. She wouldn't be here if it weren't for you. I owe you."

I laughed. "Okay, I'll take the help." I pulled into my driveway. "I'm at my house. I'll check in with you tomorrow." I scanned the outside to see if the wave breached the lower floors. Relief swept through me when I didn't see signs of flooding. My beachfront bungalow had stayed safe.

"Watch your back."

"I will." I got out of my car and sent Devon the number for phone number two. After crushing the phone under my boot, I tossed it into the garbage. I took a large gulp of the fresh ocean air before unlocking and entering my house. I glanced out the large picture window to appreciate the view while throwing my keys into the dish on the side table. Before I blinked, a sharp pain radiated from the top of my head down to my toes. Bright white dots formed, obscuring my vision. I tried to turn my body, but another debilitating blow hit my midsection. While the world turned black, the only thought in my head was Sadie.

"And then, officer, after I saw the man in the black hood and mask leave, I called nine-one-one. Did I do the right thing?" A woman's voice trembled.

"Yes, yes. Mrs. Bishop. We always need good folks like you looking out for our neighbors."

I groaned and tried to turn to my side. The stabbing pains made me rethink my decision, and I lay still.

"Did you hear that?" Mrs. Bishop whispered. "Do you think the burglar came back?"

I tried to yell out, but I didn't have enough air in my lungs.

"You stay right here, Mrs. Bishop. Don't move, do you hear

me?"

"Oh, Roger. I changed your diapers too many times to count. I told you to call me Donna."

Wasn't Donna Bishop Sadie's neighbor? I must warn her. Sadie was in danger. I cracked an eye open only to see the barrel of a Glock 22 pointed at my chest. The young policeman's hands trembled. Probably the first time he drew his weapon in this sleepy town. "Don't move!" he squeaked out.

"Don't plan on it anytime soon." I tried to reassure him, but my voice must have sounded strangled.

"I'm not afraid to shoot." He yelled at an abnormally high pitch.

I didn't believe that for a second. Even though he held the weapon with both hands, the gun still shook. If he fired now, he'd probably hit my guitar twenty feet away.

Donna peeked in through the doorway. "He's not the burglar. He's wearing different clothes. The criminal wore tattered clothes and a black jacket with its hood up."

The police officer lowered his gun. "That right?"

"Yes, this is my house. My wallet is on the table by the door." I tried to sit up. "Wait. The guy who hit me probably took it." Thankfully, my passport was locked in a safe.

The officer backed up toward the entrance. He picked up what appeared to be my wallet. He handed it to Donna and returned to his two-handed grip on his weapon. "Please, Donna, can you pull out his license?"

She opened my wallet and fished out my fake ID. After studying it for a few seconds, her shoulders relaxed, and she gave it to the young cop. He gave it a once-over and lowered his weapon. "I'm sorry, Mr. Gallagher. We have to take every precaution."

"Can I get up now?"

"Yes. Yes, of course. Let me help you." He reached down with his right hand to lift me up. "I'll call in a ten-seventy-one to get you some medical attention. Be right back." He strode out the door toward his car.

I wobbled.

Donna approached me and took my arm. "Oh, sweetie, you've taken a bump to your head. Let's sit on the couch before the aid car arrives."

Every inch of me hurt. I sat on the couch and rubbed my face. "Donna, why are you here?"

She stood straighter. "I'm on street watch. Your front door was left open, and I saw that shady-looking man run out."

"Can you tell me where Sadie is?" I asked.

"Oh, she's out with Ian. I saw them leave over an hour ago. She said she'd be back by three. Do you know my Sadie? Wonderful girl. And Ian, oh he's smitten with her! Those two are the perfect match."

Yeah. If Ian didn't kill her before I could stop him.

"Donna, think carefully. Did Sadie tell you where they planned to go?"

She pursed her lips and looked up at the ceiling. "I heard something about a picnic. Does that help?"

My head cleared, and the urgency took over. "Yes, that's very helpful." It would be if there weren't thousands of places to go on a picnic. In my calmest voice, I asked, "Is there a favorite place that might, let's say, have a great view? Maybe something out of the way? I rubbed my temples, the relentless pounding in my ears not subsiding.

"Oh, dear." Her alarmed eyes widened. "Do you think Sadie is in danger?"

Bingo.

"Maybe. It could be nothing, but I need to get to her." She obviously cared for Sadie. "Think. Anything come to mind?"

Her face brightened. "The lookout at Silver Point is lovely this time of year. There's a trail that only locals know about. When my husband was alive, we'd feel like we were on the top of the world."

"Can you show me where it is? I don't have time to get lost."

"Of course. Do you think someone is after both Sadie and Ian?"

"How well do you know Ian?" I asked in a casual tone.

She wasn't fooled by my calm demeanor. Her mouth dropped open. "But, but he's the mayor's son and so handsome. He would never harm Sadie."

I wanted to shake her by the shoulders. "Do you know anything else about him? Has he dated anyone? Does he have a job?"

She shook her head. "No dating. His father said he attends the university."

"Is he alone most of the time?"

"Come to think of it, yes. I don't remember seeing him with anyone other than his dad. Is that bad?" She wrung her hands together.

"Not necessarily. But I need to find out. Can you show me this overlook?" I stood, hoping I wouldn't fall over.

"Yes. We should get Officer Roger to come along. He has a

gun."

Officer Roger reentered the room. "I'm sorry, but I have a ten-forty-six. The aid car should be here any minute."

I waved him off. "I don't need a hospital trip. I'll be fine after a few Tylenol."

"You sure? You have a nasty bump on your head. Could have a concussion." He hesitated.

"If I get any symptoms, I'll go get it checked out."

That seemed to satisfy him, and he was out the door in a flash.

"But what about the gun? How are you going to help Sadie?" Donna watched Officer Roger take off.

"Don't worry about that. I have it covered." I turned to leave. Donna wrapped her lace shawl tight around her shoulders and shivered. She also looked pale. A pang of guilt made me stop. "Are you sure you're up for this? Maybe you could give me the directions on a map." I didn't want to ask because it'd probably take longer to write out the instructions than to just drive it.

"Oh, you can't stop me from coming with you. Sadie is the sweetest, most caring girl I've ever met. If there's even a small chance she's in trouble, I want to help. I've read every Agatha Christie novel, and I know just what to do."

Great. An amateur sleuth. "Okay, let's go. When we get there, you'll be staying in the car. You got that?"

She tilted her head and gave me a sweet smile.

When we arrived at our destination, I repeated the instructions to stay put. Donna put her hands in her lap and nodded. "I couldn't get over that fence anyway. If you're not back in fifteen minutes, I'll call for help." She tapped her purse where she held her cell phone.

"Okay." I reached over her and opened the glove box. I grabbed the handgun and the box of bullets and loaded it.

"Oh my." Donna covered her mouth.

"You wanted Officer Roger to bring his gun, but I can guarantee you, I have more experience."

"Okay." She nodded. "I can't believe Sadie is in trouble!" Her round face flushed red.

"This is just a precaution." I eyed her again. "Don't move."

She blinked rapidly. "Of course."

I hurried from the car and jumped over the two-foot stone wall meant to keep tourists out. The path led me around a crop of trees obscuring the ocean view. Donna's instructions were precise: follow the footpath over a steep hill that opened to a one-eighty view of the ocean. I climbed to the top of the hill and caught sight of two figures. I froze, not believing my eyes.

"Oh no! He's strangling her. Do something!" Donna yelled from behind.

I jumped at the sound of her voice, but didn't take my eyes off the duo. I'd deal with her later. Sadie's arm was handcuffed to a wire fence. Ian stood over her with his hands around her neck. I aimed my gun. I had about two seconds to decide where the bullet would go. Kill or maim?

CHAPTER 12

Sadie

I'M GOING TO *die.*

Ian turned his back to me. "I had it all planned out. We'd go out a few times and get to know each other. You'd learn to trust me." He stopped to rub his face.

Yeah, that trust thing vanished with the handcuffs.

"And then I'd break things to you gently. There's so much to tell you."

"You can start by telling me why I'm handcuffed to this fence." If I was going to die, I wouldn't go out being polite. But why was he talking about trust and breaking things to me gently? Was he trying to trick me into feeling safe? Maybe so he could get all the information about what happened to his Jack friends in Arizona.

He turned to face me. "I need at least an hour to explain things to you. I didn't want you taking off before I got the chance to tell you everything."

"Go on." Ugh. Might as well get this *story* over with.

"Okay. Well, um, I moved to Cannon Beach two years ago to guard you." He stood still and waited for my reaction.

"Guard me?" Did he really expect me to believe that?

"Yes. From Archer."

"And why would I need to be protected from Archer?"

"You know why." He tilted his head and narrowed his eyes.

"No." I wasn't giving anything away.

He glanced at my handcuffs. "Just trust me." His fingers raked through his hair. "I know. I know. I put you in handcuffs. Not great. But I had to keep you secured so you'd hear me out. I'm telling you the truth."

"Again, handcuffs? You could have just knocked on my door and told me everything in my living room. Now that's a novel idea. Isn't that what *sane* people do?"

He sighed. "Yes, but what we're dealing with isn't sane. And I didn't want Archer interrupting and trying to fill your head with lies. I know you met up with him in Portland. I just don't know why."

I glanced at my shackled hands. "And you think I'll tell you?"

Ian puffed out a large breath and frowned. For a Jack serial killer, he didn't seem to fit the part. And it wasn't because of his off-the-charts good looks. He hadn't killed me yet—score one. He seemed stressed and worried about my reactions—score two. He was incredibly attractive—score, wait, that didn't count.

"Okay, why don't you just spill it, and we can get this over with?" My arm ached.

"If you'll agree to listen to the end and promise to stay. If you try to escape, I have other ways to stop you." He glanced at his backpack.

"Well, aren't you the little Eagle Scout all prepared to keep me in place." Frustration and anger bubbled in my chest and spread throughout my body, making my skin hot and prickly. If I got free of this, I'd hit him over his crazy head with a rock and make my escape.

He eyed me and sat down about two feet away. "Archer is a Jack."

I kept my expression bland. "And what's a Jack? Is he a drug lord or something?" Might as well play innocent until I could figure out his angle.

He rubbed his face. "You asked about the handcuffs? This is a perfect example. Just come clean and we can get this over with."

Meaning, he'll kill me once he gets the info.

I let my eyes drift out over the stunning ocean vista. A clear day, with only tiny puffs of white clouds sprinkled over the horizon. The calm sound of seagulls overhead, along with the waves lapping on the shore, clashed with the turmoil brewing inside. Would this be my last day on earth?

"Stalling is just going to make things more difficult. We need to have this discussion." He looked down at his hands. "I can't believe I let Archer get to you before I could explain everything."

"Archer didn't get to me. I don't know what you're talking about."

"Tell me this. Did he use his Jack charm on you? Do you consider him a friend, or maybe more?"

"First of all, that's none of your business. Second, well, it's the same as the first. Why in the world would you care if I'm friends with Archer?"

"Because you have to kill him."

The air left my lungs in a giant whoosh, and I couldn't breathe.

"Sorry. Sorry. I didn't mean to dump it all on you at once." He shook his head. "I'm doing this all wrong."

"How did you... I mean, where did you get that information?" *Don't have a panic attack. Breathe.*

"Are you okay? You've gone pale as the moon."

A tingling sensation spread from my fingers, and black dots formed, obscuring my vision. Great. I've gone from a possible panic attack to on the edge of passing out in seconds.

Get a grip.

I held up a finger. "Give me a minute." What were those calming words from yoga? Namaste? Didn't that mean peace? No, divine light. Focus. Shakti meant power. That's the word I needed. I closed my eyes and envisioned ripping my hand free from the restraints and running like a gazelle far, far, away.

"Sadie."

"Don't talk for a minute." My eyes remained shut.

"I know about the vision."

"What vision?" He couldn't know about that.

"You'll be the Seer to kill the last Jack."

My eyes opened and locked on his. There was no way he should know this. I was the only person on the planet to have knowledge about the vision. "How?"

He sat perfectly still, but his left eye twitched. "My parents told me before the—" He blinked rapidly a few times. "Before the Jacks wiped out the Seers."

Ian was the last Jack! I took both hands and pulled on the handcuff that was stubbornly holding firm. Renewed anger swirled, and my stomach churned with what felt like acid. With each yank, pain ripped through my arm, but I wasn't stopping until I was free.

Ian came closer and held up his hands. "No, no, no. Stop! You're hurting yourself. I'm not a Jack. I'm a Seer, just like you. My parents gave me instructions to find you and keep you safe. Sadie, we're supposed to be together. They saw it before everything went down."

"I don't believe you," I wheezed out and kept fighting with the manacle. Stupid tears ran down my face, and I sucked in a ragged breath. The adrenaline sapped my energy, replacing it with pain, and I dropped back down into a sitting position. I drew my knees to my chest and rested my head on them. I failed. My parents would be so disappointed.

He crouched down in front of me. "Sadie," he whispered.

I shook my head and looked past him. A small fishing boat bobbed about two miles offshore. I wanted to sit on that boat all day with a fishing pole in my hands and the sun on my face.

"Look at my eyes." He leaned a little closer.

I glanced and looked away. Wait. I looked back and—

"Is this a trick? Did you hypnotize me or something?" The brown in his eyes swirled and shimmered.

The beginning of a grin turned up the left side of his mouth. "No, Sadie."

"I thought I was the only one. No. This is a trick. I've been on my own for thousands of years. If there was another Seer, I would've known."

"We were meant to stay apart until now. Do you want to hear about the vision?"

Did I? Was all this smoke and mirrors to get me to believe he was a Seer and not a Jack? "Go for it." I'd listen, but that didn't mean I'd believe him.

"Okay. My parents received the vision I'd be the one to guide you and help you find and kill the last Jack. They knew of your parents, Astriar and Zeno Sosigenes."

I sat a little straighter. Would a Jack know my parents' names?

"They said the Jacks would have another uprising and would try to take back control after the big wave. I wasn't sure what they were talking about until the tsunami. That's why I offered to help Donna. I needed the introduction. I planned to go slow, but then I saw you and Archer go into the hotel." He got up and paced. "That blew my plans out of the water. I never thought he'd seek you out."

"He didn't."

Ian stopped, and his eyes bulged. "You contacted him?"

Should I tell him? I checked his eyes. Still swirling. "Yeah. My mom told me about the vision. I wanted to contact Archer to see what he was up to. Kinda like keep your enemy's closer kind of thing."

"And?"

"And he's been working with the Readers."

He frowned. "Impossible. He plotted with the Jacks and planned to kill them all. They'd never trust him again."

"How do you know all this?"

"My dad. Or, I should say, my adopted mortal father. His family has been taking care of me since my parents died. They've handed me down with each new generation and have only shown me kindness. Every single one. Anyway, we have a file on each one of the Readers. My parents prepared everything for my adopted family."

I sighed. "You had a family this entire time?" Why hadn't my parents done the same for me?

"I'm sorry. It must have been lonely for you all these years."

I bit the inside of my cheek and said nothing.

His eyes softened. "It was set up that way on purpose."

"They meant for me to be alone?"

"It would make you become stronger, more independent." He searched my expression.

I thought about my propensity for tripping over my feet, my awkward conversation skills, and how I did my thinking out loud. "Well, that plan failed. Look at me. I trusted you, and here I sit in handcuffs, at your mercy."

"Sorry again." He reached over and rummaged through his backpack. "Here it is." He pulled out some bottled water. "Would you like some?"

"No, I don't need water. What I need are these handcuffs off."

"I have a few more things to tell you first." He bit his lip and looked down.

This would be bad.

I looked skyward and mumbled to myself, "What now?"

He cleared his throat. "It's the soul mate thing."

Oh no. I wondered which one he referred to.

"The first one was about The Lost One. You knew about that one, right?"

I nodded.

"The second one was about you."

Any doubts about him posing as a fake Seer flew away like a crispy brown leaf in the wind.

"What do you know?"

"Well, there's another vision." He sat back down and took a deep breath.

"Okay..."

"It's about the two of us."

Huh.

"It foretold that we'd join together to take out the last Jack. That's my purpose, to help you."

"Why didn't my parents tell me?"

"They didn't know. This came later after you separated from your parents. Right before the war"

"What else don't I know?"

He hesitated and closed his eyes for a moment.

"You're making me nervous. Is it bad?"

"No." But he wouldn't make eye contact.

"Why do you look all nervous, like you don't want to tell me?"

His eyes met mine. "You'll have a child that will save the world from nuclear destruction."

What the what?

Ian glanced at my handcuffs. "Now you know why I had to

use those. Are you okay to hear the rest? Do you need water?"

"Yes." Now I did. My throat went dry, and my body began to shake.

He unscrewed the cap and handed me the water. I took a few big gulps and tried to get my breathing under control.

"Okay."

"There's one more thing."

"Really? Because saving the world from destruction wasn't big enough? Doesn't the universe know I'm a klutz, and I'd most likely pass that down to my child?" *My child.* I never dreamed I'd ever have the chance. The possibility sank in, and I blinked back tears.

"It's about the father of your child." He blushed.

"Don't tell me it's you." Would that be a bad thing? Yes. No. Maybe? I didn't even know him. Ten minutes ago, I thought he was a Jack. I needed to get away to absorb this. I wasn't sure I could hear any more before I combusted.

He smiled. "I know this isn't the greatest start to our budding relationship."

A gust of wind blew his hair over his eyes. He brushed it out of the way, and I studied him. He had classic good looks, but, for the first time, I noticed what was different about his eyes. Brown with flecks of gold. It wasn't the color though. Kindness and compassion held my gaze. But before I could gather my wits, Archer's face flashed in my mind. Why did I think about him now?

I cleared my throat and asked, "Are you sure?"

"Well, not entirely. The visions stopped exactly where we are now. I didn't realize it, but when my mom explained it, she described the setting as beautiful and rejuvenating. Anyway, all the visions stopped abruptly at this point. She felt it was because, when we joined forces, it would put everything in motion. We're the only two Seers left on the planet, so it makes sense, don't you think?"

"I don't know what to think."

"I've brought something just in case you still have any doubts."

Did I? My mind was still spinning.

"It's your mom's necklace. It was transferred to my mom a few days before the Great War. Do you remember it?"

A buried memory resurfaced. My mom, dancing with Dad, wearing a gorgeous, dark maroon gown with her jeweled necklace sparkling in the moonlight.

Oh, Mom. You were so beautiful that night.

Ian reached into his back pocket and pulled out a black velvet bag. He gently removed a necklace, and I knew from a simple glance it was my mom's; I would recognize it anywhere. The multi-colored gems intertwined with gold, silver, and copper flowers left no doubt.

Tears spilled from my eyes and I held out my hand.

Ian placed the necklace in my hand, which sent waves of love and warmth throughout my body.

"Thank you," I choked out. "I can feel her."

I wasn't alone after all. I loved my new friends, but Ian was just like me.

"Another thing you should know. When you wear the necklace, it'll bring back some of your powers. Your mom searched around the world for these specific gems. They'll work with the gravitational pull of the earth and open the part of your brain that's been closed. Do you want to give it a go?"

I nodded. "Hurry."

He chuckled and draped it around my neck. "I guess it's time to take off those handcuffs."

Archer, with a gun, pointing it at—

"Ian! Duck! Right now, move!"

He hesitated for a half second before the gun fired.

CHAPTER 13

Archer

"OH, DEAR. OH, dear!" Donna's voice echoed as I pulled the trigger.

Ian flipped to his side and rolled out of range. I kept my gun raised and ran toward Sadie.

Sadie held up a hand and yelled, "No! Don't shoot him!"

What the hell?

Donna tagged after me and tugged on my arm. "Poor Sadie! He has a gun pointed at her."

I moved forward a step with my gun raised to see how far Ian rolled down the little slope.

If he had a gun, why would he try to strangle her?

"Donna, go back to the car. This isn't safe." Not wanting to take my eyes off Sadie, I quickly glanced at Donna.

She straightened and pushed her shoulders back. "You need backup. I led the White Rose Women's Club self-defense course three summers ago."

Great. An eighty-year-old vigilante.

"You." I pointed at her. "Stay out of my way. Go back to the car. I will not say it again."

Donna's cheeks flushed. "Okay, dear. You don't have to be rude about it." She turned and started walking back to the parking lot.

I turned my attention back to Sadie. She sat about ten feet away with her hand held up. "Archer, I know this looks bad." She glanced at the handcuffs. "But it isn't what it seems. Ian's here to help me."

I walked a few steps in her direction with my gun raised. Ian was just out of my line of sight, which made me nervous. "And the handcuffs?"

"He said something about me being stubborn and running off."

True.

Still not convinced, I inched toward her.

"He's a Seer!" she hissed.

That stopped me in my tracks. Another Seer? Now?

"It could be a trick," I warned.

"He proved it." Her head turned toward the downhill slope. "Ian. Don't move for a minute. I have to explain to Archer. Are you okay?"

"Yeah, but can you call off your guard dog?" he shouted back.

Sadie pressed her lips together, but a laugh escaped. Her

eyes brightened when she touched a string of multi-colored gems hanging around her neck. "He gave me this. It's my mom's necklace. Only a Seer would know about its existence. We kept it secret."

The gems sparkled, and I found myself mesmerized by the unusual shades of color.

I stared, transfixed, until my attention was caught downslope by a long arm holding a white napkin.

"Ian?" I asked her.

"Yeah." She laughed. "He's resourceful, I can say that about him."

I lowered my gun and kept my voice low so Ian wouldn't hear. "If he even sneezes in your direction, I'm taking him out."

"It's all good." She rubbed a gem. "My powers are back. Well, a little." She smiled. "A vision appeared with you and the gun, so I warned Ian."

My heart picked up speed. "Wait. You're telling me your mom's necklace has that power?"

"I guess. But remember, Seers only get the big events in our visions. I won't be able to see day-to-day occurrences."

"That's good though. No, it's great." We'd be a step ahead of the Jack clones. *Maybe.*

"Archer, do we trust him?" Donna asked. "He is waving a white flag. Or I should say napkin."

I rubbed my temples. "I thought I told you to go back to the car?"

"Not with Sadie's life at risk." She stood tall, well, as tall as a five-foot-two feisty, older woman could, and gave Sadie a wave. "Hey, sweetie." She peered downslope to where Ian's voice echoed. "Ian, do I need to have a chat with your father?" She shook her head. "I don't think he'd appreciate your manners, young man. You have some explaining to do with those handcuffs."

"I'm just fine, Donna. These will be off in a minute." Sadie turned in Ian's direction. "It's safe, can you please take these things off now?"

Ian, still waving his napkin, walked up the small embankment. "They'd be off by now if it weren't for Archer charging in on his white horse." He sent me a glare. "How about you ask questions first, then shoot. I know for someone like you that's a novelty."

Someone like me?

"You may know of me, but you know nothing about me." I shot Donna a glance to see if she picked up on Ian's hostility. She walked the few feet to sit next to Sadie, and the two women began talking.

"I know enough." He crossed his arms over his chest.

"Whatever." I wouldn't explain myself to him. "Mind unshackling Sadie?"

He rubbed his face and muttered, "Oh, that's right." He plucked the keys from his pocket and said, "Sorry about all this."

Donna clucked her tongue. "Ian, this is not acceptable behavior for a first date."

Ian rubbed his hand over his mouth. "Yes, ma'am."

She continued, "You could have gotten yourself shot. I thought you were strangling poor Sadie, not putting a necklace on her."

"We're all good now. Right, Archer?" Sadie cocked an

eyebrow in my direction.

"Maybe."

She rolled her eyes, then focused her attention on Ian unlocking her handcuffs. "Free at last." She hopped up and offered Donna her hand. "Here, let me help you." She tilted her head in Donna's direction. "What are you doing here, anyway?"

Donna's cheeks pinkened. "Archer needed help to find this place."

Sadie turned toward me. "And how did you know where I'd be?"

I pointed to Donna. "She told me."

Donna shrugged and glanced out at the ocean. "I might have overheard something about Sadie and a picnic."

Ian scratched his jaw. "And when was that?"

Donna blew out a large breath. "Okay, well, I might have accidentally listened to your phone conversation yesterday. You know, after you finished the cabinets next to the television."

Ian groaned and rubbed his face. "The conversation with my dad. I should have known better."

Donna touched Sadie's arm. "I was so excited you and Ian got together! And then I thought he was a crazy killer." She held her heart. "That gave me a fright. But now that I know he's good, I'm all for the romance." She glanced at Ian. "But you really do need better manners."

He sighed and shook his head.

"Anyway," she said, then lowered her voice. "Ian's a much better choice than Archer. He's rather cranky."

"I can hear you, Donna." What was it with old people always speaking their mind?

"Oh. Sorry, Archer. It's just that Ian's father is the mayor and, you know, respectable."

Donna didn't know about my past, but her observation was spot on.

Sadie clapped her hands. "Okay, now. Let's not worry about all that stuff. I have to get back to my cottage...to clean."

All eyes turned to Sadie. "What?" she asked. "I love to clean."

"I'll drive you back," I offered.

Ian stepped in front of Sadie. "I'll be taking her home."

We stood for a moment in a silent standoff. I still didn't trust him. Even if he did give Sadie her mom's necklace. It proved nothing.

Sadie moved to stand next to Ian. "It's okay. Ian and I still have a few things to talk about. Maybe you can come over later after you take Donna home?"

Oh, hell no.

"I have a meeting in town. Since you're going in the same direction, maybe you and Ian can drop her off?" I knew my suggestion wouldn't go over well.

Sadie pursed her lips together and glanced at Ian.

He shrugged.

Sadie glared at me before she turned to Donna. "You okay catching a ride with us?"

Donna smiled sweetly. "That would be lovely, dear. I'll just sit in the back and not make a peep. I don't want to intrude on your date."

Meddling old woman. Well, at least she'd keep Sadie safe until I could stake out her cottage.

Three hours later, Ian still hadn't left Sadie's place. I glanced at my watch. Now three hours and ten seconds. Ugh. For all I knew, he could be in there torturing her for information. My heart seized for a moment. The thought of anyone harming Sadie did terrible things to my already churning stomach.

She's just a quirky, clumsy girl.

I wish it were that easy. I wish I didn't notice the intelligence behind her shimmering blue eyes. Or her laugh and the way she scrunched up her nose when she didn't like something. I wish she didn't have the sarcastic, dry humor and witty responses that both irritated and intrigued me. Or that she was so damn beautiful, I could barely look at her without having a physical reaction. If I could quit thinking every second about touching her, sweeping her golden blonde hair from her face, and then those lips...

Enough. I got out of my car and stalked closer to her cottage. There was only one window in the back without drapes or anything blocking a straight view into her living room. If Ian wasn't who she believed him to be, I'd be ready to jump in.

The vegetation around the cottage was thick. I peeled back the leaves from a large bush, fit through the opening, and got to the side of the window without any sound.

I peered in the window, and when I saw them, my stomach dropped. Sadie leaned forward on the couch, crying, while Ian sat on the floor, holding her hand. Every few seconds he'd reach up and wipe a tear from her face and nod about something she was saying.

Sadie never cried. She was goofy and tough, and, most of the time, her guard was up. How did Ian get her to open up? Was he really a Seer? Would they be naturally bonded? I squeezed my eyes shut and regulated my breathing. With my back to the outer wall, I slid down to a sitting position.

No problem. Now I could quit thinking about her. I rubbed my temples. Who was I kidding? I had good instincts, and there was definitely something off about the picnic, an energy that buzzed with negativity. Ian shows up out of nowhere to save the day? Nope. Not buying it. I'd get Sadie out of town and into the safety of Samara. Then the group could investigate him. I stood and wiped the dirt from my jeans. Time to break up this Seer reunion.

I rounded the house and pounded on the door. After a few minutes, Sadie opened the door. Her face was wet, like she just splashed water over it. "Hey, Archer. Come on in."

She led me into the living room, where Ian lounged in a chair. I gave him a nod, and he answered, "Archer," in a clipped voice.

Sadie flopped on the couch and patted the cushion next to her. I eyed Ian and sank into the sofa. He probably wasn't too excited about me crashing their date. But Sadie invited me over earlier, so he'd have to deal.

"Ian and I have talked a lot and want to get you caught up."

I glanced at Ian, and he glared right back. Yep. I was right.

"Ian was sent to help me find the last Jack, or, in this case, the Jack clones. Isn't that great?" She clasped her hands together. "You'll get two Seers for the price of one." She laughed.

Great? Uh, no. And... "What do you mean, two Seers?"

"This is the exciting part. I reached Ann, and she and Devon think it's a great idea to have Ian come with us to Samara."

I shot up from the couch and shouted, "No."

Both Sadie and Ian jerked back, and their eyes widened.

"That will not happen." I turned and stomped out the front door. Not knowing where to go, I went back to my car about a half block away. I plopped down in the front seat and banged my head against the steering wheel. Talk about a knee-jerk reaction. What was wrong with me? Sure, Ian was an unknown, but it shouldn't be too hard for Adam to get a full background check on him before we headed out for Samara. Jacks were tricky though, and who knows if he'd gotten into the mainframe and manipulated his files.

But he had the necklace. It would be hard for a Jack to get their hands on something like that.

A rap on the driver's side window made me jump back. Sadie. My heart pounded from the scare, or was it just her?

"Can you unlock? I need to talk to you." She rubbed her hands up and down her arms to keep warm.

I unlocked the passenger door, and she jumped in. "Brrr. It's cold outside."

She smelled like lavender and honey, my two favorite scents. I cracked open the window.

"I know you don't trust Ian yet, but Ann said they'd do a full background check on him by tomorrow."

"I guessed as much. Although, Jacks have been known to mess with information."

"The necklace?"

"I'll give him that. Where did you say he got it?"

"From his parents when they told him about the two of us

joining forces."

"Do you believe him?" I leaned closer.

"Yes." She moved closer.

"It looked like the two of you were getting close." Damn. That slipped.

"I knew it!" She slapped my arm. "Stalker."

"I had to make sure he wasn't, you know, killing you or something." Yeah, I'd stick with that.

She glanced at my lips. "As you can see, I'm in good health."

"He could be dangerous."

"You could be dangerous." She licked her lips.

"I probably am." I moved toward her. Had to ask. "Are you and Ian supposed to be like Ann and Devon?" I swallowed hard.

She tilted her head. "You mean a soul mate kind of thing?"

"Yeah, like that. There were rumors before the Great War about another couple and child. But nothing concrete surfaced and now I wonder..."

She moved a little closer, so our lips were only a breath away. "He said we're destined to work together to take down the last Jack."

Warmth radiated from her, like a stone heated by fire. "Work?" I brushed a lock of silky blonde hair from her face.

"Yeah. He also thinks we might belong together."

"Is that what you think?" I held my breath and waited.

"Maybe, but there's this one—"

The passenger door flew open, and Ian leaned down to talk to Sadie. "Hey, sorry to interrupt, but your phone keeps ringing off the hook."

She straightened. "Oh, that must be Ann." She scurried from the car. After a few feet, she called out, "We'll talk later."

Ian stayed in his bent position and pointed a finger at me. "Don't even think about it. I've waited two thousand years for her, and I will not let you interfere. You got that?"

I sat back in the seat and smiled. "You're forgetting one thing."

"Yeah? And what's that?"

"Sadie."

"What about her?"

"Exactly. You don't know her at all."

He threw his head back and laughed. "Did you know Sadie was married in 1927?"

I sat up straighter.

"Yeah. It just about killed her when she watched her husband die. It wasn't old age either. Cancer at forty-seven."

"How do you know this?"

"I haven't lost track of her since the Great War. You want to know anything about Sadie, I'm your man. She's stubborn as hell, probably from living in an old Scottish convent in the 1800s, or it could be from her days nursing during World War I. She's also funny, sarcastic, witty, and is a sucker for anything furry. She vows to never get attached, but she does anyway. You've seen her cat and Donna. She thinks she's living independent, shielding herself against loss, but she does a terrible job at it. When they die, she'll spend months crying, mourning them. She'll vow never to get close to anyone again, but she does anyway. I've seen her do it over and over. She loves hard and strong. It's part of her DNA." He stopped and took a deep breath. "And I've loved her every second since I laid eyes on her two thousand years ago."

Everything stopped. The distant hum of the ocean, the sounds of crickets and frogs croaking, the wind rustling through the trees, pure silence. *Damn.* If all this turned out to be true, I needed to back off. Every cell in my body seemed to revolt at the idea. My stomach twisted, and my breathing came in labored rasps. Sweat beaded on my forehead, and my hands formed into fists. I hadn't accepted it when Ann and Devon got together, and I wouldn't repeat the same mistake. This time, I'd do the right thing. I blinked a few times and nodded. If I spoke, he'd guess what this decision was doing to me.

"Thank you." He nodded and left me sitting in the car, wondering what the hell was wrong with me.

I pick the only two women on the planet wrapped up in some stupid soul mate bond.

CHAPTER 14

Sadie

A FTER TWO LONG days of packing, cleaning, closing up my cottage, having the post office hold all mail, and a tearful yet temporary goodbye to Donna, we reached our destination. Samara.

"Isn't it beautiful?" Ann slung her arm around me while she held Henry on her hip.

"Yes. Is it possible the sky has an extra shade of blue painted on? This doesn't even look real." The buildup of Samara didn't disappoint. Snowcapped mountains jutted up from a blue-green river. The foliage in vibrant shades of green danced with the slight breeze. The cool, fresh air tickled my nose, urging me to breathe deeper. "You guys didn't exaggerate. It's lovely."

Ann grinned. "You haven't even seen the inside. Just wait."

"How do we get in?" A rusted iron bridge spread out between us and the steep mountainside across the river. A moss-covered birch tree leaned over the water, seeming to stretch its limbs to the other side. The sun played between the greenery, giving the river a speckled appearance.

Ann laughed. "It's very James Bond-ish. The guys will be here soon." She placed her hand to shield her eyes and looked down the dirt road. "There they are!"

Two Jeeps pulled up and stopped behind us. Archer and Devon exited first. Adam, Lucy, and Ian were next.

I tried to catch Archer's eye, but he looked everywhere but in my direction. I hadn't talked to him since our almost-kiss. My lips still tingled with the memory. Once Ian cleared the background check he was added to the plan, Ann called to let me know she'd be my ride to Samara. I didn't think twice about it until now. Did Archer ask her to switch? Was he avoiding me for some reason?

"Hey, Archer," I yelled, and waved. No time like the present to see if he'd answer.

He looked up for a moment and gave me a chin lift. *That's it?* He turned away and continued his conversation with Devon. Something wasn't right. His usual bright and curious eyes dimmed when he looked at me. Why? *Think.* The last time I saw him, everything was fine, and then Ian... Uh oh. Ian must have said something. But what would make Archer turn cold suddenly? Even if Ian expressed an interest in me, that would be like catnip to a guy like Archer. He wasn't one to back down. He seemed to thrive on a challenge. No. It was something else. Regret? Maybe he didn't want a relationship. Pretty sure he was over Ann, but perhaps he still carried unresolved feelings for her. Ugh. Why was I analyzing this?

Ian came to stand beside me. "Breathtaking, isn't it?"

"I was just thinking the same thing. Hey, you don't have

extra abilities, do you?" I smiled, but curiosity made me watch his face for any telltale signs of lying.

"Nope. Just the one. I'd love to know what you're thinking though." A light flush covered his cheeks.

Ian and I had become close. Fast. I didn't know what it was, but I was able to open up to him. He understood what it was like for me to be alone all those years. He seemed so familiar even though we'd just met. Were we meant to be best friends, business partners, or more?

A sudden memory of Archer's green, penetrating eyes flashed before me. Why was it every time I tried to focus on Ian, Archer's stupid face interfered? I didn't want to think about him, even though I knew he wouldn't be the last Jack. At least I didn't have to worry about killing him. But thinking about him all the time was almost killing me. Why was I so drawn to him? Why did I want to kiss him so badly my entire body felt like someone had stuffed fireworks down my throat and set them off? Archer was an unknown, a possible betrayer who might have murdered his friend Markus. He'd kidnapped Ann, for goodness' sake. Why wasn't I running for the hills? I looked at the mountain in front of me and chuckled to myself. I was at the "hills," but so was Archer.

Archer is so much more than his past. Keep looking; you'll find it.

Ugh. Were the thoughts that popped into my head my own? Could it be my parents sending me messages? In this case, it might be wishful thinking.... because, Archer.

Ian interrupted my thoughts. "It looks like a normal mountain. I'm having a hard time imaging people living in there."

"I know, right? I can't wait to see it on the inside." I scanned the entire area, not seeing any signs that would indicate over three hundred Readers lived inside.

Devon stepped in front of us. "We've done the scan, and we're good to go."

"Scan?" Ian asked.

Devon nodded. "Yes. We don't enter unless we have a two square mile buffer around us to make it into Samara before anyone can detect us. That includes land and air. We have heat-seeking drones and a network of cameras set up around the perimeter to alert us of any intruders."

"You guys thought of everything." Ian smiled and looked around.

"We try. You'll have to move back while I flip the switch." Devon waited for us, then opened a panel in the framework of the rusted bridge. I wouldn't have noticed it if I'd walked or driven past. Inside the panel, a set of switches lit up. Devon punched a series of buttons and flipped a few breakers.

Immediately after he finished, a loud scraping noise came from the area in front of the mountain. A few bushes moved in opposite directions as the mouth of the mountain squealed its way open.

Ian's huge grin stretched across his face. "That's way cool."

Devon called over his shoulder, "It's still a work in progress, but we'll get there soon."

I glanced at Archer standing next to the Jeep with his arms crossed and a deep scowl on his face. Without giving it much thought, I walked right up to him. "What has you looking so serious?"

He seemed to shake himself out of a trance. "My dad." His eyes traveled up and down the steep hillside.

"Oh. Not a happy reunion?"

"I'll be lucky if he doesn't take me away in shackles. But Devon cleared the way with the Elders and says I shouldn't have any problems." He looked at me and shifted away.

"And?" I asked.

"Coming back home isn't as easy as I thought."

I studied his face. "Why not?"

"I don't know what to expect when I walk through those doors." He rubbed his hands over his face. "I betrayed them all."

"Yeah, I guess that might be awkward." Ugh. Is that the best I could do?

Archer chuckled and mumbled something under his breath.

"Don't laugh at me. And what did you say about missing something?"

He pressed his lips closed.

"Hmm?" I coaxed.

"I just said I've missed the community. You'll see. The Readers are tight."

I tilted my head up to take in the size and scope of the large mountain. "How much space does Samara take up in the mountain?"

"They tell me almost all of it."

"Okay, everyone. Let's get going," Devon shouted.

Archer turned away from me and headed to his Jeep. He must be nervous and forgot to say goodbye.

Ann tugged on my arm. "We'll be going in first. Come on."

I let her keep a hold on my arm while she dragged me to the

car. I had hoped to ride with Archer. He always did a great job describing things and never got irritated with my excessive amount of questions. But, whatever the reason, he didn't want to continue to talk. My stomach dropped a little.

Ann took me by the shoulders. "Hey, what's the matter?"

"Oh, nothing."

"You are the worst liar." She chuckled. "Oh, wait. You don't have claustrophobia, do you?"

"No, I'm fine in small spaces."

She took in a deep breath. "The first time I entered the other Samara, I had a mini panic attack."

Ann? A panic attack? Hard to believe with her so calm and self-assured.

"Don't look so shocked. I'm a big baby with tight spaces." She flicked her hand in the air. "Childhood issues and all that."

"I'm so sorry." I didn't want to ask or intrude on her privacy.

"No worries. I'm a lot better now." She bit her lip. "Except for the hairy vermin that sometimes break in." She glanced at the back seat and stopped when her eyes rested on the cat carrier. "Eve will be a welcome addition."

I didn't like the idea of Eve bringing me rats though. "How big are these vermin?"

"Oh, about this big." Using her thumb and forefinger, she opened it to about two inches.

I slapped my hand over my mouth to prevent the laughter from bubbling to the surface.

"Yeah, yeah. Go ahead and laugh." She chuckled. "Doc told me I need immersion therapy. They'd like me to get a pet mouse to help reduce my fear. But"—she shivered—"I'm not quite ready yet."

"I'm not a fan either." Hmm. Ann had a fear about tight spaces and mice. Could they be connected?

"Time to go, everyone," Devon yelled to the group. "Ann, you and Sadie can go first."

Ann muttered under her breath. "Great." Her face turned a little pale.

"Do you need me to help with anything? A sedative, perhaps?"

"Ha. It's Devon. He always has me go first. I think he's afraid one of these days I'll decide I can't go back in."

I flopped back into the passenger seat, and Ann buckled Henry into his car seat. Then she straightened her shoulders, put the car in gear, and said, "Off we go."

The Jeep bumped and jostled us over the rickety bridge. I gripped the door handle even though my seatbelt was fastened around my lap and shoulder. I turned to see if Eve was doing okay. She'd been asleep the entire trip. I reached back and stuck my finger between the mesh and tried scratching behind her ear to wake her up. "Are you excited, Eve?" She opened her beautiful green eyes and licked my finger with her sandpaper tongue. I loved that feeling.

"She'll love it. This will be like kitty heaven." Ann laughed. She stopped at the entrance.

"You mean chasing around the two-inch mice?" I kept a straight face.

"Yes, that, and she'll have some kitty friends to play with."

"That'll be nice for her. She's only played with me. And, of course, Donna loves to spoil her."

Eve meowed and scratched at her enclosure.

"See? She's raring to go." Ann laughed, then took a deep breath. "We're about to go in. You ready?"

I gazed at the gaping hole at the foot of the mountain. "Yes." I clapped my hands. "This is an adventure."

Ann eyed me for a moment and shook her head. "I wish I'd felt that way when I first went in. But I was shot at the time, so that probably influenced my initial reaction."

"What? You were shot?"

"Long story." She waved me off. "Once you get settled, I'll tell you everything."

"Can't wait."

Ann gunned the engine, and we entered a tunnel-like road that weaved around a few corners. The shiny tiles that covered every inch reflected the headlights while she navigated around each bend.

"This is fantastic! Reminds me of a ride at Disneyland." I loved it already, and we hadn't even arrived yet.

Ann chuckled. "Except this ride ends in a parking garage." The last curve proved her right. It opened into a large, lighted space about the size of an average-sized garage or parking lot in the city. "Wow. It looks like you can fit over a hundred cars in here." I scanned the space. "And someone loves Jeeps. I've never seen so many in one place. Not even at a dealership."

She pulled into a parking spot and killed the engine. "Yep. They're easy to maneuver on the dirt roads around here."

I hopped out of the car and watched the other Jeeps pull into spots along the wall right next to us. I started toward Archer's car but hesitated.

"Why don't you grab Eve so we can get you settled into your

room." Ann motioned to the back seat.

Eve. I'd almost forgotten. Instead of grabbing the carrier, I reached inside and unlatched the top so I could hold her against me. I held my backpack in the other hand.

"So, this is the famous cat. Steve, is it?" Archer said from behind.

I felt it before I heard the low growl and hiss.

"Whoa." Archer held his hands up. "Is that thing rabid?"

Her growl deepened. And her body stiffened "No, of course not. I've never heard her growl before. You probably scared her by coming from behind like that." I dropped my backpack so I could pet her head. "And calling her Steve didn't help. I'm sure she'll be fine if you pet her."

"Uh, no thanks. I already told you, I don't get along with cats." He took a step back.

Ian put down his bag before he reached us. "Do you need some help? I can grab a few bags so you can focus on getting Eve settled."

Eve relaxed and purred, rubbing against my shoulder.

"That would be great. She's a little off-balance from the trip." I put her back in her carrier so she could get a little more sleep.

"Off-balance or feral," Archer muttered, and walked toward what looked like an elevator with tall, shiny metal doors and a panel of multi-colored lights on the right side.

"I heard that!" I shouted at his back. He just shrugged and kept walking.

Ian scratched under Eve's chin. "Cats have good instincts about people. I'd stay away from Archer as much as you can." He held my gaze. "I don't trust him."

The group gathered in front of the elevator. Devon motioned to us. "Let's get going. There're a lot of people waiting to meet both of you."

I whispered to Ian. "Doesn't this seem weird? It's all happening so fast."

"Yeah, but in a good way. I've been waiting—I mean, I'm tired of pretending and being alone for so long."

A thrill ran through me. "I know what you mean. We're with a group of people that will never leave us." A tear slipped from my eye, and I swiped it away. Where did that come from?

How embarrassing. I hope he didn't notice.

Ian's expression softened, and he gave Eve a final scratch on her cheek. "You'll never be alone again, Sadie." He brushed my hair off my face and smiled. My stomach dipped and fluttered.

"We don't have all day," Adam said.

Ian picked up his bag and mine, and we joined the group.

"What type of elevator is this?"

Devon opened the panel and pushed a series of buttons. "It's a magnetic levitation elevator. German technology. We can use it vertically or horizontally. It's quite convenient."

"Ah. A transverter," Ian said almost with reverence.

"You know what it is?" Devon's eyebrows raised.

"Sure. My dad and I have followed the technology for years. It runs on magnets and motors, correct?" Ian asked.

"Yep." Devon finished tapping the code into the panel and the doors slid open. "They've tested it in a few high-rise towers, but we built the first functioning one thirty years before them."

Ian grabbed my hand and tugged. "Let's give this a spin."

I laughed as he pulled me into the large enclosure. My heart raced not knowing what to expect. Everyone entered except Archer. He stood frozen at the door staring at... Oh, Ian still held my hand, and Archer's eyes were locked on them.

"Come on, Archer," Adam called. "Don't tell me you're afraid of the elevator you helped build." He snickered. Lucy gave him an elbow to the ribs. He jumped back and pressed his lips together.

What's with Adam? Always taunting Archer at every opportunity.

"I just remembered. I left something in my car. You guys go on ahead without me." Archer turned away.

"Oh no, you don't." Devon stepped out of the elevator. "We have a meeting with the Elders in a few minutes. I don't want you coming in late. You know how they hate that."

"Fine. You win. I'll get my stuff later." Archer huffed and stepped inside.

Devon returned to the elevator and punched in more codes. "We have to stop at the Hub to drop Henry off with a babysitter. Then we'll head to the tribunal chamber for our meeting."

"Great." Archer rolled his eyes.

"Don't worry. I've cleared the way with the Elders. The other Readers don't know we're coming back yet. After the debriefing, they'll be filled in. You might want to stay out of sight in the back of the elevator in case a Reader sees you before the Elders have a chance to update them."

Archer pursed his lips and nodded.

The elevator stopped, and the doors opened to—Wow. *What in the world?* A huge space opened up in front of us, almost the size of a concert stadium. The ceiling reached up at least thirty feet, and thousands of tube holes of individual lights illuminated the room, giving it a natural, outdoor feel. The vitamin D I packed wouldn't be needed. I stood there, mesmerized by the tube-like structures that channeled the light into the room, until I heard Ian say, "I've never seen anything like this."

My gaze drifted down to the rest of the space. About thirty people stopped what they were doing and stood like statues, staring at us. Wait. They stared at Archer. He'd stayed back in the corner of the elevator, but once the doors opened, he was exposed.

Ian reached over and squeezed my hand. "Can you believe this place? It's fantastic."

"No," I whispered back. Would these Readers form a mob and go after Archer? For all they knew, he killed one of their own and plotted against them.

"This is like the fanciest hotel lobby I've ever seen." Ian's eyes darted around the room. "On steroids." He chuckled. "Look, they have a restaurant and pool tables. Is that authentic artwork by Monet?" He took a step forward.

I searched the expressions of the group. Devon, Ann, Lucy, and Adam all seemed unconcerned about the possibility of violence. I let my shoulders relax a little until I heard a scream. Or was that a squeal?

"Archer! Is that you?"

A girl with wavy blonde hair ran toward the elevator. She hesitated for a moment at the entrance and held her hand over her heart. "I knew you were alive."

This girl was not normal. Her thick, blonde hair almost sparkled, and her perfect features seemed to glow beneath her flawless skin. I already hated her a little.

Before another thought entered my mind, she catapulted herself at Archer, wrapped her legs around his waist, and kissed him on the lips.

"Oh, God. I totally forgot about Susie." Ann eyed the figure wrapped around Archer. "I should've warned you about her."

My entire body turned cold, and my hands formed into fists. I tried to keep my expression blank, but my narrowed eyes probably gave me away. Hating her a little morphed into all-out loathing. Susie. Even her name irritated me.

CHAPTER 15

Archer

A T LEAST ONE person wasn't angry with me. Susie's lips on mine brought back the familiar feeling of home, back when the days of harmless flirting and goofing off were part of our daily life. Susie had liked to pull stunts to get our attention. Normally, I wouldn't mind playing her game, but I wasn't in the mood. I tried to peel her off me, but with her monkey hold, it was difficult. I glanced over at Sadie and thought twice. If looks could kill, Susie would be in ashes at my feet. *Interesting.* Maybe I'd let this Susie thing drag on a bit longer. "Hey, Susie. Great to see you. I see you haven't changed."

She smoothed the hair back from my forehead. "Oh, but I have changed. Come by my room later and I'll show you."

A snort erupted from Sadie.

Susie jumped down and noticed the two new arrivals. "Who

are *they*?"

Her expression would have been more inviting if she had bitten into a lemon. She kept her eyes locked on Sadie.

"Long story. We'll fill you in later." I tried to lead her out of the elevator. She stopped in front of Ian, taking her time to look him up and down. Ian and Sadie stood still, like they were watching a train wreck.

"You're not a Reader. You're too good-looking," she said to Ian.

Sadie's face went from pale to flushed red.

"Hey, now." Devon laughed.

Susie waved him off. "You know you're great looking. But this guy, nope, he's a different race. Look at those high cheekbones, and are those dimples?" She clapped her hands together. "Is he a leftover Jack?"

"No, Susie." Devon sighed. "We have a meeting in a few, so you'll have to wait to find out like everyone else."

A tall girl with brown hair and a paper bag approached from the side. "It's so nice to see everyone. Henry, you must have grown a foot!"

Henry gurgled and laughed.

"Thanks so much, Briana. Are you still able to watch him during our meeting with the Elders?" Devon asked.

"I'd do anything for my little Henry." She smoothed the top of his head. "I have a snack for you." Her eyes flicked over to me. "Hey, Archer."

"Hi, ah, hello, Christine Lee Gribble." Her casual greeting threw me off. *I'm an idiot.*

She smiled and looked me straight in the eyes. "You have a

good excuse for how everything went down?" She tilted her head.

"Not sure yet. We'll be doing some research while I'm here."

"Good luck then. For the record, I never believed you capable of all the—"

"I know. Thanks." My throat tightened. The Readers always wanted to believe the best. How could I ever have thought of destroying them? Atarah. Even her name filled me with a hatred so intense, I could barely breathe. "Hey, can you do me a favor?"

"Sure."

"Can you put Sadie's cat in her room?"

Sadie clutched the carrier with Eve inside.

"She'll be safe."

Sadie looked back and forth between Briana and the cat.

Briana smiled. "I'll take good care of her. I'm in charge of the cat army around here."

Sadie raised an eyebrow. "Cat army?"

"Yep." Her eyes darted to Ann. "We like to keep Samara mouse-free."

"Okay. Um, I should let you know, Eve is scared of loud noises." Sadie put her finger inside the carrier and let the furball lick it.

"I'll keep it nice and quiet for her." Briana plucked Henry out of Devon's arms and gently pried the carrier out of Sadie's closed fists. She headed back toward the kitchen with a "See ya!"

Susie snapped her fingers and blinked a few times. "He's...he's a Seer!"

We all froze. "Why would you think that?" I asked.

"Because of the vision. Don't you remember? It was the second soul mate pairing that saves the next generation with some super child. A Seer"—she glanced at Ian—"and a Reader will get together." She smoothed back her hair.

I could see where this was going. "Susie, that vision has always been nothing more than gossip and never proven." I also heard a version it would be two Seers, not a Reader and a Seer. But I wasn't about to spill that info.

"Maybe, maybe not." Susie giggled and joined the others now gathered around the main dining area. She turned back. "See ya, Archer. And Ian? It was really nice meeting you." She batted her eyelashes and did a hair flick followed by her famous hip-swinging walk back into the Hub.

The elevator doors closed, and we stood in silence for a few moments. Ann laughed first, followed by Devon, Lucy, and Adam. Ian and Sadie still looked a little shell-shocked.

Ian wiped his brow. "What was that? I mean, who is that?"

"I think *what* was that is more accurate." Sadie scowled.

"She's nothing," Ann said and raised an eyebrow in my direction.

"Oh, she's something all right." I laughed.

"You like her?" Sadie's eyes challenged.

"She's harmless. Maybe you'll end up liking her."

Lucy snickered. "Archer, don't get delusional. The day a female likes Susie is when the conspiracy theorists prove the earth is flat."

"You haven't taken the time to get to know her. She can come off a little—" I tried to think of something diplomatic.

"Like a man-eater? Or maybe a bimbo?" Sadie slapped her hand over her mouth. "Did I say that out loud?"

Ann and Lucy broke into peals of laughter. "Oh, yes. Yes, you did," they both said at the same time.

"Ugh. Sorry, guys. It's my dysfunctional sporadic filter. It doesn't work sometimes."

"You mean all the time?" I joked.

Sadie cocked her head and waited a few beats. "Did you hear that?"

"What?"

She grinned. "It's working."

"You stepped right into that one," Adam said while punching in the code for the floor.

I asked Devon, "You didn't change the codes?"

He shrugged. "Never really thought about it." He rubbed his chin. "But now that you mention it, I should have."

"It's because we instinctively knew you wouldn't come back to harm us." Ann patted my arm.

Adam made a groaning sound.

"What's that for?" Sadie called him out.

His eyes widened. Then he put on his mask of bored nonchalance. "Just clearing my throat."

Lucy tugged on Adam's sleeve. She lowered her voice, but I heard her say, "We need to talk."

"It's okay, Lucy. I don't blame him." Even though I didn't like Adam, I didn't want to cause friction with her relationship with him.

Adam's head shot up, and his eyes narrowed as he studied

me.

"I'm being serious. I've had two years to think about everything that went down, and I still can't explain it. If I can't clear myself through our research, I'm willing to face the consequences." I hadn't decided until that very moment that's what I'd do. If I did anything worthwhile in this life, it would be taking responsibility for my actions two years ago. My heart raced, and my stomach churned at the thought of the Colorado Compound, but I'd accept the outcome.

Lucy slapped my arm. "Oh, no you won't. Anyway, we'll research this until we find conclusive proof. Let's not discuss it anymore."

I met her eyes, and they glistened with tears. *Aw, Lucy.* I tried to give her a little smile, but it came out lopsided.

Her lower lip trembled, and she launched herself at me, wrapping her arms around my neck.

"If you're not careful, I'll be dead before we get a chance to clear my name." My effort to make a joke made her cry harder onto my shoulder.

Lucy let go and took a step back. "Sorry." She blinked rapidly. "It's just that, being here makes me nervous. I'm worried about what will happen to you."

"I can handle it. I promise."

A tear escaped from Lucy's eye and tracked down her face. Her voice quiet, she said, "But what if I can't?"

Adam wrapped an arm around her. "It'll be okay."

Lucy sighed and nodded. "Thanks, Adam." She rested her head on his shoulder for a moment and perked up. "Okay, everyone. I'm not going to wallow, I promise. Let's get this party started. We'll go meet with the Elders, then we'll find those darn security tapes."

Good. She was back to her feisty self.

The elevator came to a stop. Devon waved us forward. "The meeting is in the evaluation room."

"See, Lucy? It's not the execution room." I winked.

She pushed her elbow into my ribs. "Very funny."

Sadie wiped her palms on her jeans. "Why am I so nervous?" she asked Ann.

"Oh, I'm always nervous when I go in front of the Elders. They can be an intimidating bunch."

"Great." Sadie crossed her arms.

Ann patted her back. "You have nothing to worry about. This will be a brief, *hi, how are you*. The hard stuff will come later."

"Hard stuff?"

"You know, finding the evidence and clearing Archer's name."

Sadie bit her lip and looked my way. I pretended to be fascinated by the elevator panel, even though I had designed it. I punched in the code to open the doors.

Lucy tucked her arm in mine, with Sadie on the other side. "We're off to see the Wizard." She pulled on both of us, and we exited the elevator.

Sadie laughed, not paying attention until she ran smack into an Elder. "Oh, I'm so sorry! I didn't see you there."

He scowled at her.

Her face flushed. "I don't know the area well. It's my first time and—"

He held up his hand. "Stop."

She froze.

"I don't need to hear your excuses." His icy stare landed on me. "Archer."

"Dad."

Sadie gasped, then hiccupped. It took everything in me not to laugh.

My dad turned back to Sadie and crossed his arms. "This is the Seer."

"Yes?" She clasped her hands in front. "Although my visions don't flow; they're more sporadic."

"I can see why." His glare turned to Ian. "I hope you have a better handle on your gift."

"No, sir," Ian answered and glared right back. My opinion of him just shot up a few points.

"Great. Two useless additions."

"Dad, you don't need—"

"I'm talking." He pointed his long finger at me. "I voted to ship you off to the Colorado Compound with the rest of the criminals. You are not to speak unless I ask you to do so."

I straightened my shoulders. "No, Dad. I'll speak when I have something to say. Now, if you're done judging everyone, we have a meeting to get to." I walked right past his gaping mouth.

Sadie bounced up beside me and raised her right hand. "High five! That was great."

I stopped and raised an eyebrow.

"What?" She covered her mouth and giggled. "Come on,

you're not too old to high-five. That was epic." Her vivid blue eyes sparkled, and the energy around her seemed to crackle.

My pulse sped up, and a warmth spread throughout my body. Intense feelings of, what was it? Friendship? Affection? In a flash of a millisecond, I knew what it was. A lump in my throat formed, and sweat beaded on my forehead. This was nothing like what I felt for Ann. No, it couldn't be love. My heart pounded, and an overwhelming impulse to put my arms around her almost took over, until Ian stepped beside her. The heat spreading inside me turned cold.

Ian watched my father walk away. "Hey, man. I don't want to diss your dad, but he's a jerk. What's his problem?"

It took me a second to tear my eyes away from Sadie to answer him. "It goes way back."

Devon shook his head. "He's in rare form, even for him."

Lucy touched my arm. "I'm sorry, Archer. Maybe one day he'll see how wrong he is."

"I'm not going to hold my breath." He'd never change. And since I'd been exposed as half Jack, he wanted to get rid of me as fast as he could. Just an unwanted reminder his child was a half-breed.

"We're here," Adam announced as he tapped in the code and turned the door handle.

We walked into the room. Wow. Almost exactly the same as the original Samara evaluation room. Replicas of the destroyed original paintings hung on the beige walls, and potted plants and flowers were scattered haphazardly throughout the room. Ten upholstered chairs were strategically placed in a straight line on the floor under the platform holding the fifty-two Elders. My father sat in his usual spot in the middle. I'd hoped we'd make it in before him. He probably slipped in the back entrance so he'd be able to tower over all of us. With his pinched mouth, flat expression, and narrowed eyes, it wasn't hard to guess how he intended the meeting to go. I scanned the other fifty-one Elders, but I didn't sense the same animosity. A few tilted their heads or raised their eyebrows, nothing out of the ordinary for the situation.

The gavel pounded on the table and the Head Elder, Explesor, spoke. "Let's get this started." His intense eyes zoned in on me. "Archer."

"Yes, sir."

"We've heard you were instrumental in saving the lives of five of our Readers."

"Not really. It was Sadie who told me about the tsunami."

His attention shifted to Sadie, and he smiled. "A miracle. It's an honor to meet you."

She blushed, and her eyes darted to me. I nodded.

"Thank you, sir. I'm happy to have helped."

Explesor turned to Ian. "And the other Seer, is it Ian?"

Ian wiped his forehead. "Yes, thank you for having us. Sadie and I would like to continue helping until we find the remaining Jack clone."

Of course, he made it sound like they were already a couple.

Sadie cleared her throat. "I want to make it clear how much Archer has helped, not only the Readers, but also myself and Ian."

His expression gentled, and he smiled with his eyes. "Yes, dear. Devon has filled us in." He tented his hands on the table. "Archer, we'll have a private debriefing later, after you get settled."

Yeah, knew that was coming. "Of course."

"Devon, do you have anything else to inform us of since your last report?"

"No, it's been quiet."

"Okay. We'll expect updates on an hourly basis now that you're back. We have Adam set up in the data room to track any suspicious activity over the internet. We all assume the clone has instructions to draw you out again."

Adam stood. "I'm on it."

"Good. Before you go, I'm assigning Devon and Lucy to make our guests comfortable. We want them to feel like this is their home." He smiled warmly at Ian and Sadie.

Ian and Sadie said, "Thank you," in unison. They're even thinking alike. Acid churned its way up my throat.

We filed out of the room and paused for a moment.

Sadie chuckled. "I felt like I needed to curtsy. Are they always so formal?"

"Yep. And they're exceptionally good at it," Devon answered.

Ann laughed. "Well, that wasn't so bad. Your dad calmed down to a slight scowl."

I took a deep breath, happy to leave. "He's all for appearances. I'm sure it's burning up his insides to have his outcast son return."

Ann placed her hands on her hips. "Well, it's time to change his mind, isn't it?"

"Be my guest. What's the plan?"

"The surveillance tapes. They'll be the key to everything if we can locate them."

"You'll never find them," Adam blurted.

Lucy cocked her head. "What makes you say that?"

He cleared his throat. "I meant the old recordings have probably already been destroyed. I can ask around, but there'd be no reason to keep them. We're short on storage as it is."

Adam might be right.

Lucy shrugged and asked Ann, "Where do you want to look?"

She pursed her mouth. "No idea. Devon?"

"The basement storage where they do the library restorations should be a good start." He rubbed the back of his neck and didn't make eye contact.

Sadie's eyes brightened. "Can I come?"

Ann and Lucy glanced at each other. Ann shrugged. "Why not?"

"I can also help." Ian's gaze flicked to Sadie.

The writing on the wall was clear. His strategy was to not leave her side. Hmm, I wondered how that would go over with Sadie.

Lucy shot me a quick look. "No, thanks. Too many cooks and all." She smiled sweetly.

I wanted to hug Lucy. I knew exactly what she was doing. Too bad she didn't know I'd already given up. Been there, done that.

Then why couldn't I quit thinking about her? Why did I want to touch her so badly it made me weak? *Maybe, if we shared one kiss, I'd be able to get her out of my system.* As the thought swirled through my head, heating my body and making me almost insane, Sadie caught my eye. She didn't break contact for a few seconds before she glanced down at my lips. Realizing what she'd done, a bright red flush crept up her neck while she bit her lip. If the others weren't around, I would've grabbed and kissed her until we both forgot our names.

Stop. She isn't destined for me and never will be.

CHAPTER 16

Sadie

"SADIE. ARE YOU listening?" Ann shook my shoulders.

"What? Um, yeah. You said something about the Hub?" The memory of Archer's intense gaze made my brain fuzzy and my body tingle.

"You zoned out. I was telling you the Elders sent a text informing the Readers about you and Ian, so we might as well hit the Hub for dinner. You okay with catching a bite first before we go to your room?"

"Sure. Sure. Sounds good." Brain. On vacation.

Ann studied my face. "You're one person I wished I could read. I bet it's very interesting up there." She tapped my head.

"No. I don't have any interesting thoughts. Really. All boring up there. I actually don't even think that much." Only about Archer. Ugh.

"Okay. If you say so." Ann chuckled and linked her arm in

mine. "Let's go meet the gang."

"Where is everyone?" I scanned the empty hallway. Lucy, Adam, Archer, Ian, and Devon seemed to have vanished.

"They went on ahead while you did your space-out thing."

"Did anyone notice?"

"No, I think hunger got the best of them, and they took off a few minutes ago."

I closed my eyes and let out a deep breath. "Thank goodness. I seem to always be embarrassing myself."

"Nonsense. You're unique and interesting. Never change. Now come on before they eat all the good food." She tugged at my arm.

"Ann," a voice called from behind us.

Ann turned, and her face brightened. "Doc!"

"How's my favorite patient?" He grinned.

"Perfect." She gave him a hug and motioned to me. "I want you to meet my friend,

Sadie."

I raised a hand. "Hi. Ann's told me so much about you. I feel like I know you already."

Doc was Ann's first friend when she came to Samara.

He cocked his head. "You're the Seer?"

"Guilty." I smiled.

"Come by my office after you get settled. I have many stories about your ancestors right up here." He motioned to his head.

"I'd love that." Maybe he knew my parents.

He smiled and turned to Ann. "Remember to bring Henry

by for his checkup tomorrow."

"Of course. Henry has been asking about 'Wok' for days now." She laughed. "Do you want to join us at the Hub? We're going to grab a bite to eat."

"I have a patient in ten minutes. You two go enjoy yourselves." When he smiled, his eyes crinkled.

We both said goodbye and watched him leave. "There's something about him. He's so..." I couldn't place it.

"Real? Genuine?"

I snapped my fingers. "That's it."

"He's someone you'd want on your side if things go wrong. Not only is he a doctor, he has multiple degrees in psychology and counseling, too. You have a problem, make sure to visit Doc."

"I will."

She hooked her arm in mine. "Let's go meet up with the group."

I let her tug me down the hall and into the Hub. I already loved this room. It had a comforting vibe, almost homey. Ann was right, the group sat at a long table with about six plates of delicious-looking food being passed around. A butterfly war was going on in my stomach, so I gave the group a little wave and ventured out alone to check out the space.

"Don't be too long," Ann called over.

The large room was sectioned into different areas of interest. A game room with ping pong tables, video games, and a pool table were in the east corner. A small movie screen with about thirty overstuffed recliners sat tucked away in the west section, and oh, a popcorn machine. My stomach growled. I glanced at the kitchen bustling with energy at the north end of the room, and at the south end of the spacious area, tables and chairs were scattered around. The center of the room showcased a huge see-through wood-burning fireplace. An upholstered rocking chair sat close to the warmth, and it had my name on it. I plopped down and closed my eyes. Ahhhh.

"I've been through this before and lost. I don't plan on losing again. Especially to you."

That voice. It could only be one person. I glanced over to the chair next to mine where the she-devil, Susie, sat in a high-back chair, glaring at me.

"You lost something?" I might as well play dumb. Ann and Lucy had already filled me in on her obsession with Devon and Archer.

She stiffened and leaned in. "I wouldn't have thought you were stupid, but I'll explain. I will get Archer." She flung her blonde tresses over her shoulder. "That ninny Ann snagged Devon, but I won't let some silly little girl get in my way this time."

"Okay."

"What do you mean, okay? Are you trying to trick me?" Her face flushed red.

"No, have at it. If Archer wants a *ninny* like you, I'm sure he'll get what he deserves."

She huffed. "You may be protected by the Elders for now, but that could change. Don't let their friendly welcome give you a sense of security." Her eyes narrowed. "Once you step out of line, I'll be right there making sure you get tossed out like the day-old trash you are."

"Aww. Isn't this sweet, Ann? Susie is welcoming Sadie into the fold." Lucy stood next to Susie's chair.

Ann positioned herself on the other side. "Yes, I'm sure she's showing our guest how kind she is." Ann raised an eyebrow that morphed into a menacing glare.

"Whatever." Susie catapulted out of her chair and stomped off.

"I heard the entire thing. You okay?" Lucy plopped down in the vacated seat.

"Yes, I expected it after our first meeting. But it seems like she's out to get me."

"Don't worry. She's all bark. Mostly. She'll try to cause trouble, but I think she's just trying to scare you off." Ann shook her head and kept her eyes trained on Susie as she weaved around the tables in Archer's direction.

Lucy leaned toward me. "For now. But don't trust her. Watch your back, Sadie. We'll also keep an eye on her. If she continues, we'll file a complaint with the Elders. That should set her straight. She wants to appear like a perfect Reader and get voted to an upper-level position, stuff like that."

"That's good to know. Hopefully, that'll keep her in line." I followed Ann's line of vision to see what Susie was up to next. My empty stomach clenched. "I think I'll throw up."

"Why?" Lucy asked and then looked over at Archer. "Ooohh."

Susie had scooted her chair right next to Archer, and her hand smoothed his hair back off his face.

"I'm gagging." I wasn't joking. Not only was she falling all over Archer, he wasn't pushing her away. He smiled like he enjoyed it.

"Archer has always held her at arm's length," Lucy said. "He tolerates her. She never shows him her true side."

"Has anyone told him, you know, about her spawn-of-Satan side?"

Lucy sighed. "Plenty of times. He thinks she's funny and harmless."

"Has she ever followed through on one of her *harmless* threats?" Pretty sure she was part evil.

Lucy shook her head. "Not that we know of, but she likes to stir up trouble."

"Great."

"Let's get some food in you. Then we can go check out your room. You'll love it." Lucy's eyes brightened.

"Why?"

"You're just going to have to wait and see."

"Never mind about food. Let's go see it now." I'd never been a patient person. We all stood, getting ready to head out.

A tap on my shoulder made me jump back a foot.

"Sorry, I didn't mean to scare you." Ian smiled, showing off his dimples.

Was that a sigh coming from Lucy and Ann's direction? It was almost impossible to look away from his handsome face.

He cocked his head. "What are you going to see?"

"My room. There's a surprise in there. Right, Lucy?"

Lucy laughed. "Can't get anything by you, Sadie."

Ian glanced at the kitchen. "I'm going to grab some ice cream and head to my room."

"Ice cream?" I looked at Ann and Lucy. "You have ice cream here?"

"Yes, Sadie. We also have all the other food groups." Lucy

put her hands on her hips. "You think you're in the outback or something?"

I covered my mouth to stifle a laugh. "Well, sort of. When you said we were going inside a mountain, I thought maybe it'd be a little like camping." My eyes did a sweep around the room. "Obviously, I was wrong."

Lucy nodded. "Very wrong. Wait until you see the waterfall room."

"Oh, and the rainforest room. That's my favorite." Ann placed her hand over her heart.

"I'll grab some extra ice cream if you want to stop by my room later," Ian offered.

"I'm terrible with directions, and I don't know where your room is located." Too excited to see my room, food would have to wait.

"Well, it should be easy because my room is right next to yours."

"Oh." My breath caught.

"With a connecting door." He smiled and waggled his eyebrows.

Was he flirting with me? I stood frozen in my spot and stared at him.

He chuckled. "Don't look so excited about it. I promise I won't come through the door, unless, of course, I'm invited." And then he winked.

Definitely flirting.

Lucy giggled and choked at the same time.

Ann pounded her back. "You okay there?" She shot me a quick look with widened eyes and mouthed, "Wow."

My cheeks flushed red. The best way to break the awkwardness of the moment was to play it off as a joke. Ian must be teasing me...*I think*. "Ha ha, very funny. Okay, girls, let's get going."

Ann linked her arm in mine. "Nice seeing you, Ian. We'll take it from here."

He gave a little bow and waved us forward.

As soon as we got out of earshot, Lucy grabbed a napkin from a table and fanned herself. "That guy, good grief. I think my ovaries just gave a standing ovation. He's too good-looking to let loose on the female population."

"That's what I thought when I first met him. But once you get to know him, he becomes a regular person. Does that make sense?"

"No." Lucy kept fanning herself.

"Does someone have a little crush?" Ann winked, and nudged her.

"Of course not!" Lucy's face matched her red hair. "I can appreciate beauty from afar. I'm with Adam. And even if I weren't, Ian looks at Sadie like she's holding the last hot dog at a World Series game."

"No, he doesn't." I waved her off. "He likes to hang with me because we're both Seers. He'll branch out now that we're with the Readers."

"And I suppose you don't know Archer feels the same way? Except he might have it worse. I haven't quite figured him out yet. He seems to run hot and cold." Lucy shrugged. "I'll get back to you on that."

"Gee, thanks." I rolled my eyes. The mention of Archer always made my stomach take a dive. I wondered if that was a good or bad thing.

"Just remember, when you leave the Hub, take the first right, the third left, then three hallways down, another right." Lucy fast-talked the directions.

"You lost me at the third left. How do you guys do it? I'll be hopelessly lost if I leave my room."

Ann stopped for a moment to admire the paintings. "It was worse before, when all the walls were beige."

"I was just going to ask you who did all these beautiful murals." Each wall featured a famous painter. Famous works imitating Monet, Gauguin, and Rembrandt covered the three walls we'd passed by.

Ann ran her fingers lightly over the Rembrandt. "We have a lot of talented Readers who've studied the masters for centuries. Some even surpass the originals in technique and talent."

Lucy slowed to keep at my pace. "We brought color back into Samara when we built this one."

"What do you mean?"

"The original Samara had beige walls for security. If there was a Jack invasion, the Elders figured they'd get lost with all the twists and turns. Our plan was to escape through one of the emergency exits."

We traveled around another corner. "Oh, that makes sense."

Lucy's shoulders sagged. "We thought the Jacks were gone for good."

"Only one clone left." Ann put her arm around Lucy's shoulder. "He can't stay hidden forever. Adam will find him."

Lucy's face brightened. "You're right. Adam can do just about anything."

And once the Jack clone was located, somehow, I'd need to find a way to kill him.

"Here we are." Lucy stopped in front of door 777. My flowered duffle sat against the door.

"If there are only three hundred forty-two Readers, then why the number 777?"

"Oh, that. The Elders assign a number for each Reader, in your case, a Seer. Most of the time it relates to one's purpose in the group. Your number is all about your journey. When you see three sevens, it means something beautiful and awe-inspiring is happening or is about to happen in your life."

My heart stumbled, then melted. "Oh, that's sweet." I noticed Ian's luggage the next door over. "Ian got 999. What does that mean?"

"That's the number for completion. Something in Ian's life will end or be completed soon."

Interesting. "It sounds like the Elders have a little of the Seer gift in them."

Lucy tilted her head and paused for a moment. "Not really. It's more like intuition."

Archer came bounding around the corner and screeched to a stop. "Oh, hey." He panted and brushed the hair back from his eyes.

Stomach. Dive.

"Susie chasing you or something?" Lucy winked.

"Funny girl. No, I forgot I left cupcakes in the oven."

Silence. We all stood together, staring with our mouths open.

"What? Do you think I spent the last two years staring at the ocean?"

"Yes." Oops. That slipped out.

He smirked. "I love the ocean." He stared at me a beat longer. "Just like you, Sadie."

I took a long swallow.

"We are similar that way." Jerk. He knew I spent two years watching him.

"And you make time to learn new things, like writing books, gardening, and spy techniques. You know, the usual stuff." A mischievous twinkle in his eye gave him away.

"Whatever." I flicked my hair over my shoulder. I knew I looked like a brat, but I didn't care.

He leaned over and punched numbers on a pad.

The pad that was right next to my room. "Wait. That's not your room, is it?"

"Yeah. Why?"

Lucy pointed to the door. "This is Sadie's room. Right next to yours."

He quirked an eyebrow.

"I guess they wanted to group us all together." I shifted my purse to the other shoulder, but before I could get it hooked on, it dropped to the floor, dumping all my girl stuff.

He ignored the mess. "All of us?"

"Oh yeah." I shot my thumb over my shoulder. "Ian's on the other side."

"Well, isn't that cozy?" His jaw clenched.

I casually picked the tampons and lipstick up off the floor and stuck them back into my purse. "I guess it makes sense."

"Do you also have a connecting door to Sadie's' room?"

"Also?" His eyes narrowed.

"Yeah. Ian was flirting with Sadie and mentioned the connecting door between their rooms," Lucy proudly informed him.

A sudden urge to put my hand over Lucy's mouth took hold.

Archer's lips tightened, and a crease formed between his eyebrows.

"It was just a joke." I laughed but didn't pull off the levity I was shooting for.

Without a word, he pushed the last button and disappeared behind his door.

"Uh oh." Lucy bit her lip. "I didn't think it would make him that upset. I've always teased him about stuff. He usually takes it a lot better."

"I'm sure he's fine, Lucy." Ann studied his closed door. "It's been a long day for everyone."

Lucy nodded. "Okay, if you say so." She turned back to me. "Your room is equipped with a fingerprint pad. It's not only easier than trying to remember a code, it has better security."

"Why do I need more security?"

"Well, the Elders are still concerned about the vision not being certified. You know, the process of ten Seers documenting the results. The war began before it could get done."

"Which vision is this?"

"It's the one that said someone who lived with the Readers would betray us. We thought if the vision were true, it would've been Archer. But now because of Atarah, it's up in the air. The Elders are concerned that you might be in danger. Most of them are convinced it's not Archer, so it might mean anyone living in the Reader Compound could feel threatened by you and Ian. You might see their plan before they can carry out their sabotage."

"I didn't even consider something like that."

Lucy tapped her finger against her lips. "Now that I think about it. That's probably why the Elders grouped you together. They're expecting Archer and Ian to keep you safe."

"What about Ian? There could be someone after him. Who will watch his back?"

"Why, you, of course." Lucy grabbed my finger and placed it on the pad outside my room. The lock clicked, and the door opened.

"Cool. And how am I supposed to protect Ian?"

"I'm sure that's why you have the connecting door. Come on, I'll show you." She took me by the shoulders and led me to what appeared to be a painting by Monet in the foyer. She picked up my finger again, pressed it against a water lily, and a huge steel door opened.

"Wow. It looks like a regular door." Inside, weapons of every size and shape hung on hooks on three walls. AR-15s, knives, pepper spray, guns, a Kubotan, and drawers with who knows what else.

Ann clapped her hands. "Oh, the Kubotan. My favorite."

"We should practice together. I love the Kubotan." It appeared benign, but could inflict a lot of damage if you knew how to use it. It was the normal size, a small, carved stick about six-and-a-half inches long. The ridges fit between each finger with the end coming to a point.

Lucy leaned over and whispered, "You don't want to do that unless you love pain and misery."

Ann laughed. "I heard that. I'll go easy on her."

"Could we schedule it after I get a refresher? It's been years." I picked up the second Kubotan and enjoyed the smooth surface in my hands.

Lucy tugged on my arm. "I'd practice eight hours a day for a couple hundred years. Then you might not get smashed to the ground." She laughed. "Now for the tour."

We walked from the foyer to the living area, where I stopped dead in my tracks. "Oh! How did you... I mean, what in the world?" The room was the replica of my cottage living room.

Ann and Lucy wore huge grins.

"I never thought it'd be something like this. I mean, maybe a cozy blanket or something. Wait. What is that?" I pointed to a large structure with carpeting.

"That's a cat hotel, silly. Don't tell me you've never seen one before."

My eyes started at the bottom and worked their way to the top, where Eve lounged, sound asleep. "Eve sure looks relaxed." I laughed.

"That's because they put catnip in every room, so she'd explore around."

"You drugged my cat?" I kept my face straight.

Lucy adjusted her shirt. "Um. No." She cleared her throat. "It's more like a recreational substance for enjoyment."

Eve stayed curled up, not moving. Hmm. Maybe I should tease Lucy a little more. I looked closer. "Is she still alive?"

Lucy went for the distraction technique. "It's harmless. Let's go exploring, shall we?"

After I tore my eyes from Eve, I took in all the special touches they'd done to help make me feel at home. "Some of my furniture was from the eighteenth century. How'd they put these replicas together so fast?"

"Archer sent pictures after the first time he was in your house. He didn't tell you because he'd taken a vow of secrecy."

I laughed. "I won't give him a hard time then."

"They also stocked your kitchen with all your favorite foods." Lucy waved her hand around the kitchen. "Adam broke into security at that cute little Cannon Beach mom-and-pop store you like to shop at."

My stomach grumbled again, and a shot of excitement ran through me. I didn't even mind the invasion of my privacy. "Hot Tamales and Fritos?"

"Yes, they put the disgusting processed food in your junk food drawer over there." Ann pointed to a large drawer next to the sink.

"This place is impressive. I would've never thought I'd get my own kitchen, let alone have stainless steel appliances and granite countertops. The blue and pale-yellow colors make me feel like I'm home."

"Wait until you see your bedroom. They did a few things different."

Lucy strode across the room and swung open a door. "Ta-da!"

Ann started to walk into the bedroom but jumped back and screamed. "Oh my God, it's a rat!"

I covered my mouth before a giggle could escape. I didn't

want her to think I was making fun of her phobia. "Maybe Eve went hunting before you catnipped her." I pressed my lips together in another attempt not to embarrass her.

Lucy walked into the bedroom and picked up a note off the bed, scanned it and said, "Uh oh. Ann, call Devon right away."

"What is it?" I tried to peer inside. Lucy pushed me back out of the room.

"You don't want to see it," she said as she kept urging me out.

I stopped in my tracks. "Yes, I do. What's going on? A dead rat isn't a big deal. I can handle it."

Lucy looked down at the floor. "It's not the rat I'm worried about."

"Look at me." I lifted an eyebrow and waited.

"The rat came with a note." Her eyes darted around the room.

"Okay. What does the note say?"

She took a deep breath and met my eyes. "It says: *This is your first and only warning. If you don't leave, you and your cat will be next.*"

My hands clenched, and my nostrils flared. "Cat! Someone's after Eve?" I sprinted back into the living room, picked up Eve, and held her close. Her breathing remained slow and steady, oblivious to my inner turmoil.

Just as my heartbeat slowed, the adjoining door next to the couch burst open. Archer ran in holding a gun and wearing...an apron?

CHAPTER 17

Archer

WITH MY HEART beating out of my chest, I bypassed security on the connecting door. My hands shook as I punched in the emergency code. Who'd screamed? Was it Sadie? Sweat broke out across my forehead. No. It couldn't be Sadie. Not her. I pushed everything from my brain and went into warrior mode—focused only on neutralizing the situation and making sure Sadie stayed safe.

I burst into the room and found Sadie clutching the damn cat like it was her lifeline. I pointed my gun away from her and pivoted around the room. Ann was talking to someone on the phone. Probably Devon. Lucy approached Sadie and rubbed her back.

"Anyone in the room?" My eyes and gun were aimed at the bedroom door.

"It's clear." Lucy turned to me. "I pressed the silent alarm just in case."

Sadie continued to clutch her cat. "They threatened Eve!" Her face reddened, and she stomped her foot. "Why would anyone do that, harm a vulnerable animal?" Her entire body shook, her skin paled, and her lips and chin trembled. "I'll find them. They'll be sorry they ever tried to scare me like this."

Lucy glanced around and grimaced. "Uh, Sadie, they also threatened you."

"Pfft. I'm not worried about that. Bring it on." Her hands clenched around the cat's fur. "She's a defenseless cat. What kind of monster would go after a cat?"

"How was Sadie threatened?" I asked.

Ann shivered. "A note's attached to a dead rat, threatening both of them."

Adrenaline still coursed through my veins, but it didn't stop me from saying, "You've got to be kidding me. You're worried about that...fur, I mean, cat?" A chuckle escaped.

Sadie's eyes narrowed.

I held up my hands. "Okay, the situation isn't funny." The person who did this will wish they were never born after I got through with them. "But you're hanging onto that furball like her life is more important than yours. That's a little out of whack, don't you think?"

"No." She held her chin high, but seemed to calm down. "Eve's been...she's been the only cat I've adopted since 1825." She took a deep breath. "I couldn't live with myself if she died because of me."

"Nothing will happen to either of you." Ann gave her a side hug so she wouldn't squish the cat. "Look at her. She slept through the whole thing." She petted Eve's head. "I'll go wait by the door for Devon."

"Lucy?" I asked.

"Yeah?"

"Do you still carry plastic gloves in your purse?"

"Sure do. I have just about everything in here." She rummaged through the disaster she called a purse.

"You might as well bag the note. This is a crime scene now."

Sadie perked up. "Do you have Reader police?"

"We call them Reader patrols, but yes, they're like police, and they also have a forensic unit that will process the scene."

"Do you think we'll be able to find who did this?"

"We should be able to if the cameras are functional, and there's at least some microscopic evidence left behind."

Sadie kept petting Eve's head and nodded. "That's good."

The door burst open on the other side of the room, and Ian dashed in. "Everybody okay? The red light was on."

Sadie forced a smile. "We're okay."

Ian in Sadie's room didn't feel right, and irritation took hold. "A little late for the party, aren't you, Roberts?"

"It's Ian."

"Okay, Robbie."

Ian's eyes shot daggers at me. "Again, it's Ian."

I shrugged. Maybe he got to have Sadie, but that didn't mean I had to be happy about it.

Ian approached Sadie as Devon came through the foyer to where we all stood in the living room. "Okay, everyone out." He pointed to the door. "The Hub is still open. I'll meet everyone there after the patrol team arrives."

"Sadie, you okay?" Devon asked.

"Just peachy." She scowled in my direction.

I tried to smooth things over. "Okay, maybe I shouldn't have laughed at your off the charts reaction to your cat being threatened."

"Her name is Eve." Still glaring.

"Uh, okay. Eve. Anyway, I'm sure they'll beef up security after this. Eve will be fine."

"I know she'll be fine, because I don't plan to leave her again. Anyone see my cat carrier?"

Great.

"Devon, is it all right if I get her carrier out of the closet?" Ann asked, and then turned to Sadie. "I helped put your things away."

"That's sweet. Thanks, Ann."

"The rat is still in there. I'll get it." Devon always looked out for Ann. I waited for a few beats. Nope. No knife in the heart pain.

My eyes shifted to Sadie. She'd turned pale, and even though she was trying to act brave, her lips trembled, and her eyes were glazed over.

"Someone get Sadie a chair. Right now. She needs a glass of water." I'd seen shock too many times to ignore the signs.

Lucy jumped into action by taking Sadie's arm and guiding her to a kitchen stool. She handed Sadie a glass of water and sat beside her. "You okay, honey?"

Sadie closed her eyes and drank the entire glass. She rubbed her temples and looked up at me. It started as a small laugh and escalated into peals of laughter. By this time, Devon had returned, and we all watched Sadie lose it.

"It's the shock," I mouthed to the group.

Sadie covered her mouth, looked at me, laughed harder, and turned away.

Ian lowered his voice and asked Devon, "Do you think she's having a mental breakdown from the shock?" That made Sadie laugh even harder.

She wiped her eyes and settled down. "Sorry, everyone." She pressed her lips together even though she still laughed. "I'm not losing it, I promise."

Ann approached her like she was a wounded animal. "Can I get you anything? Maybe more water?"

"No." She started full-on laughing again and looked down. "I'll be fine in a minute."

I kept my eyes glued to her to look for more signs of shock.

"It's Archer's fault," she said with a hiccup.

"My fault?"

"If anyone were to tell me Archer would rush in to save me with a gun and..." She snorted and laughed some more. "A gun and a pink...a pink Barbie apron, I'd never have believed it in a million years."

Oh hell.

All eyes turned to me.

"It was the only one in the laundry," I said, which, again, only made Sadie laugh harder. Ann, Devon, and Lucy joined in while Ian wore a blank expression and crossed his arms over his chest.

"Okay, enough of this." Devon clapped his hands. "I'll wait

here for the team. You'll have to ridicule Archer at the Hub." He winked at me.

"Thanks, Devon." I removed the apron and went back into my room. A few wisps of smoke came from the oven, so I flipped the switch to off and rejoined the group.

Sadie put her cat in the carrier, and everyone started out toward the Hub. Ann stayed behind with Devon, and Lucy and Sadie kept up with their intermittent laughing while Ian walked beside them with a puzzled expression.

Sadie broke free from the pack and sidled up to me. "Thanks, Archer."

"For what?"

"Well, risking your life to save me. I'm sorry I laughed about your apron." She looked away, and her shoulders shook.

"You're still laughing?" I couldn't help it. Her laugh was contagious, so I joined in.

"Really, though." She hiccupped. "You look good in pink."

I gave her an elbow, and that shock thing happened again. "Geez, do you eat static every day?" I rubbed my elbow.

"No, it's your fault." She massaged her arm. "It must be the carpet."

Ian joined us. "What must be the carpet?"

"Oh, just some static electricity thing." She touched his arm. "Nope. It's gone now."

Ian's eyes widened just a fraction, and he glanced at me with a crease slicing his brow. We walked a few more feet before he excused himself and said he'd be right back.

Sadie waved. "See you in a few."

We found a large table in the center of the room and settled in. Sadie scooted the cat carrier under the table and leaned forward. "Should we start to plan or wait for the others?"

Lucy reached into her purse and pulled out a notebook and pencil. "I'm prepared for every situation. We can fill them in later."

"Okay," Sadie started. "While we wait for the Jack clone to make his move, we should focus on clearing Archer by finding the security tapes."

"Yep. That's what I was thinking." Lucy scratched her chin with the pencil. "We need to use this time wisely, because who knows when the Jack will make his next move. We have a lot of areas to search." Lucy motioned to a waiter and turned to Sadie. "The eggplant parmesan is wonderful. They also have a killer macaroni and cheese."

Sadie tilted her head for a moment. "I think today is an eggplant day."

Lucy called to the waiter, Noah, "One eggplant for my friend. Archer, you want anything?"

"I'll take a hot fudge sundae. Thanks, Noah," I yelled.

"What happened to your cupcakes?" Sadie kept her lips pressed tight.

"Burned. And I don't want to hear about it." I tried to make my expression intimidating, but she laughed anyway.

"Here's the deal." Lucy leaned in. "We have to locate the security tapes from two different time periods." She held up a finger. "One, from the day Markus died." A second finger joined the first. "Two, the day of the explosion."

It sounded easy, but we had our work cut out for us.

"Are they stored off-site, like, in the cloud?" Sadie asked.

I shook my head. "No. Too many ways for a security breach.

Everything we do has to stay under the radar. The security files are small, about the size of your small toe. They carry about a year of data for each file." They'd be easy to hide. I didn't want to bring everyone down, but the chances we'd find them were slim.

"How many square feet is Samara?" Sadie's eyes roamed around the room.

"Three hundred fifty thousand," I answered.

"Wow. Really? I need to tour this place."

"I can—" I started.

"I'll take you on a tour. I have the map already memorized." Ian came from behind and sat next to Sadie.

"You're kidding?" Sadie's eyebrows rose.

"Nope. Photographic memory right here." He tapped on his head.

"Okay, everyone," Lucy interrupted. "We need to stay focused. Does anyone have an idea where we should start?"

I shrugged. "Maybe in the library? It'd be easy to hide the files in an old book."

"It'd be too risky for someone to come across them by accident." Lucy shook her head. "How about the obvious place? The safe?"

I rubbed my temples. "Too many Elders have access. If someone, specifically the betrayer, took the files before the explosion, they could've hidden them anywhere. They might be sitting right in front of our faces."

"And we don't know if they destroyed them either." Lucy sighed. "Maybe the process of elimination will help. Let's think of all the places they wouldn't be."

"Well, the waterfall and rainforest rooms are out. Too much moisture." I ran through the footprint of Samara in my head. "Also, the kitchen and bathroom areas, and laundry rooms."

Lucy nodded. "I don't think it would be in any of the personal rooms. Whoever stole them in the first place wouldn't want to be implicated if sensitive security files were found in their space."

"True," Sadie agreed.

Lucy tapped her pencil on the table. "Okay, now let's talk about where they could be."

"Right here in the Hub." I pointed at the ping pong table. The files could be hidden in a panel on the underside.

"Yeah, they'll probably be somewhere we wouldn't expect." Lucy's gaze zipped from the floor to the ceiling.

"How about the storage room?" I asked.

"Nah," Lucy said. "It'd be too easy for someone to come across them."

Ian offered, "How about behind one of the paintings? The files could be taped to the back."

"Yeah, but they'd have to keep up with the restoration sessions. They'd want to find a place where they wouldn't have to check on them." Lucy continued to tap her pencil as she thought. "How about outside somewhere? They could've dug a hole and put them in a watertight container."

"That's a good one." I wouldn't have thought to look outside. "The classrooms and gym might be worth a search."

"Eggplant parmesan?"

"Oh, me, me." Sadie held her hands out for the plate. "I didn't know I was so hungry."

"Hot fudge sundae goes to Archer." The waiter set the glass bowl in front of me. I grabbed a spoon and dug in.

Sadie stopped eating and stared at my ice cream.

"Um. Do you want a bite?"

"You'd share?" She wiggled and bounced in her chair.

I rolled my eyes and handed her the spoon.

She leaned over and scooped up the ice cream with a large glob of hot fudge. She closed her eyes and put the huge bite in her mouth. About a second later, she spit it out into her napkin. "There's something wrong with the ice cream."

"What do you mean?" I hadn't noticed anything.

"It tastes like it's carbonated or something. Maybe it went bad?" She gasped. "Oh no. Do you think someone is trying to poison you?"

Devon and Ann arrived and sat across the table from Sadie. "Sadie, they're done with your room. You can go back now if you want." Devon looked around the table. "What's wrong?"

Lucy grabbed the bowl of ice cream. "We think someone might have tampered with Archer's ice cream. Sadie said it tasted funny."

"Yeah, like all bubbly in my mouth," Sadie added.

Devon raised an eyebrow and shot Ann a quick glance. "Here, let me try it."

"No!" Sadie shouted, and her face flushed. She scanned the table. "Isn't anyone else worried about it?"

"How do you feel?" Devon asked.

She bit her lip. "Okay, why?"

Devon took the spoon and put a bite of ice cream in his

mouth. "Tastes normal. Did you eat some red sauce right before?"

"Yes." Sadie drew out the word.

"That can happen sometimes. The acid in the tomatoes can interact with the dairy."

She wrinkled her nose. "Oh. I've never heard that before. Sorry for shouting."

Devon smiled. "No worries. I don't blame you. I'll send it to the lab just in case."

"I don't think you'll find anything. Sadie's just a little on edge," I said.

"Oh, I am?" Her eyes narrowed.

"The note?"

She checked the cat carrier again and sighed. "You're right."

Lucy plopped her notebook on the table. "I don't know about you, but I'm beat. How about tomorrow we start our task force and split up into groups?"

"Sounds good." Sadie turned and asked Ian, "How about you help me find my room? I don't think I'll make it past the third turn."

Ian shifted in his chair and asked Lucy, "Hey, can you help Sadie to her room? I have an errand I need to do."

Sadie's eyes widened, but she smiled and nodded.

Lucy stood. "Sure. I want to make sure she knows where everything is in her room. I'll get a to-go box for your eggplant."

"Thanks. Let me get Eve." Sadie grabbed the carrier from under the table.

"Is that cat ever awake?" Lucy raised a brow.

"You've never heard of cat naps?" She hooked her arm in Lucy's and headed out.

Devon took Ann's hand and started to leave.

"I'll join you." I started to get up.

"Wait." Ian sat rigid.

"What's up?"

"I thought you said you'd back off." His fingers drummed an impatient beat on the table.

"I have." A sinking feeling edged in. "You're not suggesting I can't even have a friendship with her."

"That's exactly what I meant. You're just going to confuse her. Can't you see that? She'll be stuck right in the middle. Do you really want to put her through that when we both know what the outcome should be?"

I sat back in my chair, closed my eyes, and tried to process. I was kidding myself. I couldn't be just friends with Sadie. I'd want more, and she'd sense it. She'd be torn, but ultimately, she'd sacrifice everything for the Seers and to fulfill one of their final visions. I rubbed my forehead. "I get it. I'll back off." The stabbing pain returned. This time for a different woman. And this time it was much worse.

CHAPTER 18

Sadie

I PICKED UP a glob of mud and considered flinging it at Archer's head. Instead, I flung it a few feet away from the hole we were digging.

Lucy wiped dirt and sweat from her face with her arm. "It's been two months searching the entire compound and three days digging and still nothing."

Archer and Devon had mapped out the digging sites two hundred feet from the rooftop exit. It rained the night before, so it turned our area into a mud bath. Lucy put down her shovel, flopped onto the grass, and lay on her back. "Are Archer and Susie still digging?"

A glance in their direction about thirty feet away proved my suspicion. Archer fervently dug a hole while Susie sat next to him on a dainty, little chair, filing her nails. "Ugh. She's doing exactly what she's done for two months."

"What's that?" Lucy asked.

"Nothing," I replied.

"That sounds like Susie." Lucy sent a glare in their direction. "I don't know why her uncle insisted she be included on the dig. I can't imagine her volunteering."

"I mean, she's supposed to like Archer, and she's not even trying to help him," I said. The past two months had been hell. Between Archer acting like I didn't exist and searching for the digital files until my mind went numb, I was ready to jump ship. I lay down next to Lucy and stared up at the blue sky. At least it was beautiful here. The fresh air and smell of the pine trees, along with a scattering of wild mountain flowers, made me almost enjoy digging for the hidden treasure—*Archer's* treasure. Proof he didn't kill his friend Markus and had, in fact, been under Atarah's control.

"Susie will only participate if it helps her. She's always been like that."

Maybe I'd throw the mud at her instead.

"Do you think Archer will marry her?" I held my breath, waiting for an answer. Lucy sighed. "When we all came here two months ago, I would have said you and Archer would get together. The chemistry, wow, it was smoking. And then poof! Nothing. Did you have an argument?"

"We always argue. But I don't think that's why he's giving me the cold shoulder. Maybe he just likes Susie better." Saying the words made me gag.

"Nah. He's trying to distract himself. I've been watching him. His eyes look sad." Lucy frowned. "Have you noticed that?"

Yep. I noticed. "Maybe a little. Do you think it's coming back to Samara and feeling guilty or something? It probably sucks a little of his soul each day we don't find the files."

"True. If we're frustrated, he must feel a thousand times worse."

I rolled onto my stomach. "Maybe we should approach this from another angle."

Lucy turned on her side. "What do you suggest?"

"We should dissect the visions, even the ones that weren't confirmed."

"Okay, let's start with the first one about Ann. The vision stated there'd be a lost Reader who'd decide the outcome of the war between the Readers and the Jacks."

"Yep."

"That one was confirmed, and we know how that turned out." Lucy smiled.

"Okay. Let's talk about the next one."

"How about the one about a Reader and Seer match? They'll have a child that will save the earth from nuclear war. This one wasn't confirmed, and when the Seers were wiped out... Oh, sorry, Sadie."

"It's okay." My throat tightened a little.

"Anyway, we all dismissed it. Now that you and Ian are here, we'll have to consider it as a possibility." She pulled a few blades of grass. "There's also a vision about a two Seer match. I wonder if that could be you and Ian?"

"I haven't heard that one before." *Interesting.*

"And the next one. The person who'd betray the Readers. Again, we need to rethink this one because we assumed it was Archer. Now with everything in doubt, we'll need to be open to all possibilities."

"I vote for Susie." I chuckled.

"Yes, she wins the Obnoxious Award. Keep your eyes and ears open. Finding the person who's the possible betrayer might lead us to the hidden files."

That made sense. "Because if we could prove it wasn't Archer, the attention would fan out to all the Readers. Do you have any suspicions?" I asked.

"Not one." She sighed.

"I haven't had any visions pop up since Cannon Beach when Archer almost shot Ian. I'd hoped my mom's necklace would help things along. It's frustrating. Do you think the Jack clone could be interfering?"

Lucy pursed her lips. "I don't know. That's what we should talk about next. The clones must have been programmed with instructions to draw us out. Devon worries that, with each week that goes by, he'll get stronger. If the Jacks were able to tap into Archer's limbic system, the clone might have some of his memories. That could be a dangerous thing."

"The Jack clone won't have any memories of me, right?"

"That's right, Archer didn't know you back then. But if the clone is connected with the betrayer, there might be some surface stuff he'll have learned about you. You'll need to be careful and watch out for that when we leave the mountain."

"Maybe a code word might work."

Lucy nodded. "Excellent idea."

"The word *beach* would be appropriate and simple enough for us both to remember." I said.

"Just make sure you discuss it outside the mountain in case some or all the rooms are bugged. We can't take any chances."

My brain couldn't keep track of everything. "Okay. How many threats do we have right now?"

Lucy held up a finger for each. "We have the betrayer, the Jack, whoever planted the bomb in Arizona, and whoever they talked to in Portland."

"Could the betrayer and the Portland or Arizona connection be the same person?"

"Possibly. I'll ask Devon or Adam to research every Reader to see if any were off the mountain at the time of the explosion. We can examine each one and eliminate as we go."

"I'm glad we talked. Maybe we won't have to dig for the next hundred years." I sat up.

"Before we go, I wanted to see if you were open to working with Ian on getting the visions to come back, if you were to come outside and have some sort of séance-type thing? How about it?"

I shook my head. "I've never tried that before. In the past, the visions just came to me. I didn't have to work for them, but it's worth a try. We could sit together and concentrate on a specific thing. Like where the files are hidden."

Lucy clapped her hands and stood. "That's a great idea! Let's get cleaned up and track Ian down. Where is he searching today?"

"The classrooms. He's combed through them once already, but is going back to see if he missed anything."

"If you get a vision, let's keep it between the two of us. Just as a precaution. We know Devon, Ann, Ian, and Adam are off the list of possible betrayers. But if the building is bugged, it's best not to say anything."

"That's a good idea." I got up and wiped the dirt from my pants with a renewed sense of determination. "Let's blow this popsicle stand."

Lucy tilted her head and stared.

"You know, let's get out of here."

"Popsicle stand?" She laughed.

"I keep forgetting you only go out a few months a year. It's a slang term, started around 1920. My hus—I mean, someone I knew always said it."

She took my hand. "Sadie. You know you can talk to me about it."

Tears formed. "I broke every rule," I blurted.

"Aw, honey. What happened?"

I wiped my face and took a deep breath. "I fell in love with a mortal." The tears streamed so rapidly, I couldn't wipe them away fast enough. "I tried so hard not to fall for him. He smiled at me, and it was over." I laughed and cried at the same time. "I knew it would end, but…" I shook my head. "I was powerless. He didn't even die of old age. It was cancer at forty-seven. There should have been so many more years together."

"Is that why you're avoiding Archer and staying clear of Ian?"

"Maybe. But it's Archer who's avoiding me. I'm keeping Ian at arm's length because I don't know how I feel."

I glanced over at Archer just in time to see Susie wrap her arms around his neck. It was like watching a train wreck in slow motion when they kissed. The mystery of why Archer avoided me was solved. I turned my back because if I continued to watch, I'd throw up. A kick in the stomach would have felt better. Why would he go for her? Why did I feel like a part of me had died?

Lucy must have seen the kiss because she said, "You should give Ian a chance. You two have a special bond."

I pushed my shoulders back. "That's true. I should at least spend some time with him. He's been asking me to go to one of the movie nights." I blinked and tried to keep my breathing normal. I wouldn't let Archer get to me.

Too late.

She hugged me. "Good girl. You deserve to have some fun."

"Thanks for the talk. I'm going to find Ian. After my shower, of course." I pushed my muddy hair back from my face, grabbed the cat carrier with Eve sleeping, and headed inside.

After thirty minutes in the shower, I still didn't feel better. A nice cleansing cry would usually lift my spirits, but I couldn't get the horrible picture of Archer kissing Susie out of my mind. Instead, an ugly cry, along with an abundance of snot and a rip-roaring headache, were the results.

I turned the water off, grabbed a towel, and walked into the bedroom. Eve slept curled in a ball on my bed. "Hey, Eve." I sat close. Her furry face always soothed my soul. "I'm so glad you're with me." She loved it when I scratched under her chin. With a stretch and a yawn, her beautiful green eyes opened. "I need to talk to you about something." She blinked. "Okay, here goes. I can't figure out why I'm so upset about Archer." I wiped my nose with the towel. "I mean, it's weird. At first, I thought I'd have to kill him. You'd think that would be off-putting, right? But no, my crazy brain liked him right off, even though I tried to deny it. He's everything I don't want—bossy and cocky. Oh, and stubborn. It's almost impossible to change his mind. His mood swings could make anyone want to scream. I never know what he's thinking because he's closed off." I tapped my finger against my lips. "What else? Oh, and he kissed Susie." I shivered. Eve meowed and rubbed her face on my shoulder. Tears welled again. "No, I will not cry anymore." I got up and started to change into clean clothes. "Maybe it's because he's so handsome?" I pulled a sweater over my head. "No. That couldn't be it. Ian is just as handsome. Hmm. Perhaps it's because he makes me laugh, or when he smiles it's like the best thing in the world. His face lights up, and he has this twinkle in his eyes. Does that sound stupid?" I wrestled with my too-tight jeans and flopped back onto the bed. After tucking a pillow under my head, I whispered, "I think it's his eyes. When he lets his guard down, even if it's only for a minute, it feels like I can see right into his soul. His pain, his hopes and fears, and his heart are so pure and vulnerable." A tear escaped. "Eve, I think I lo—"

Eve jumped, her back arching, and she hissed.

I shot up off the bed and scanned the room. "What is it?" My heart raced while I tried to pinpoint the danger.

A knock on the door startled me. I walked slowly as I checked for a mouse or anything else that might spook Eve.

A check through the peephole put me at ease. I opened the door. "Hi, Ian."

"Lucy said you wanted to talk?"

"She did?"

"Are you all right? You seem distracted."

I let out a deep breath. "Eve saw something in the room and hissed. It freaked me out."

He looked around the room. "Do you want me to check it out? You might have a mouse friend in here." He smiled, and I relaxed.

"Maybe under the bed?" I shivered. "I don't want to be nose-to-nose with a mouse."

He chuckled. "Yeah, no problem."

Ian was so nice and thoughtful and kind and sweet and helpful and...ugh. Once I accepted the fact Archer had chosen Susie, I'd be able to appreciate Ian. He was about as perfect as they came.

He kneeled and lifted the bed skirt. "All clear."

My racing heart slowed down a little. "Phew."

He approached Eve. "Hey there, don't scare your mom like that."

Eve purred and rubbed against his outstretched hand. He scratched under her chin just how she liked it.

"Wow. She might like you better than me." Eve's purring sounded like a motorboat.

"I haven't had a cat in years. I forgot how affectionate they can be." He leaned down, and she licked his nose.

"Okay, that's it. I'm getting jealous now." I laughed.

"You know what they say." He straightened and backed away a little.

"What's that?"

"Animals are a good judge of character." He grinned and winked, which caused my heart to flutter a little. He really was very charming.

Hmm. Every time Archer was in the room, Eve would stop purring and even hiss.

"I do believe you're right." Our eyes connected, and he took a step closer.

"You wanted to see me?" he asked.

"Oh, that's right. I did." His closeness had my mind jumbled a little. Did I want him closer? "Lucy and I were talking, and we thought...um..." Now that I'd started, the idea sounded a little ridiculous.

"You thought…?"

"Well, it sounds a little silly now, but we thought, if we held a mini séance-y thing outside Samara, it might help bring on a vision. Maybe if we concentrated just on the files, we'd be able to figure out where they're hidden."

"You had me at séance-y thing." He pressed his lips together.

"Okay, now you're just making fun of me." My face warmed.

"No, no, I'm not. I promise." He put an arm around my shoulder. I stiffened a little, and he backed away. "Sadie?"

"Yes?"

He stepped in front of me and took me by the shoulders. "I really like you."

"Oh?" I'd stopped breathing and was pretty sure my heart seized at the same time.

"A lot."

"I like you, too," I choked out. Did I want him this close?

"What I mean to say is, I more than like you." His expressive blue eyes held me captive.

I stood frozen, like a freak. Why couldn't I just be normal? Why the conflict? Archer obviously wasn't interested in me. Ian was easy, like soft butter on warm cornbread. I loved cornbread. If I loved cornbread, maybe I could love Ian.

"Sadie."

"Yeah?"

"I want to kiss you." He squeezed my shoulders a little. "I mean, I think I might die if I don't kiss you right now."

"Okay." What? What did I just agree to? Before I could retract permission, his lips were on mine, and oh, it was nice. I was right; I melted into him like butter. His arm went around me, holding on tight, and his other hand held my face.

When we parted, he breathed into my neck. "It was better than I dreamed about for all those years."

I pulled back. "What do you mean? All *what* years?"

CHAPTER 19

Archer

A CHILL RAN down the length of my spine the moment Susie put her lips on mine. I peeled her arms from around my neck. "Susie, I told you already. I don't mind hanging out with you, but I'm not interested in anything more." I shot a look over to where Lucy and Sadie were digging. Sadie's back was to me, and Lucy's eyes hurled daggers at me.

Susie's bottom lip jutted out. "What are you going to do, be alone for eternity?"

If the only choice remained Susie, then yes.

"Maybe."

She stomped her foot. "Hmpf! You're impossible. You could have this." She took her hand and displayed herself like one of those presenters on a game show. "Or, that freak Seer. What's her name again?"

She knew what her name was. I gritted my teeth. "Sadie. And she's not a freak."

"Oh, yeah, Sadie." She twisted some hair around her finger. "Her eyes creep me out."

"Why, because they're beautiful?" Couldn't help it. Susie was annoying me. And her sour expression was anything but beautiful.

"No. Because of the color. Haven't you noticed she has that weird shade of blue, or is it gray?"

About out of patience, I answered in a barely civil tone. "You mean an unusual shade? A shade no one else on the planet has?"

"Yep, it's weird." Susie went back to examining her nails.

"Well, this conversation has been fascinating. I'm going to clean up and go inside." I got the hose and sprayed the shovel.

"Whatever. I'll go on ahead and find Ian. Now he's unusual, but in all the right ways." She lifted a brow and waited for me to object.

"Good idea."

She frowned. "You'll be sorry. Everyone knows I'm the prettiest Reader. You're blowing it."

"Susie, I'll say it again. I've lived enough to know physical beauty isn't important. It's what's on the inside. Like integrity, kindness, compassion... A person's beauty shines from the inside and finds its way out."

"That's stupid. Would you ever date a troll?" Her eyes dared me to say yes.

"Over you?"

Her eyes narrowed, and she held up her hand. "Okay, you've

made your point. I still think you've made a poor choice. I could be all those things, but you haven't given me a chance."

"You mean two thousand years hasn't been long enough?" I almost laughed.

Her lips pressed together. "You know you don't have a chance with Ian around."

"I guess that means you don't have a chance either." I had a quick moment where I thought about turning the hose on Susie.

"Unless we find a way to break them up. Then everyone would be happy." Her eyes seemed to glow.

"Susie, I hope you're joking. Don't you dare try to interfere." I narrowed my eyes and tried to look intimidating.

"Yeah. Just joking. You're no fun." With the signature flip of her hair, she left to finish cleaning up.

I darted another glance to where Sadie and Lucy were digging. Gone. My heart sank. The best part of my day was the sound of Sadie's laughter.

Get a grip.

Not going there. I would not spend more years obsessing about a woman I couldn't have. Destiny was a bitch. Sadie and Ian would most likely leave after we catch the Jack clone. At least I wouldn't have to watch them anymore. But they didn't seem to be a couple. Yet. Sadie almost avoided Ian. They'd have lunch together on occasion and sometimes work together. But Sadie's body language said, "Don't get close." I wondered what that was all about.

"Hey, I'm glad you're still here." A familiar voice startled me.

"Hi, Lucy." *Here comes the lecture.*

"I'm not going to lecture you, so you can take that defensive look off your face and relax." Her body language didn't match her words. She stood with arms crossed and a crease between her eyebrows.

"You don't look very relaxed." I rolled my eyes.

"Don't you roll your eyes at me. Susie? Really?"

"And the lecture begins."

She took a deep breath. "Okay. I guess you need a mini lecture. What the heck are you thinking? Not only are you ignoring Sadie, you kiss Susie right in front of her? How insensitive can you be?"

"Sadie saw that?" An ache started in the back of my throat and made it difficult to swallow.

"Duh. You were standing in clear view."

"If you'd stayed to listen, you'd have heard me tell Susie to back off and I would rather spend eternity alone than be with her."

"You did?" She covered her mouth, but a laugh escaped.

"Yeah. And she wasn't happy about it." I combed my fingers through my hair. "I don't trust her. Her plan is to go after Ian next, and I wouldn't put it past her to do anything to get her way, including lying, cheating, stealing, or whatever, to break them up."

She tilted her head. "You think Sadie and Ian are together?"

I shrugged. "If they aren't now, they will be."

"What do you mean?" She leaned forward a little.

I hesitated a moment, but I trusted Lucy. "Before we came here, Ian and I had a little talk."

"Go on."

"You can't mention this to Sadie. You promise?"

"Ugh. I hate promises. I always have to keep them. Do I have to?"

Nodding, I said, "This information comes at a price. I trust you, or I wouldn't bring it up."

Her shoulders sagged. "Oh, okay."

"Apparently, Ian has been watching Sadie to protect her since the Great War when the Seers were wiped out. He's been in love with her for over two thousand years."

She crossed her arms again. "So?"

"What do you mean, so? I've known her for a few months. I can't mess with that. I don't want to. It's destiny." Every time I thought about the talk with Ian outside Sadie's cottage, it brought back an overwhelming feeling of loss. Almost like someone had died. But instead, a dream or hope had died that day.

Lucy tilted her head. "Just because they're the only two who survived?"

"Yeah. And because there's a vision about two Seers who have a child that will save the world. You know, a small, little thing." I couldn't believe she'd overlook that.

She threw her hands up. "Oh yeah? Well, there's also another vision about a Reader and Seer. Why couldn't it be you and Sadie?"

Lucy loved a good argument, but she wouldn't win this one. "Because I'm also a Jack. I'm sure the vision didn't cover a half-breed like me."

She looked up and exhaled. "Both visions weren't certified. If they had been, we could have more confidence in the content. You know Seers' visions weren't always spot on. Is this because of Ann?"

"No." I thought for a moment. "Maybe." Another few seconds. "Yes."

She stared off toward the trees and valley below. "You don't want to interfere with a soul mate pairing again."

That annoying pang in my chest returned. "I'd be insane to get caught up in it a second time."

Her gaze shifted back to me. "I get it. But I'm not convinced they're soul mates yet. Sure, she likes him, but she doesn't look at him the way she looks at you. And if you had observed her these past few months, you'd have noticed she tracks your every movement. She's very subtle about it, but I'd bet she knows your favorite meals, your moods, and even the type of soap you use."

Speechless. My thoughts scattered, and adrenaline coursed through my body. A small glimmer of hope peeked through, and then... "Lucy, Ian's been in love with her for two thousand years. I can't compete with that."

"You're impossible!" She stomped a few feet away, then stomped back and pointed a finger at me. "First, you wouldn't be competing. Second, you know love isn't always based on time. You can't measure love in hours or minutes, or even thousands of years." She crossed her arms. "And... and, what about Sadie? Have you considered what she wants?"

My heart thudded in my chest. "That's all I think about. If Sadie is fated to be with Ian, she'll do what's right for the Seers. I can't risk it. Don't you see? I can't trust what I'd do if I were rejected again."

Lucy's expression softened. "I understand. You're afraid history will repeat itself. We need to get that fixed. How about we find the files and you can decide then? Once it's confirmed

Atarah was responsible for everything, I think you'll view this differently."

"Will we ever find them? They could be destroyed, for all we know." An emptiness formed in the pit of my stomach.

She pushed up her sleeves. "Don't you dare do that. We will not give up until we find them and prove you're innocent."

A comfortable warmth released the tension in my neck and shoulders. "Thanks, Lucy. For being there for me."

"Anytime." She wrapped her arms around me in a big hug. "Oh, I almost forgot to track down Ian."

"Why Ian?"

Her eyes sparkled. "I have an idea. I think if Sadie and Ian put their minds together and focus on the digital files, maybe a vision would come through. I figure two Seers are better than one, right?"

"Sure. It sounds promising."

"Great!" She turned and ran right into Devon. "Ouch. Don't sneak up on me like that."

"Maybe you could look where you're going? Ever consider that?" Devon smirked.

"I have things to do." She looked back at me and smiled, then looked back at Devon. "What are you doing up here? I thought your assignment today was the storage room."

"I'm trying to gather everyone for another brainstorming meeting. We're getting nowhere, and I'm worried the Jack clone will make his move soon."

Lucy rubbed her arms and looked around. "It has been quiet. I've been concerned about the same thing."

"Where and when?" I asked.

"The conference room in an hour. I need to gather everyone else." He glanced at Lucy. "Do you know where Sadie is?"

"She's probably still in her room. Do you want me to get her?"

"Sure. We'll be meeting in conference room one."

"Okay, see ya." With a wave of her hand, she was off.

Devon turned to me. "We need to figure out what the clone's strategies might be before the meeting. C'mon."

I grabbed the shovel and followed him back into the Samara.

Devon stopped and glanced at my clothes. "On second thought, why don't we meet after you shower and change your clothes."

I looked down at the mud and grass that covered me head to foot. "Yeah, maybe we can figure out a more efficient way of searching. Digging these holes has grown old fast."

"You volunteered." He laughed and shook his head.

I rubbed the back of my neck. "Two months ago, it seemed like a decent plan. Now, not so much."

His eyes scanned the hillside with dozens of filled-in holes. "I agree. If someone went to the trouble to bury the files, it would've been close to the exit if they needed them quickly."

"And we've covered almost every square inch along the exit path."

He nodded. "Let's nix this area for now. At this point, it's just a time drain, and we need every second."

"I'm good with that." We'd entered the hallway leading to the elevators. I veered right, Devon left. A quick shower and a change of clothes and I'd get to the meeting early so I could jot down some notes.

An hour later, I entered the conference room. Uh oh. Sadie sat at the table, scribbling something in a notepad. I hadn't been alone with her since before Samara, and my body instantly reacted. Warmth flooded every cell, and my fingers tingled with the need to touch her. What was with my breathing? Great, now I was lightheaded, and my chest tightened. I took a deep breath and ordered my body to get a grip. God, though, she was so freaking beautiful.

Sadie lifted an eyebrow. "Well, you're looking in my direction, and there's no one else in the room. Does that mean I'm not invisible anymore?"

I cleared my throat. "Uh, well, um…"

She got up from the table and stood in front of me, so close, I could smell the familiar scent of her lilac shampoo. I breathed in.

"Why are you avoiding me? I know you're with Susie, but can we at least be friends?" She held still and waited for my response.

"About that—"

Devon barreled into the room. "Hey, I'm glad you're both here. We have a lot to talk about."

Lucy, Ann, and Ian followed right behind.

"Okay, everyone. Thanks for coming on such short notice." He looked around the room and asked Lucy, "Where's Adam?"

"Right here," he said as he entered the room.

I sat down across from Devon. Sadie grabbed her notebook and chose a seat next to me. Not good. I wouldn't be able to think with her so close. Ian sat next to her on the other side and tried to hold her hand, but she pulled away. Ann sat next to Devon, and Adam approached Lucy, gave her a kiss, and took his seat next to her. What was with the PDA all the time? If Lucy loved him, I guess I had to tolerate him, but it was a challenge.

"Great, let's get started. I've checked for bugs, and we're all clear. But, just in case, don't mention anything too specific."

"Sure," Ann said, and the rest of us nodded.

Devon took in a large breath. "We're going to shift some of our energy from the search to the last Jack clone."

Sadie sat up straighter. "But we'll still look for the digital files, right?"

"We'll shift some manpower to the clone search. It's been too quiet, and I have a feeling he'll strike soon."

Sadie stood and shouted, "No!" Her face flushed red, and she looked down for a moment. "Sorry, what I meant to say is, we need to clear Archer first. If we do that, the Elders agreed to start an all-out search for the betrayer. If we find the betrayer, he or she will most likely lead us to the people who are orchestrating this."

Devon's eyes softened. "We could spend years and come up empty. We'll need to focus short term on possible motives for the Jack clone. I promise, we won't stop looking for the files."

"That's easy. The clone wants us dead." Adam scowled.

"But why us specifically?" Ann asked.

Adam gave Devon a brief glance. "The Jacks would go after Ann first and foremost. Think about it. How many immortals have all three talents? The Jacks believed you were the strongest and most likely to save their race if you chose them. You chose the Readers instead, and I'd bet my life they want your power extinguished. That way, once they get enough clones, they can go back to their evil doings."

Devon frowned. "I hate to say it, but that makes sense."

Adam scratched his face and continued. "They drew us out to Arizona, knowing Ann would be there. They would've been successful if Sadie hadn't received the vision." He turned to smile at Sadie. "When they try to draw us out again, we should keep Ann here in Samara, so she stays safe."

"No way. I'm not staying behind." Ann's pleading eyes turned to Devon. "Right?"

He tried to ignore her. "Let's bounce around—"

Ann tugged on his shirt. "You aren't going to leave me here, are you?"

He smiled. "No. I've been at the other end of a Kubotan."

Ann relaxed back in her chair.

"The Kubotan wouldn't have protected her from the explosion," Adam reminded Devon.

Ann glowered at him.

He shrugged. "Just sayin.'"

Devon continued, "We'll talk about risks later. Anyone have any ideas or guesses about what the Jacks are up to?"

Lucy bounced in her seat and raised her hand. "Oh, pick me."

Devon shook his head. "Go ahead, Lucy."

She leaned forward, her red hair touching the table. "I think they were programmed to take out our core group."

"Why, though? Why not the entire Reader community?" Devon asked Lucy, then scanned the table.

Adam took Lucy's hand in his. "Sorry, but I think they're gunning for Ann. And after, maybe the rest of us." He glanced at Sadie and Ian. "Perhaps not the Seers because we didn't know about them two years ago. Anyway, if the Jacks got rid of our group, then things around here would get chaotic. The Elders would probably shut the Readers off from the world for protection, and if that happens, the Jacks could build up their army again within a hundred years."

Lucy shivered. "We have to stop them."

"Another thing." Devon paused, and his lips tightened. "We have to entertain the thought that at least one or two Jacks lived after the explosion."

Ian leaned forward. "Why?"

Devon rested his hands on the table. "Think about it. When we were in Arizona, they were in contact with someone from Portland. There needed to be someone in Harmony besides the clones to keep an eye on us. We used fake names to check into the hotel, and they knew when we'd all be there. The only reason we aren't all dust is because of Sadie."

"They made a mistake with Adam. He was out getting sandwiches, remember? Could they have used a satellite and maybe missed him leaving?" Lucy asked.

"That's an interesting thought," Devon said, then turned to Adam. "Did you get sandwiches every day at the same time?"

Adam shifted in his seat. "No, we ate at different times."

Devon sighed. "Okay, a satellite could be a possibility. But they'd still need someone to plant the bomb."

We all stayed quiet for a few minutes.

"Could the Arizona Jack clones have planted the bomb?" Sadie asked.

Devon shook his head. "They wouldn't have known which rooms we booked."

"Anything weird about our check-in?" Lucy directed her question at Adam.

A crease formed between his eyebrows. "Not that I can remember."

Ann glanced at Devon. "Do you think it's possible they planted bombs in all the rooms?"

Devon shook his head. "Highly unlikely, but we should send a team back to make sure there's no one else in danger."

Ann rubbed her face, took a deep breath, and sighed. "I didn't want to mention this, but I'm worried that Atarah may have survived."

My blood ran cold. "That's impossible." A darkness, black and evil, crept up my spine.

Devon frowned. "When we find the files, we need to search all exits the night of the explosion." He put a hand on Ann's shoulder. "Atarah was devious, and if anyone could find an escape, it'd be her."

I exhaled a long breath. "Then she'd be after me and Ann for sure."

"Yes," Devon agreed. "She was all about revenge. She wanted the Readers to suffer."

"What's our approach going to be when the clone makes a move?" Adam asked.

Devon hesitated a few moments. "We should keep it on a case-by-case basis. We don't want to barge into a situation with only a single plan. I think the explosion was to get rid of us and possibly switch places with Archer. If they'd have pulled it off, they'd have access to take out the entire Reader population." He wiped his forehead. "As a precaution, we'll need to seal all doors like we did when the Jacks were alive. There are too many things pointing to them having assistance once they were 'born.'"

The pounding at my temples shot stabs of pain through the rest of my head. My hands fisted, turning my knuckles white. "If Atarah is alive, please let me have the honor of destroying her."

Devon sighed. "Let's not jump to any conclusions. This place was locked up tight. It would have been impossible for her to escape. You had her handcuffed, right?"

"Yeah. To the refrigerator door."

Ann bit her lip. "I hate to bring this up, but if Atarah did have Archer under mind control, couldn't she have planted a memory of the handcuffs?"

Everyone went silent. My stomach churned at the thought. But if it turned out to be true, there would be one good outcome and another unthinkable one.

Sadie summed it up, "That would mean Archer is innocent like we all believe, and Atarah is still alive."

Devon nodded. "That's a possibility, but hopefully not probable. Let's get back to the Jacks' motives. Let's assume Ann and Archer are their targets. We need to operate from that angle. We should keep them far apart when we go out. Agreed?"

"Sure" and "yes" and "good plan" rang out from the table.

"I'll stay with Ann." Devon's eyes darted around and landed on Adam. "Would you stick with Archer?"

Adam frowned, then sighed. "Okay, I guess."

I chuckled. "Don't be so excited about it."

Adam shrugged and appeared bored.

Devon closed his notebook. "We have the start of a good plan. We'll end the outside search. I don't believe it's productive to continue digging. I'll reassign everyone to different areas for tomorrow. We'll continue to come up with different strategies based on the possibility of one, maybe two Jacks surviving the explosion. Does anyone have anything they'd like to add?"

No one spoke, so he continued. "Okay. Adam and I will focus on all the Reader whereabouts during the Arizona trip. We'll also expand our search for incidents in other countries in case they try to draw us out in another region."

We all stood to get ready to leave. I glanced over at Sadie just as Ian attempted to hold her hand again. She grabbed it back and crossed her arms while glaring at him. Hmmm.

"Are we still getting together later?" Ian asked.

"Yes." She sighed. "But you have a lot of explaining to do."

They tried to keep their voices quiet, but, unfortunately for them, I had excellent hearing.

"I'm sorry I didn't tell you sooner," Ian said.

"Are you?"

Oh. Ian hadn't told Sadie about his two-thousand-year stalking until now. I almost laughed.

Wrong move, buddy.

CHAPTER 20

Sadie

"I WANTED TO wait for the right time." Ian scrubbed a hand over his face. "I didn't want to freak you out before we got to know each other."

"And two seconds after we kiss is good timing in your book?"

He stared down at the floor. "No, it's the worst possible timing. It slipped out." He raised his head and met my angry stare.

His eyes, ugh, they were usually so clear and bright. Now they looked dull and sad. I didn't want to feel bad for him. I wanted to stay angry.

I huffed. "Let's get out of here. Are we still going to the rooftop to see if we can conjure up a vision?"

He perked up. "Sure. Whatever you want."

"And I'm going to ask you to quit trying to hold my hand. I

don't know how I feel about all of this."

He said nothing, just nodded, and looked down again. Geez, I felt like I'd kicked a puppy.

"I didn't say forever, but for now, I need to process this." I thought for a moment. "All those years alone. Did you ever think about contacting me?" I took a deep breath and tried to forget all the lonely years.

"My instructions we implicit. I couldn't contact you until after 'the wave.'"

I nodded. "I get it." I would have done the same thing. The rules were set in place for a reason and we never questioned them. But it still hurt.

He let out a deep breath. "Thank you. I promise I won't ever keep anything from you again."

I studied his face. Everything about him appeared to be sincere. "We need to sit down and have a long talk about everything. But right now we need to focus on finding the files. Let's get going."

"Sure. Lead the way." His usual grin returned.

Don't get too relaxed. You're not off the hook yet.

Once we entered the outdoor terrace, I let myself unwind a little. This would be the perfect spot. The sweet smell of moss, pine, grass, and dirt made me take a few deep cleansing breaths.

"You love it out here."

"That obvious?" I laughed.

"You've always loved...God, sorry. I'm doing it again." He shook his head.

I waved him off. "The cat's already out. Oh look, someone

left the fireplace on. Let's go sit at that table." The rooftop terrace could match any fancy hotel's. It had a gas fireplace with comfy green lounge chairs, potted plants, and an outdoor grill. I stashed Eve's carrier under the table, then grabbed a blanket off one of the chairs, and put it around my shoulders.

"Are you cold? I could turn up the fire."

"No. I'm good. These blankets are warm." I turned my chair to sit in front of his. "Shall we?" I sat and waited for him.

"How's this supposed to go?" he asked.

My stomach flopped, and my mouth went dry. *Good question.* "I have no idea. I brought my mom's necklace. I guess we'll figure out the rest."

"Okay. I'm game. We're going to focus on the location of the files, right?"

He rubbed his hands together.

"Yes. Maybe we could hold hands?"

Ian grinned. I guess it was okay with him.

His hands felt warm and comforting. We smiled at each other. "Let's close our eyes and focus on the files."

"Okay."

We waited for a few minutes.

"Anything yet?"

"Not yet."

Just as he said, "yet," a vision flashed. A metal box with a lid. Darn. It looked like it needed a key. Another hoop to jump through. Where was it? I kept my mind blank and my focus laser sharp. The box was tucked away in a cupboard with the door cracked open. Florescent lighting made the box almost glow. *Concentrate and look around. Oh, a wooden desk. Had*

I ever seen a desk like this at Samara? Think. Was it familiar? Definitely not one of the desks in any of the conference rooms. I mentally walked through each room in Samara.

"Anything yet?"

"Sshh. Yes."

Why wasn't Ian getting the same vision? Wouldn't worry about it now. My eyes squeezed tighter. A cluttered room with desks, chairs, and beige walls. One desk displayed a photo. Black frame with... I strained to see who was in the photo. Nothing but fog.

"Maybe if you told me about it, I could help."

I kept my eyes closed. "Ian." And then it vanished.

I raised my head and met his eyes. He interrupted the vision twice. Even a young Seer knew that wasn't allowed. It was Seer 101.

"Why did you do that?"

"What?" His head cocked to the side.

"Interrupt me in the middle of a vision."

"Sorry, I could see you were struggling and wanted to help."

"Have you forgotten?"

"Forgotten what?"

"Never mind."

"Were you able to see where the files are hidden?"

I thought for a moment. Should I tell Ian? We were outside, safe from any bugs. "All I saw was a shiny box that needs a key."

"That's it?"

"Pretty much. It was a crowded room. Could be in any

office, but the box was in a cupboard. I don't think it's here in Samara. There's too many people looking for it."

"Do you want to keep trying?"

"No. I'm lucky to get as much as I did. You didn't see anything?"

He shook his head. "Nope. Maybe you can loan me your mom's necklace sometime."

"Sure. Shall we try again tomorrow?"

"You can count on me, Sadie. I'll do whatever you need."

Ian was a good guy. I mean, it really wasn't his fault his parents gave him the burden of looking after me all these years. How bored he must have been. I rubbed his arm. "Thanks, that means a lot."

He took a step forward.

"Not that much," I said with a straight face.

He stepped back quickly.

I laughed. "Sorry, you had that coming. But I need a little distance to take everything in. These past three months have been overwhelming, to say the least."

"I get it." He made a zipping motion across his lips. "No more talking until you're ready."

"Thanks. Now I need to find Lucy." I glanced at the door leading inside.

"Lucy?"

"We're working together."

"On what?"

Wasn't sure if I wanted to say. "Lots of stuff, why?"

"Just curious."

"Curiosity killed the...oops." My eyes darted to the cat carrier. "Sorry Eve."

Ian threw his head back and laughed. "If I see Lucy when I hit the Hub, I'll let her know you're looking for her." He rubbed his stomach. "The food is great there. I may never go home."

"Why aren't you going home?" Lucy, as usual, came from behind and made us both jump. "You two are awfully jumpy. What's going on?"

Ian drew a cross over his chest. "I've been sworn to secrecy." He grinned, and those distracting dimples appeared. After a wave, he disappeared into Samara.

Lucy coughed into her hand, and her face turned beet red. I hit her on the back. "Tell me I don't have to perform the Heimlich on you."

"No. No. I just swallowed the wrong way."

"I hate when that happens."

A few minutes later, the cough had settled from alarming to intermittent. Lucy eyeballed the door where Ian exited. "It sounds like things went well."

"Yes and no. I had a vision of the storage box where the files might be kept, but not an idea of where it could be. Asia, Africa, Australia...no clue."

Lucy rubbed my arm. "It's a start." She picked up my mom's necklace. "It's stunning. What a wonderful keepsake from her."

My throated tightened, and I blinked rapidly. "I still remember everything about her."

"Aw, honey." She wrapped me up in a tight hug. "You can cry."

"I'm not, I'm not...a young child anymore." And then I burst into tears on Lucy's shoulder.

She rubbed my back and sang me a song about how love never dies, which made me cry harder. What was wrong with me? "This is so embarrassing. I never cry." I wiped my eyes. "Well, I mean, almost never."

"I'm sure the past few months have brought up a lot of difficult memories for you. Don't fight them. It might be the reason your visions are blocked."

"What did you say?"

"Your visions might be blocked because you're repressing painful memories."

"Lucy! You're a genius. I remember now."

"What?"

"The Seers always needed to clear their minds and meditate before each session. The important visions would come through no matter what. But the smaller ones would only come with an acceptance of the past. It's kind of a purity thing. Any disagreements needed to be resolved and forgiven."

"Okay, who do you need to forgive?"

My shoulders sagged, and I let out a deep breath. "The Jacks."

"Wow. I mean, that's a tough one." Lucy bit her lip and sighed.

"More like impossible. How do I forgive evil?"

Lucy wrinkled her nose. "You don't. But maybe you could forgive Archer."

"What do you mean? There's nothing to forgive. He didn't take part in the Great War. He was already with the Readers."

"But he's part Jack. Do you think you could forgive that part of him?"

"Ohhh. I see where this is going." I closed my eyes. "Okay, done."

Lucy's eyes widened and then she laughed. "That was fast. I'm impressed."

I shrugged. "By the time I got to know Archer, I knew what made him tick. His heart is pure; I can feel that. This was just a formality. I hope it works." I pointed to the chairs where Ian and I had been sitting. "Would you help me? I'd like to try again."

Lucy bounced on her feet. "Are you kidding? Let's do this thing." She practically skipped to the chair and flopped down. Her hands stretched out to me.

I bit my tongue so I wouldn't laugh. We didn't need to hold hands because she wasn't a Seer, but I did anyway. I closed my eyes and focused on the metal box. The mental picture of it came in a lot clearer this time. I kept my heart steady by breathing in and out slowly. *Come on box, show me where you are.* The frame came into focus. A girl with beautiful blue eyes and freckles. My eyes popped open.

"It's here somewhere."

"What is?"

"The box with the files."

"Where, where?"

"I don't know the exact place. But there's a desk with a picture of Ann. Does that sound familiar?"

"What the... What? You've got to be kidding me."

"What?"

"Oh my gosh. This is unbelievable." She sank back in her chair and rubbed her temples. "It's so obvious. We're so stupid!" She quickly added, "Not you or Ian. Us. The Readers. How did we not figure this out?"

"What is it?"

"The files are in the technology center. Devon has his desk back there. I've only been there once, because, you know, technology." She stuck out her tongue. "Anyway, the room is always super clean. No clutter. I'm sure that's why Devon didn't think about searching there."

"Can anyone get in?"

"No, that's the thing. There're probably two Elders, Devon, and Adam who have the door codes. It's not a huge security risk because they erase all their search data every day. If someone broke in, they'd just find a bunch of empty computers." Her brow furrowed. "Why would someone hide the files in there?"

"Maybe they were placed there accidentally during the move?"

"The Readers had only a little time to grab a few personal items before the evacuation. Whoever put the box there knew it would be overlooked. I think it was deliberate."

"Okay. Are we still keeping this just between us? Ian knows about the box, but not that it's at Samara. Devon or Adam could get us in the room with the code."

"I don't know why, but something keeps telling me to keep this quiet. Is that okay with you?"

A door squeaked shut.

"What was that?" Lucy asked.

We both bolted toward the exterior door and went inside.

Nothing. An empty corridor.

"Maybe we're just getting spooked." Goose bumps traveled up and down my arms.

Lucy put her hand on her chest. "That almost gave me a heart attack."

"We're just jumpy. Let's sit back down." I tried to relax my shoulders. "I trust your instincts to keep this quiet for now. How do we get into the room?"

She paused and pursed her lips. "I got it. The technology room is next to the library. I'll sneak in there and stake out the door. When either Devon or Adam go in, I'll pretend to be passing by and ask a question. They won't think twice about punching in the code because why would I ever want to go into a place that has—"

"Technology." I laughed.

"Exactly."

"Got it."

"You got the code for the door and the computer password?"

"Easy-peasy. I just asked Devon a few questions about Henry's next birthday when he was going into the center."

"I thought Henry turned two a few months ago?"

She rubbed her hands together. "It's never too early to shop for gifts. And besides, any chance Devon gets to talk about Henry... well, just forget about it. Ann and Devon think the sun and moon rise with that kid. I already knew his password— Annhenrylove. Isn't that sweet?" She laughed. "Anyway, I digress. Now that everyone is asleep, it's the perfect time."

"Once we get it, what do we do with a locked box? I assume we can't just pry it open."

"We'll need the key." She pursed her lips. "Or maybe a drill?"

"Any drills lying around?"

"No, and it would raise suspicion if we asked for one." She closed her eyes. "Let me think."

"Never mind. We'll cross that bridge later. I just want to get my hands on it before someone moves it."

Lucy grabbed my arm. "Let's go get that sucker."

We took the transvater to the fifth level and exited on tiptoes. "We don't look suspicious at all do we?" I chuckled.

"You're right. Let's just saunter our way there." Lucy slowed her pace, and I matched it.

We stopped in front of the technology center door. I took a deep breath. "Are you ready?"

Lucy pushed up her sleeves and gave a curt nod. She pressed in the code and the door clicked open. "See? Easy. Let's get the box."

Some of the automatic lights flickered to life. We went back to tiptoeing through the corridor, passing a few offices until Lucy came to an abrupt halt. A cupboard door, open with light eerily reflecting from one of the overhead lights, marked the spot. "There it is," she said in a reverent tone.

I peeked over her shoulder. "Wait a minute."

"What?" she whispered.

I moved around her and took the box out and put it on the desk. "The shape of this lock looks familiar." A cross shape with two ends that tapered into a curved point.

"How so?" She peered at it.

"Just a second." I closed my eyes and tried to remember back. "Oh."

"What? What?" Lucy grabbed hold of my arm again.

With shaking hands, I removed my mother's necklace and examined the antique clasp. One side held a unique scroll design. I turned it over and the other side had a serrated edge.

Lucy's eyes widened. "Oh my gosh. That looks just like the lock."

"Here goes." I put the clasp into the lock and, with a pop, the box opened. Inside laid hundreds of flash drives in rows with dates.

"Oh! Oh!" Lucy jumped up and down.

"We can celebrate later. We'll need to work fast before someone comes." I studied the dates. "I know the year, but I'll need the exact dates. Do you remember them?"

"Of course. April nineteenth was the night Markus died. May twenty-ninth was the day of the explosion."

I ran my fingers over the flash drives. "Okay, found the 19th. What time?"

"Between 8:00 p.m. and 11:00 p.m."

"And his room number?"

"Sixty-seven."

I glanced back toward the exit. "This might take some time. Can you watch the door while I go through them?"

Lucy clapped and bounced at the same time. "Sure thing. Oh, this is exciting!"

I powered up the computer and inserted the flash drive.

This is it. The mystery surrounding the death of Markus would finally be solved.

Twenty minutes later, I had the answer. It left no doubt. I sat back in the chair and rubbed my eyes. I wished more than anything in the world I could unsee every minute.

Murmuring voices coming down the hall interrupted my thoughts.

"No, Archer, Sadie is just doing a little research for me. We're looking for a, um, a salon to do our nails." She shot me a glance and shrugged.

Lucy was the worst liar on the planet besides me.

They entered the room and Archer asked, "Is that the security tape?"

I stood to face Archer. Tears streamed down my face, and I couldn't stop crying if my life depended on it. "Yes," I whispered.

"Okay, I'm going to leave you to it," Lucy said. "I'll be at the entrance, and this time, no one will get past me." She made sure to narrow her eyes at Archer when she passed.

He moved closer and his eyes softened. "Thanks for caring. I'm sorry you witnessed the murder." He shook his head. "I'm ashamed to let you down. I know you believed I was innocent." He reached over to wipe a tear from my face, then jumped back. "What the...?" He bent over, holding his hand and swearing under his breath.

My hand flew to my chest. "What's the matter? Are you okay?"

Beads of sweat formed on his forehead. "What are you, radioactive or something?" His face twisted in pain as he leaned back against the desk.

"No. I don't know what's going on." My heart raced, and panic fogged my brain. "How can I help?"

He held his hand under his arm. "It's getting better." His head snapped up. "Why would you want to help me after what you've seen?"

"Oh, Archer." I shook my head. "I was crying for Markus and all the time you lost. I watched the whole thing." I squeezed my eyes shut, collected my thoughts, and blurted, "You're innocent."

He stared at me, still and silent.

"Archer, did you hear me? You didn't kill Markus."

He tilted his head and continued to stare into my eyes. "Why do your eyes shimmer like that?"

"Um, Archer, are you okay? I just said I watched the security tapes and witnessed everything. That awful woman—it must have been Atarah—killed Markus, then brought you into the room. It looked like you were hypnotized. You had this vacant stare—"

"I'm innocent."

I threw up my hands. "Yes! That's what I've been trying to tell you."

"This changes everything." He took a step toward me.

"It does? I mean, yes, it does." My heart pounded and raced and squeezed in my chest.

With one more step, we stood toe-to-toe. He picked up a lock of my hair and ran it through his fingers. "Your hair feels like silk." He rubbed the strands between his fingers. "And when the sun hits it, it bursts into different shades of white gold and silver. It almost sparkles."

"Oh, yeah, well, I washed it today." *Stupid. Stupid.*

His smile started slow and ended with a full grin. He placed a hand on my back. "Do you feel that?"

My lungs contracted, but I managed to say, "It feels warm and kinda tingly." I left out the part where my pulse raced, stomach fluttered, and a blast of euphoria surged through every cell, making my knees weak.

He ran a finger down my cheek. "Did you ever wonder why, every time we touch, there's a spark?"

"You don't use fabric softener?" I swallowed and took a huge breath. *Body, don't desert me now.*

He leaned closer, until our lips almost touched. "Sadie."

"Yeah?"

"Are you ready?"

"For what?"

"I don't think this will feel normal." His breath whispered against my lips.

I took a step back. "What do you mean?" It took everything in me to appear as though my breathing was calm and even. What was going on with my heart? It thudded out an uneven rhythm that swooshed through my ears. I balled my hands into fists and crossed my arms, so I wouldn't touch him.

Oh, how I wanted to touch him.

My head and heart were engaged in a silent battle which probably reflected through my

alarmed eyes. There would be no going back. Could I handle it?

Archer grinned and took a step closer, so our bodies touched. "This." And he gently swept his lips against mine.

Definitely can handle it.

Heat and sparks and flames took over every sense. "Oh. Wow. Okay. Can we do that again?"

He took my face in his hands, and his eyes stared intently into mine. "There's something you need to know. I love you, Sadie."

I tried to take a step back, but he held firm.

"Look at me."

"Please don't make me love you. It'll kill me if, if some—" Tears filled my eyes, and my heart sank.

"Nothing will happen to me. And anyway, it's too late." That cocky grin of his made an appearance.

My lower lip trembled, and I nodded.

"Hey." He lifted my chin. "It could be worse."

I wasn't sure if I wanted to laugh or cry, but a giggle slipped through.

Archer chuckled. "Life will never be boring, that's for sure."

CHAPTER 21

Archer

I DIDN'T WANT to move from this spot. Sadie, soft and beautiful. I hadn't let myself dare to dream. Not knowing if I'd killed Markus and Ian's two-thousand-year obsession and possible soul mate connection, I didn't feel worthy. *Atarah*. She tried to destroy me even after her death.

"Archer?"

"Yeah?"

"I'm ready." She grabbed my T-shirt with both hands and tugged.

I didn't need to be asked twice, but after the incident with her tears, going slow seemed the best route. "I think we should—" Before I could finish, her lips were on mine, and any ideas of restraint left my brain. In its place was an overpowering desire that ripped through every fiber of my soul. I grabbed and pulled her into me. A soft moan came from her lips, and that was it. I let go and kissed her like I did in my fantasies. Hard and passionate. My hands traveled up and down her back, feeling every inch of her as she melted into me.

Her hands reached into my hair, and she mumbled, "I didn't know it could be like this."

Soaring. I lost all sense of time and space. Just the two of us, and everything else fell away. An unfurling in my chest made me pause for a moment, and I held her closer. Close enough to hear her heart beating in the same rhythm as mine.

"Did you feel that?" Her eyes widened. "My heart and yours, they're connected or something."

"Soul mates, Sadie."

At the very moment I spoke, a piercing, shrill sound came from the speakers and flooded the hallways.

"Did we set off an alarm or something?" She pulled away and checked the exit doors.

"No, I doubt they'd care if we're in here. Can you grab the flash drive with the night of the explosion before we go? It's May 29. I don't want to risk leaving it here."

"It's already in my back pocket. I also sent a group email with the death of Markus to every Reader, so they can see with their own eyes that you're innocent."

"Thank you for believing in me." My chest expanded, and the tingling warmth stayed even after the kiss ended.

She stood on tiptoes to press her lips against mine. The same tingling warmth spread through me again.

I stepped back. "Oh, no you don't. Next time, I don't think I'll be able to stop."

"That's okay with me." She smiled.

"How about we save the world from the Jack clone first?"

She bit her lip and sighed. "Okay, I guess."

I held her next to me for another moment before I let go. I didn't know how long we'd be apart if the Jacks set up another attack.

"Why do you think they sounded the alarm?"

I shrugged. "This alarm isn't for evacuation. We'll need to meet in conference room seven."

"Does it mean something bad?"

"It's never good when an alarm sounds. Conference room seven is our strategic planning area. Kinda like a war room."

"Great," she said under her breath. "The Jack clone."

"This is a good thing. Jacks are always impatient. I'm glad we don't have to wait years. Let's get Lucy and head out."

"I'm here." Lucy entered the office. "Sounds like the Jacks are up to no good again."

"Yeah. Most likely."

Sadie hooked a finger in my belt loop as we walked down the hall. I took it off and kissed it. "Don't worry. This will be over soon."

We rounded the corner just as a group of ten Elders, Devon, Adam, and Ann reached the door. At least my dad didn't come to this one. I wouldn't miss his judgmental scowl. We filed in without a word spoken. I checked out the Elders' expressions to see how bad the report might be. They sat stiff and quiet, their faces void of expression. *Not good.*

I liked this room better than the evaluation room. Less intimidating than the raised platform with the Elders looking down on us. A large table sat in the middle with twenty hardwood chairs circled around, leaving everyone on a level playing field.

The Head Elder, Explesor, addressed our group. "It looks like either the Jack clone or the betrayer has made his or her move. We need a plan to neutralize this situation." His gaze landed on Devon.

Devon stood and placed his hands on the table. "He's hit locally."

Adam leaned forward. "What's he up to?"

Devon clenched and unclenched his hands. "It appears he wants worldwide coverage on this one. He has ten hostages sitting on the edge of the Space Needle roof, six hundred feet up." He cleared his throat. "The hostage negotiators are reporting he's threatening to push one over the edge every hour starting at 2:00 p.m. if his demands aren't met."

"What?" Lucy held her chest.

"They wanted to make sure we got the message," Devon said. "This is the showdown we've been waiting for."

Adam sat back in his chair. "How do we know it's the Jack and not some whacko?"

"He's made a demand." Devon shot a glance at Ann. She nodded and clasped her hands together.

Devon looked down at the table. "The note says they want the child."

Lucy shot up. "Henry? They want Henry?" She shook her head and repeated, "No, no, no."

Ann grabbed Lucy's hand over the table. "I promise you, Henry will be safe."

Lucy's cheeks flared red. "How do we save the hostages and keep Henry safe? Will the clone really push them over the side?" Her eyes darted around the table. "Those poor people must be terrified. We have to do something."

Devon placed a hand on Lucy's shoulder. "We will."

"Do you know who's behind this?" she asked between gritted teeth.

"It could be the clone, the betrayer, or a surviving Jack." Devon looked around the table. "We still don't know what part the betrayer possibly has in this. Everything we talk about in this room stays in this room. Got it?"

A pounding on the door made me jump.

Explesor sighed. "That's probably Susie. She's been asking for more responsibility. She's requested to work in the field with you on this one. Does anyone have a problem with that?"

Lucy bolted to her feet. "Uh, yeah. Susie is a self-serving bi—"

Devon cleared his throat. "What Lucy meant to say is, maybe Susie could start out a little slower and work her way up." He shot Lucy a glance. "We don't want to imply your niece isn't capable."

"Darn. Forgot about that," Lucy said under her breath and sat down.

If the subject matter wasn't so serious I'd probably laugh. Lucy's personality matched her red hair in every way.

Explesor studied the group with pursed lips. Made me wonder what kind of screws Susie put to her good old uncle to get him to consider adding her to such an important mission.

He pressed a button on the desk, and the door clicked open.

Susie came barging in. "Finally. What took so long?"

He pointed a finger at her. "Take a seat, and don't say a word unless you're spoken to."

She huffed and sat down in an empty chair.

With a warning look, Explesor ordered, "You will go on this assignment as a shadow. No interaction. You understand?"

She rolled her eyes. "Yeah. Yeah. No interaction. Got it."

Devon looked around the table. "Where's Ian?"

"I left him in the library. Why?" Susie said while examining her nails.

Lucy leaned toward Sadie. "By the way, has Ian had any visions since you've met?"

"No. But that's not unusual. The Seer's visions can be quite unpredictable."

Explesor cleared his throat. "Lucy and Sadie, is there something you'd like to share with the group?"

The two girls pressed their lips together, both shaking their heads.

"It'd be wise for the both of you to pay attention," he admonished. "Go on, Devon."

"As I was saying. We'll need to fan out. Because we don't know the clone's real intentions, we'll have to make things as difficult as we can. Also, we don't know where the betrayer is located. It could be here in Samara or another location. I've talked to the Elders and because Samara has limited security and defense, we'll evacuate until we extinguish the threat." He took a deep breath and looked at me. "Archer, we'll need your expertise after the mission. You set up the last security system. We'll need to have another put in place. Are you game?"

I nodded. "Sure." It was understandable the Readers hadn't seen the need for extra security because everyone believed the Jacks were dead. But what really hit me about his question was the amount of trust it expressed.

Lucy rubbed her forehead. "What's the plan?"

Adam took Lucy's hand and whispered, "Don't worry. We've got this."

She put her head on his shoulder.

Devon leaned forward with his hands braced on the table. "Here's how it will go down. The Readers will spread out around the continental states. Our team will split into two groups. The Space Needle group will be myself and Archer. Sadie, we've outfitted your house with enough security to guard the White House. A specialized unit has also placed guns and ammunition in your garage with instructions. Ann, Henry, Ian, Lucy, and Adam...and I guess Susie, will go with you. If the Jack clone is stupid enough to come after you, we'll have a team ready for him."

Sadie and I wouldn't be together. Her alarmed eyes met mine. I gave her a half-smile and mouthed, "No worries."

Easier said than done.

Ann shifted in her chair. "They could be using this situation to lure you out by leaving the hostages on the roof."

"What would their end game be?" Devon asked.

"Maybe they want to split us up this time. Their plan to take us out in one explosion didn't work."

Lucy got up and began to pace. "But someone needs to save the hostages. We can't leave them there. Right?"

Ann bit her lip and glanced at Devon. His furrowed brow and tight expression softened.

He spoke directly to Ann. "We'll go to the Space Needle and get a read on the crowd. Once we kill the clone and the hostages are free, we'll meet at Sadie's house."

Ann tried to smile, but her watery eyes gave her away.

Adam leaned back in his chair. "We'll need to flush out the betrayer once we get back to Samara."

"At least we all know it's not Archer." Lucy smiled at me.

Adam groaned. "We have to validate the video first before we jump to conclusions."

Next to me, Sadie straightened. "What do you mean, validate?" Her eyes bored into Adam. With cheeks flushed red and hands clenched into fists, she was a sight to behold.

I'll have to remember never to get on her bad side.

"We can get into all of this later." Devon smiled at Sadie. "I have no doubts about the integrity of the surveillance tapes." He cocked his head and said to Adam, "We're all going to need to work together on this. You have a problem with it?"

Adam pursed his lips and shook his head.

Explesor stood. "It looks like we have everything settled here. I'll sound the evacuation alarm in the next hour. That will give you a chance to pack and be on your way."

Devon spoke directly to Explesor. "Once the mission is complete, we'll contact you through our emergency network."

The rest of us stood to leave.

"Thank you. All of us appreciate your willingness to put your lives in danger." Explesor looked up at the ceiling. "Maybe this will be the last time."

"We'll get them. I promise you," Devon said.

I left the room with a swirling mixture of adrenaline, determination, and dread. The Jacks were clever, so we all knew the stakes. One wrong move and we'd all be dead.

Sadie gave my sleeve a little tug. "Can you come to my room while I pack?"

"Sure, I have a couple of minutes before I meet Devon."

We made the trip to Sadie's room in silence. She opened the door and waved me in. As soon as the door closed, she jumped into my arms with such force I stepped back to keep my balance. "I like your enthusiasm." I laughed, but when her lips trembled, and her cheeks turned pink, I stopped. "What's the matter?"

"I have this feeling I won't see you again."

My heart stopped. "A vision?"

"No. No. It's more like a gut feeling. Maybe it's fear?"

My shoulders relaxed a little. "Yeah, I'm sure it's just fear. You haven't gone into combat before, right?"

"I haven't, but my parents made sure I received specialized training. I can hit a Jack at a hundred yards with any automated weapon and take out the exact section of the brain where they reside. It hasn't been put into practice, but if it's done right, the human host has a shot of surviving."

I kissed her cheek. "Well, well, well...I've fallen for a Seer warrior. What other things haven't you told me?"

Her eyes widened, and she looked away.

I pulled her into me. "Don't worry. Whatever you don't want me to know, I'm sure there's a good reason for it." The warmth and exhilaration surged again, spreading throughout every cell in my body.

Don't kiss her. Too many things to do.

She wet her bottom lip with her tongue and blinked slowly.

My resolve shattered, and I didn't care if she held every secret in the world. I pulled her to me, our lips collided, hands explored, and our bodies melted together.

I'm lost. This is better than the first time.

We broke apart, breathless.

"Sadie, you feel that?"

"Yes. I'm scared." A lone tear tracked down her cheek.

I reached to wipe it away, but stopped before contact.

She laughed a little. "Smart guy. I guess your job in life is to never make me cry."

"I don't want to leave you," I blurted. "I mean, everything will be okay, but I'd feel better if we were together."

"Same here. Oh, I thought of something, just in case."

"Just in case?"

"Yeah, in the event the clone tries to pass himself off as you."

My stomach sank. "What do you have in mind?"

"Your eyelashes."

"What?"

"Yeah. You have the most beautiful eyelashes of any man I've ever seen."

"Okay." I chuckled.

"I'm going to cut a few. The Jack clone would never notice something so subtle. If it's just between you and me, I'll be able to identify the clone even if he has all your memories. And we agree that 'beach' is our password, right?"

"That's right." I blinked rapidly. "Since you're jealous of my eyelashes, you can go ahead and cut away."

She ran her hand lightly over the ends. "No, they're like a work of art." She smiled. "I'll cut about ten lashes off your right eye. No one will notice except for me."

CHAPTER 22

Sadie

EMPTINESS SETTLED OVER me when we arrived back at my cottage. Everything appeared the same, but everything had changed.

Lucy jumped out of the Jeep and stretched. "I'm glad we have a few minutes before the others arrive."

"I hope they weren't too cramped." At the last minute, Lucy asked Ian to ride with Ann, Susie, Henry, and Adam. Girl talk was the excuse.

"We need to discuss Ian. Is he trustworthy?"

"He's a Seer who returned my mother's necklace. I can't think of one time he hasn't been kind or helpful."

"Maybe too kind and helpful?"

"What do you mean?"

She shrugged. "He's outrageously handsome, I'll give him that. But he could be a Jack who somehow ended up with your mother's necklace. It wouldn't be the first time a Jack has stolen from the Readers or Seers."

"I hadn't thought about that. But he knows all about me. He said he's been protecting me for two thousand years."

"Sadie. Think. Wouldn't you have noticed someone who looked like *that* in two thousand years? My girl radar would have been shouting code red."

"Let's keep a close eye on him, okay? In the meantime, let's see if we find anything on the digital files about the night of the explosion. Maybe we'll get lucky and learn the identity of the betrayer."

"Good idea. Let's unpack and get started."

We entered the front door, and the smell of apples, cinnamon, and flaky pastry floated in from the kitchen.

"Have I died? Pinch me." Lucy immediately searched out the origin.

"Donna must have smuggled in one of her famous apple pies." I chuckled. "The SWAT team has instructions to leave her alone." I made it into the kitchen just in time to witness Lucy taking a bite too large for her to handle. Crumbs and small pieces of apple dusted the kitchen counter. It didn't stop her, though. She picked up the stray pieces and jammed them into her mouth. "Canth wasth it."

The note next to the pie said, *Welcome home! The mayor said you'd be back today.*

Donna. I needed to talk to Ian about the let's-keep-it-only-between-us plan.

I shook my head watching Lucy try to cram more pie into her mouth. "I'll check out the artillery they left for us. We'll need a plan."

"Yeah, right after another bite. Two minutes is all I need."

"You'll love Donna. Pie isn't even her specialty."

"Where is she? I think I need to marry her." She broke out laughing.

I rolled my eyes and chuckled. "When the others get here, can you get Eve? I left her in the car because with all the coming and going I'm worried she'll get spooked and take off."

"Sure thing."

I left the kitchen and headed to the garage. As promised, there was enough ammunition to equip a small country. We'd be safe here. I put my safety plan into motion and plopped onto the sofa next to Lucy.

"I'm dying. Why did you let me eat so much?" She rubbed her stomach.

"Could I have stopped you?" I asked.

She paused. "Nope." She closed her eyes and asked, "I heard you moving from room to room. What were you doing?"

"On the off chance the Jack clone makes a visit, we'll be more than ready for him."

"Okay, good." Her eyes remained closed. "You need me to brief me right now?" She cracked open an eye. "Please say no."

We both laughed. "No, it's under control. The security team did a thorough job."

The other Jeep arrived. I flung open the door and waved as they unloaded their suitcases. I remembered Eve and ran out to get the carrier from the back seat. "Sorry, girl. We had to get the house ready." I poked my finger through the mesh, and she licked it. "You are the sweetest cat on the planet, you know that?"

Adam walked by with a smile and shook his head.

"Well, she is." Maybe I should talk to her when other people weren't eavesdropping. I grabbed the handle and lifted.

Lucy poked her head out of the front door. "Hi, everyone. The refrigerator has a pie and some other goodies thanks to Sadie's neighbor." She noticed I held the carrier. She hit her head. "I'm sorry. I forgot Eve."

"That's okay. She was just sleeping." I smiled so she'd know I wasn't upset. "It's not like we have much going on right now."

"True that."

"Oh, Adam, you're here." She launched herself off the porch and grabbed him into a big hug.

A little twinge of something twisted in my chest. It wasn't jealousy or even envy. I missed Archer already. Wow. I had it bad.

"Hey, Sadie. Can I help?" Ian smiled and cocked his head.

Oh, Ian. We never had the chance for "the talk." Now it'd be a different conversation. I didn't want to hurt him, but my connection with Archer was undeniable. "We're all set. Let's see what's in the fridge besides sugar treats." *Stall. Stall.*

"Sure thing. I'll stow my things in one of the bedrooms. Is that okay?"

"It's good with me. There're three bedrooms, so we'll have to bunk in twos. Ann and Henry. You and Adam. Me and Lucy." Almost forgot. "Oh, and Susie."

His eyes cast downward for a moment. With a deep breath, he seemed to shake off any disappointment and was back to his regular good humor. "Adam isn't the prettiest, but I guess he'll do."

Relieved, I smiled. "Come on in. We'll get everything locked down and firm up our defense plan."

His eyebrows shot up. "We aren't expecting company, are we?"

"No. This is just precautionary."

He scoped out the bushes surrounding the house.

"There's been a perimeter check, and Devon positioned sharpshooters around the property. You probably have six guns pointed at your head."

"In that case." He stepped through the doorway, smiling.

We walked into the kitchen in time to get a few scraps put together, somewhat resembling a sandwich.

Adam chomped on a roast beef sandwich. "We'll need to make a grocery run."

"I thought the plan was to chill out until Devon and Archer returned?" I asked.

"Devon's guys only left enough food for today. I'll make a quick trip. Then we can settle in."

Lucy put her arm around Adam's shoulder. "Good idea. I'll tag along so we can get in and out."

Adam picked up his wallet from the counter. "No need for that. The fewer people who come and go, the better."

"And I could use your help with the last video file from May twenty-ninth. I hope we can find something." Eve rubbed against my leg, so I threw her a piece of turkey.

Ann laughed. "This isn't that boring."

Ian and I looked at each other. "Who said anything about boring?"

"Oh, I thought you said it. Sorry."

"No, I said I hoped we could find something on the video files."

"Definitely not boring." She gave Henry a sandwich already cut into pieces.

Susie entered the kitchen and flopped onto a stool. "Who'll make me a sandwich?" She drummed her fingers on the counter. "Ian? How about it?" She removed her sweater, revealing a skintight T-shirt beneath. "I'd *really* appreciate it."

Lucy took my arm. "Geez. She's at it already. Let's go stare at the screen for a few hours."

We walked to the front door with Adam. Lucy leaned in and kissed him. "See you in a few. Don't get lost in the ice cream section."

He grabbed her waist and planted a passionate kiss on her lips. "I'll only get five flavors this time."

Lucy laughed as she pushed him out the door. Once he was out of earshot, Lucy's laugh faded. "He's acting casual, but he's nervous about all this."

"You're right. He does a good job covering it up. I wouldn't have guessed."

"I can tell by the way he doesn't stay still. Ever since the wave, he keeps asking about the plan every five minutes and fidgets constantly. He's worried about me. Well, about all of us. You've probably noticed he's an emotional guy."

"I did." I smiled to let her know it was a good thing. "Do you think that's why he doesn't like Archer?"

"We've talked a lot about Archer. Subconsciously, I believe he blames him for this latest attack. Like Archer could prevent Atarah from stealing his DNA. I'm sure he'll come around once we authenticate the video from the night Markus died. Can't argue that."

"Nope." Hopefully, we'd see if any Jacks had escaped the explosion. "I'll set it up so we can look at our own screens. It'll go much faster that way."

"Great. Let's get started."

I called into the kitchen. "Hey everyone, we'll be viewing video files in the den if you need anything."

Ian and Ann waved because their mouths were full, and Henry smooshed his food on his plate. Susie either didn't hear or ignored me. She was too busy batting her eyelashes at Ian. I thought about trying to save him, but I figured he could take care of himself.

After I switched on the computer and monitors, I took a deep breath. "We have five hours of digital tape to go through. We should start with the explosion and work our way in reverse."

"Good idea. If anyone escaped, it would've been during the last few minutes."

"Yep. Here goes."

We both studied our monitors while the recording worked its way backward from the explosion. "Wow," we both said at the same time.

Lucy pointed at the monitor. "Keep your eyes on the exterior exits. We'll study the five on the south side, then the remaining five on the north and east sides."

A half hour later, I rubbed my eyes. "I've seen nothing, no shadows, nothing."

"Same with me." Lucy looked toward the hall. "Has Adam gotten back yet? I haven't heard the door open."

"It takes about ten minutes each way to the store, so he

should be back soon," I reassured her.

Her shoulders relaxed, and she went back to the video. "Hey, wait a second."

"What?" I stood up and walked to her monitor with my heart pounding.

"These two shadows coming from the laundry vent. What do you think?"

"They're so small. What are they, mice?"

"Yes, mice that made an exit before the explosion. Mice who didn't have a reason to scurry out of the building at record speed."

"You're not saying..."

"I think we witnessed two Jacks making a hasty retreat."

"Jacks can take animal form?"

"Yes, but they normally wouldn't. Too many natural predators. But to escape an explosion? I'm sure they would."

"Keep looking. We have to find out if there're more than two."

Eve jumped up on my lap. "Look at this, Eve. Two rats escaped Samara. Too bad you weren't there. They could have been a snack for you."

Lucy stood. "We should let Devon and Archer know about this."

Ann poked her head in the door. "Heard anything from Adam? He's not back yet."

"Oh no." Lucy jumped up. "It's been over an hour."

"It's been that long? It does seem like a long time. Is he usually a slow shopper?" I stood next to her and rubbed her arm.

Lucy bit her lip. "Sometimes. I even joke about him getting lost in the ice cream section."

A knock on the front door startled me. "See? That's probably Adam."

Lucy bolted to the door and swung it open. "Oh, hi."

"Hi, sweetie. I noticed a lot of you coming in today, so I baked another pie." A familiar voice.

I smiled to myself. I wondered how long it'd take Donna to come over to check things out.

"You're the Pie Lady?" Lucy grinned, but still looked over Donna's shoulder to see if Adam was on his way back.

"Yes. I'm Donna. I also knit." She held up a huge knitting bag.

"Are you going to knit us pajamas?" I winked and laughed.

"No, dear. But that's not a bad idea. I knitted a kitty sweater for Eve." Her eyes darted around the foyer.

"Where are my manners? Come on in, and I'll put the sweater on Eve." I stepped aside and enjoyed the scent of cinnamon and talcum powder as she walked past me. "This is Lucy." We walked into the living room. "And you know Ian." He waved. "Ann and Henry, this is my neighbor I was telling you about, Donna. Where's Susie?"

"Watching a sandwich being made for her must have been oh so tiring." Ann fanned her face and said with a southern drawl, "I do believe she's resting until the next meal." She bit back a smile.

Ian excused himself and went down the hall toward the bathroom.

Ann picked up Henry. "It was nice meeting you, Donna. This little one needs to go down for his nap or we'll all suffer." She squeezed him. "Won't we?"

Henry giggled and gave her a sloppy kiss.

"Yeah. He looks vicious." Lucy ruffled his hair.

"Be back in a minute. Please make yourself comfortable." I needed to clear my head. I also needed to get Donna out, but I didn't want to make it obvious. But the situation was fluid, and I didn't know if any of us were in danger. Where was Adam anyway?

Devon and Archer kept burner cell phones for emergency use. Was the information about the escaped Jacks an emergency?

As I passed the den, Ian stood over the desk, working on something. I walked in slowly and peered over his shoulder and froze. Ian held pliers in his hand and was prying open the flash drives. There could only be one reason for this. I swiveled and grabbed a set of handcuffs placed under a laundry basket I'd hidden earlier. I approached Ian on silent feet. When we were a foot apart, I moved swiftly.

"Hi, Ian," I said.

He froze, and before he could react, I handcuffed his wrist to the bookcase.

"No, Sadie. It's not what it looks like."

"Did you do something to Adam? Why isn't he back?"

"I don't know." His face drained of color. "Please, listen before you talk to the others."

"Too late." Lucy stood at the door with arms crossed and a scowl on her face.

"I caught him trying to destroy the video files."

"I can explain."

"You'll need to wait." I turned to Lucy. "Is Donna still here?"

"Yes, she's knitting and talking to the cat."

"She might be in danger. Let's get her home without frightening her." If anything happened to Donna because of me, I'd never forgive myself.

CHAPTER 23

Archer

DEVON PUSHED HIS fingers through his hair. "It's a zoo around here."

"You're not kidding." Wall-to-wall people were in and around Seattle Center due to the media's decision to broadcast live. It didn't help two of Seattle's largest television stations were located right across the street.

"We're going to need a way to get through the crowds." His eyes scanned the connecting streets. "If I remember right, there's a costume store about two blocks west. Let's go check it out."

Within a block, Devon stopped short. "What do we have here?"

I followed his gaze. "The dry cleaners?"

"Yes. Look at the carousel on the left."

I squinted. "Good catch. Real police uniforms will work much better. Let's go."

We crossed the street and paused outside the building. "Hear anything?"

"Yep. They're having lunch in the back. The only problem is, the bell will chime if we enter. Any ideas?"

I nodded. "Follow my lead." I opened the door and stepped in.

A heavyset woman walked briskly to the counter.

"Hi, I'm picking up an alteration job for Wellnitz."

"Alteration?" *Why do these stupid people have to come and interrupt my lunch?*

"Yes. Is it ready?"

No. Because I don't want to have to go all the way to the back of the store for one job. "I'll check." *I'll go finish my lunch and tell him it wasn't ready.* She turned and walked away.

Devon's mouth dropped open. "Did you hear her? How did you know that would happen?"

"They make the dry cleaning more assessible than the alterations. I waited over twenty minutes for a tailored jacket. Anyway, let's grab them and get out before she changes her mind."

Devon jumped over the counter. "Let's take all three." He tossed them to me and maneuvered back over the counter. "Next stop, the bathroom at McDonald's?"

"You read my mind."

"Ha ha." He shook his head. "Always the joker."

After we changed and stuffed the third uniform in the trash, we headed back to the area around the Space Needle. With our emergency supplies strapped to our wrists, and the lockpick secured on my waist, we were ready to go. Helicopters buzzed, police barricades were in place, and crowd control was in full swing.

"Can you read anyone?" I asked.

"Too jumbled. How about you?"

"Same. We should walk the perimeter and see if there's anyone not paying attention."

I pulled at my collar to loosen it. "This is one time I'm glad the crowds are thick. It'll be less likely for anyone to notice we aren't wearing badges and department-issued shoes."

"Hey! You over there. Need some help." An older, overweight police officer waved us over. *God help me, a couple of rookies.*

I bit back a smile and kept my face expressionless. "Yes, sir?"

"Two women, over there." He pointed to an area about a hundred yards away. "O'Malley needs some help. They insist they know one of the hostages."

"On it." Devon nodded to me, and we walked briskly to the altercation. We ducked under the police tape and stood next to the two women having it out with O'Malley.

A woman dressed in a business suit dabbed her eyes with a tissue. "And we saw our dear Teddy up on the edge of the Needle right on our television screen."

The other woman, wearing similar attire joined in. "And Teddy has a fear of heights!" She cried into a napkin. *If this guy doesn't let us pass, we'll never get the lead story tonight. KPLZ better appreciate our acting skills.* "We need to talk to him. He's probably so scared. Are you just going to leave his family out here with the crowds?"

Officer O'Malley wiped his forehead. "Listen. I'll see what I can do, but you need to stay here."

Devon took a step forward. "I don't think that'll be necessary. These two women work for KPLZ, and I doubt they have a relative by the name of Teddy." Devon cocked his head and dared them to deny it.

"Well. That's not... I mean, how did you... " She closed her lips tight. *If he weren't so good-looking, I'd kick... him.*

The second woman asked me, "Have we met before?" *There's no way I'd forget a face like that.*

"Yeah. It was a couple of years back. We did crowd control at one of the concerts."

"Which one?" *Selena Gomez.*

"Selena."

Her eyes widened. *I wonder if they're single.*

"She's my wife's favorite singer."

Damn. The first girl thought.

Oh hell. The second girl groaned to herself.

"Off you go." I gave them a shooing motion.

Maybe not rookies. "Hey, Sergeant needs some help in the northwest quadrant. Can you head over there?" O'Malley asked.

"Sure thing." Devon nodded, and we headed north. "I studied the newest Space Needle schematics online after the big restaurant remodel last year. There's a utility door around the corner. It'll lead to the stairwell. That's our best shot if the clone is still hanging around."

"He's here. I can feel it." An ugly sensation of evil weaved up my spine.

Devon motioned to an alcove away from the crowds. "Break out your tools and we'll take a look."

We ducked out of sight and I turned away and took out the lockpick.. With a quick turn and a click, the door unlocked. Apparently, not many people wanted to break into the Space Needle.

"How long before the first one gets pushed over?" I asked.

Devon looked at his cell. "An hour."

"Not much time. Let's head for the stairs." We turned the corner and two police officers blocked our way. A sergeant and a lieutenant looked us over.

I hope these are the fresh batch of hostage negotiators.

"Hey, we're the crisis negotiators. Do you know the location of the subject?"

"He's up there with the hostages, having a great time torturing the poor souls. Keeps tellin' 'em how they're gonna go splat on the sidewalk below. I'd push him off myself given the chance."

"What's he wearing?"

"Jeans, a blue T-shirt, and a mask. Blond hair, about six-foot-two."

Hmm. This time, he didn't want anyone knowing his identity.

Another outer door swung open, and a five-man SWAT team and a man wearing a business suit and hat charged in and headed up the stairs.

The two cops left to continue their sweep of the ground floor gift shop and reception areas.

Devon sighed. "I had hoped we'd get to him before they arrived."

"He'll be able to read them, so I don't think they'll be able to get a shot off."

"Wait. He's your clone. Tell me step-by-step what you'd do with the same instructions."

"The problem is, we don't know what instructions he's been given. The entire thing could be a setup to flush us out. If that's the case, we'll need to be a step ahead of him."

More officers entered through a side door and headed up the stairs. I took a quick look to see if we could plan our strategy without interruption. My eyes landed on what looked like a storage room. "Let's go in there and plan our next move." Again, with the pick, I opened it within seconds. We entered a room full of miniature plastic Space Needles, postcards, magnets, and water globes.

"Okay. We have to assume we'll be stopped before we're able to intercept the clone."

"I agree. We can only go so far before someone realizes we aren't wearing badges."

"Not only that, but hostage negotiators aren't usually in blue. We've slipped by because of all the confusion. Now that the SWAT team is here, they'll mobilize and get a strategic plan in place."

"If we go up now, we'll probably be discovered."

"Yep."

"We need a Plan B."

Devon sighed. "We have to hope he's not going to follow through on his threats. We'll stay here, out of sight, until he starts down the stairs. He's clever enough to get past the police, but not us. We'll intercept him there."

"And if he decides to push a hostage over?"

Devon rubbed his face. "He's had more time to mature than the Arizona clones. I have to go with the knowledge he's advanced past the infant stage and hope your DNA kicks in."

"And you don't think I follow instructions well?"

"That, and I also don't believe you to be a murderer. The Jacks couldn't even get you to kill Markus with all their sophisticated brainwashing capabilities."

"Thanks. If it weren't for Sadie, Markus's murder would have hung over my head for eternity."

"Ann and I were thinking that you and Sadie—"

"It's already happened."

He grinned. "Ann will be happy to hear it. She still worries about you."

"I'm surprised, after everything I put her through." I shook my head. "Kidnapping, allowing you to get blamed for Markus's murder, attempting to force her to marry me. You know, just a few small things."

He laughed. "She always had a gut feeling it wasn't as it seemed. I'm glad she was right." He tilted his head. "You know this won't go over well with Ian. He's been following her around like a puppy since they arrived."

"Yeah. I told him I'd back off. I'm sure he won't be happy with the change in plans."

"Why'd you do that?" He tilted is head.

"It was back in Cannon Beach. He told me the story about how he'd been protecting her for thousands of years. He also said he's in love with her." My chest tightened.

"There's something about him that doesn't add up. He appears to be sincere, but I think he's harboring a secret."

"A dangerous secret?"

"No. But I think he knows more than he lets on."

"After we rid ourselves of the Jack clone, we can investigate him further."

He put up a hand. "Hang on a sec. Did you hear that?"

"No, what was it?"

He closed his eyes. "There's confusion, and the SWAT commander is shouting orders. This is his opportunity for escape." His eyes popped back open. "They've lost him."

"The only way out is the stairs."

"Right. He won't attempt a rope drop with the crowd outside. He also has to know he'll be exposed if he takes the stairs."

I scratched my cheek. "But it's his only way out."

"Did you notice all the steel rods in the center? He could attempt a slide down those." Devon opened the door and peered over toward the stairs.

"It might be difficult to hit him with the dart in that case." The lethal dart secured to my wrist itched to be released.

"Let's go while there's still time to catch him," Devon said.

"Anyone around?" I asked.

"No, it's quiet on the main floor. Everyone is converging to the roof."

We walked out of the storage room like it was the most natural thing in the world. Good, the stairway remained empty.

We started our sprint up the stairs. About halfway, we

encountered the guy in the business suit. He nodded, but we stopped him before he could pass.

Devon narrowed his eyes. "I don't hear anything."

"Neither do I." I examined the man closer.

The man tilted his head. "I guess we're kind of like brothers. Nice to meet you, Archer," he said with a grin on his face. He peeled the plastic mask from his face.

My stomach dropped, and I wanted to throw up. It wasn't just his looks; his soulless green eyes were vacant. *Eerie.*

Maybe we could reason with him. "You're being used, you have to know that."

"Of course I am. I'm not stupid. When I finish here, I plan to dispose of Atarah and her little helpers."

Atarah is alive? Oh my God, I have to get to Sadie "You plan to go live in peace after this?" I knew the answer. He was a Jack; he loved chaos and torment.

He grinned. "Yes. After I rid myself of another few annoyances, Sadie will be mine."

What the hell?

Within a blink of an eye, he put a dart in his mouth and shot Devon. Before I could react, he whipped out a stun gun and aimed for my chest. I fell to the ground and hit my head. The world started to go black, but not before I watched him kick Devon in the chest, sending him over the railing. Dear God, we were over three hundred feet up.

No, no, no.

Electrical currents ripped through my body. The crippling, physical pain was nothing compared to the anguish of losing my best friend. The clone would finish me off next. The agony increased as blackness set in.

CHAPTER 24

Sadie

I WAS SO stupid! Of course Ian was the Portland connection. He'd dropped me off at the Heathman before the Arizona trip. He was at the scene.

Ann joined Lucy and me. "I double-checked the handcuffs, he won't be going anywhere."

"I'll stay here for a minute, just to make sure he doesn't escape." Lucy stood guard at the den door.

"Thanks." I wiped an errant tear that'd slipped down my face.

Ann shook her head. "Don't go feeling bad you didn't know about Ian. We all believed he was who he said he was."

"I know. He had my mother's necklace and knew things about me since the Great War. I feel naïve to have believed him."

"He was convincing. My radar usually picks this kind of

thing up." Ann glanced back at the door. "I really did believe him. I'm not just saying it to make you feel better."

"Thanks." It didn't help the horrible sensation of dread snaking through my body.

"And I also think he loves you. You can't fake that type of devotion. Seer or Jack, that man has it bad." She sighed deeply.

My cheeks flushed. "Jacks are known for their deception. He played a role in a drama. He made us all believe him. I bet he's laughing at all of us."

Her eyes flicked to the den door. "Do you think Ian could be Atarah?"

Oh no. "What do you think?" I asked.

"It would be bad. She's one of the strongest, most clever and evil Jacks of that race." Cold fingers of fear tracked up my back. "We have to get Donna out of the house. I don't want her caught up in any of this."

Ann leaned and peered down the hall. "She looks like she's here to stay. Look at her."

I kept my back against the wall and took a quick peek. Donna sat in a wingback chair with her feet on the ottoman. She held her knitting bag close and furiously worked on her latest project. A scarf maybe?

"We have to try. Come on." I motioned to Ann. We walked into the living room together. I started, "Hey, Donna—"

The front door swung open, startling me. Adam entered with a girl who appeared to be either drunk or drugged. He held on to the arm of the girl, guiding her to sit on the couch. She sat quietly, her stare vacant.

Lucy came out of nowhere and launched herself at Adam,

wrapping her arms around his shoulders. "I was worried. What happened?" She pulled back. "What's going on? Why do you look so..."

"So...what, Lucy? Happy?" Adam's tone sounded sarcastic.

"No. Just weird." She turned, just noticing the girl. "Who is that?"

"She's the girl who went missing after the tsunami. Remember that?" He snickered. "No, of course you don't. All you care about is getting rid of the Jacks."

Lucy's eyes bulged. "What are you saying?"

Oh no. Something strange was going on while Donna happily knitted away. "Donna, I was about to suggest you take Eve to your house. She loves it there. It must be the kibble you buy."

"I wouldn't miss this show for anything." She looked up and smiled.

"I'm sorry, what show?"

Susie barged into the room. "Does the word *quiet* mean anything to you people? I said I needed a nap, and this is what I get? Do you hear me? I need my sleep. You people need to shut up." Her eyes flashed at Donna. "Why is there some old person here? Can someone get rid of her?"

"Well, this one is quite rude, isn't she?" Donna reached into her knitting bag, pulled out a Glock 19, and shot Susie in the shoulder, sending her flying back into the dining room table. Susie turned, hit her head on one of the chairs, and fell unconscious to the floor. Adam whipped out his own handgun and pointed it at Ann.

Lucy, Ann, and I stood frozen as the real world took a hard shift into crazy town. The bookcase in the den fell over. Most likely Ian trying to get free.

"Adam, tie them up," Donna ordered. "Any of you make a move, I'll kill Ann first."

Oh no. Donna had been Atarah the whole time? Was there ever a Donna? Was she faking all these years? My eyes flicked to Eve. My stomach dropped. *Stay calm.* Or she might use her for leverage. That's why she always brought caviar. Ugh. Why didn't I see it?

"Adam?" Lucy whispered. "Are you okay? What's going on?"

He smiled wide. "Never been better."

Donna waved the gun. "Tie them to the dining room chairs."

Adam scanned the room. "Where's Ian?"

Donna snickered. "The girls here already took care of him. He's handcuffed in the den. Thanks for making it easier for us."

Ian wasn't a Jack after all?

"Nice." Adam chuckled.

Donna rapped her gun on the table. "Hurry up. Make sure those ropes are nice and tight."

Adam put his gun back in its holster and motioned to me first. "Don't even think about trying to make a move. Donna has a twitchy finger."

Time to plan an escape. *Think.*

A crazy idea flashed. My mom's necklace was in my jacket. When I turned away from him to sit in the chair, I shifted it to my back pocket. "What do you get for this, Adam? You're a Reader. Why would you help the Jacks? For power?"

"Shut up and put your hands behind you."

I obeyed. "You do know Atarah uses mind control. We proved it with Archer. Does that concern you?" I wanted to throw up. The ropes tying my hands together sent jabbing pain up my arms. "Too tight."

Adam cocked his head. "Good news. We haven't killed you yet. Don't test me."

Adam retrieved his gun and pointed it at Lucy. "You're next. Don't try any of your moves. Right now, you're planning to take me out. I know your fiery temper, but it will cost Ann her life. You really want us to take her out before the show?"

"What show?" Lucy's face flamed, and her hands clenched tight at her sides.

Donna pushed back an errant strand of white hair. "We decided to wait and see if Archer and Devon can make it past our clone. If they get here, we'll make sure they get to witness the executions before we kill them." She sneered. "I'm especially excited to see Devon's face when his beloved dies." Her face contorted in rage, and with bared teeth she hissed at Ann, "You, the sacred Lost One, not so powerful now are you?"

Ann turned away.

Her voice returned to saccharine sweet. "Don't worry, sweetie. We'll take good care of little Henry. With a little mind erasing, he'll be more than happy to do whatever we want. That boy will be very useful to us."

Ann's hands formed into fists and she lunged forward. Lucy took hold of her arm and grabbed her back into a hug. I heard her whisper, "Not now. Take a deep breath."

Lucy tried to hold Ann's hand before Adam ripped it away and tied her up. Ann was next.

"What about Sadie? She's a Seer. She has nothing to do with this." Lucy pleaded.

Donna sighed. "You're right. We're going to keep Sadie for our clone. They'll have lots of little super babies." Her eyes lit up. "Who will grow into the most powerful breed on the planet. A mix of Jack, Reader, and Seer. No one will be able to defeat us ever again."

I choked back the bile creeping up my throat.

She noticed my disgust. "Oh, don't worry, Sadie. He looks exactly like Archer. You'll love him."

These Jack people are freaking crazy.

"Oh, and he's already taken a liking to you. You'll have good chemistry with all the Reader/Jack mix. You know, because they share the exact DNA with Archer.." She clapped. "It should be fun to watch!"

"Why the hostages at the Space Needle?" Ann asked through gritted teeth.

"Oh, just some dramatic fun. We knew the two strongest would try to take care of things at the Needle. As a group, it'd be easier to overpower you in small numbers. And I was right! Now, it'll be exciting to see who won the showdown."

Ann's cheeks flared red. "You get pleasure from this."

Donna rolled her eyes. "Something you Readers have overlooked because it doesn't fit your logical brains—we get energy and all sorts of enjoyable endorphins from torturing and destroying humans, and especially Readers. This is fun, isn't it Adam?"

He smirked and nodded.

Susie stirred on the ground, moaning.

"Get her tied up. Now," Donna said.

Adam yanked her up and tied her to a chair before she could resist.

"Where am I?" Her eyes widened. "What's going on? Why am I tied up?"

"Oh dear. I'm so sorry to have inconvenienced you in any way. It's just that, your race decided to kill the Jacks and, sweet darling, we just didn't appreciate it. So now we're going to kill all of you." Donna's sweet tone gave me the creeps.

Susie's mouth formed an O.

It was strange to hear such foreign words come from Donna's mouth. My heart sank, and I blinked back tears. It was my fault for not noticing the evil that lurked within her. I wanted to see what I needed and wanted in a friend—a sweet, loving woman with a gentle soul. "Is the real Donna still in there?" I asked.

"Oh, I forgot you know about that. Yes, and she's quite annoying. Always wanting to help people. She's absolutely no fun at all."

I stared at the drugged girl on the couch. "Why is this girl here? If she's the one that went missing after the tsunami, she can't have anything to do with this."

"Oh, we have plans for her. Another fun surprise." Atarah sent Adam a quick smile.

Eve came sauntering into the living room without a care. Fear and loathing made me break out in a sweat. *Don't show emotion.* Donna would notice and most likely use it.

"Oh, look who's here," Donna cooed.

My stomach twisted in knots. I squeezed my eyes shut, but I couldn't keep quiet. "Don't you touch her." Tears streamed down my face, even though it would give her ammunition.

Adam laughed. "Wow. You are just as naïve as Atarah said."

My cheeks heated, and I put every emotion on my face to

make sure he'd understand the depth of my loathing.

Adam picked up Eve and ran his hand down her back. "So, Eve. Or should I say Atarah? Do you like this human?" He pointed to the drugged girl on the couch. "Will she do? She's quite beautiful."

Why was he talking to Eve? *Oh no.* It wasn't true. I started shaking my head.

Donna threw her head back and laughed. "That was the best thing I've seen in centuries. Your face when you discovered your beloved pet is the evil Atarah." She glanced at the cat. "Sorry, Atarah. I couldn't resist."

Eve meowed and jumped up and sat next to Donna.

Wait. My mind scrambled to make sense of it. "If you aren't Atarah, who are you?"

Donna sat up, appearing almost regal. "Now that you ask. I am the High Priest Cyneric, leader of all Jacks. Present and future."

Ann took a huge intake of air and began coughing.

Not good.

At that moment, Archer came busting through the door, bleeding from his head.

"Archer." I struggled with the ropes.

Donna eyed him. "Which one is it, Adam? Can you tell?"

Adam peered closely at his face.

Archer took a step back. "What's going on here?" His head turned toward me. "Why are you tied up?" His eyes shifted to Donna. "Donna? Why does she have a gun?"

Donna groaned. "Tie him up. Ugh. It's Archer. What'd you do with my clone?"

"*Your* clone?" His head whipped to me. "Sadie, what's going on?"

"Don't answer him if you want your friend Ann to remain alive the next few seconds," Donna, or Cyneric, ordered.

All I could do was shake my head at Archer.

Ann leaned forward. "Where's Devon?"

Archer looked down. "I'm so sorry, Ann. I couldn't save him."

No! My heart raced, and a lump formed in my throat. Devon. What would Ann do without him? I hung my head, and the sadness and grief washed through me.

"Don't tell me that. You're wrong." Ann wrestled with the ropes. "Let me out of here. Now! Devon needs me." She sobbed.

We sat for a few moments until Ann could catch her breath. I wanted to comfort her so much my arms ached. Lucy struggled with her ropes. I knew she felt the same.

"What happened?" she whispered, looking down at the floor.

"The clone got him with a dart and shoved him off the stairs." Archer's voice broke.

"The stairs at the Space Needle?" I asked.

"We were halfway up." He blinked rapidly. "The clone almost tasered me, but I was able to kick him off. We fought and rolled down one of the flights of stairs. I was finally able to push him over the railing." He took a deep breath. "It's fitting since that's what he did to Devon." His sad eyes looked at Ann. "I'm so sorry, Ann. I would have died in his place if I could."

Ann's face crumpled. Racking sobs made her shoulders shake.

"No more talking," bellowed Cyneric. "Tie Archer to the other chair. Move it."

Adam motioned with his gun to the chair and smiled. "Been wanting to do this for a long time."

Archer sat in the chair, scowling. "You do know Atarah uses mind control."

"Yeah. Yeah. Heard it all before."

Archer glanced at Lucy. "Why? What about Lucy?"

Adam shrugged. "It was an act. Never loved her. She was a puppet."

Lucy's eyes popped open wide, and she sat up straighter in her chair. "It's you. You've been the betrayer all this time."

"Yep. I've loved Atarah in all her forms for centuries now." Adam gazed at Eve.

Oh, the names. Adam and Eve. They probably thought they were clever. Ugh.

"Love?" Archer scoffed.

Adam's eyes narrowed. "Hard for you to believe?"

"You're delusional." Archer stared Adam down.

Adam broke eye contact and said, "At least I'll be alive. Can't say that for the rest of you."

"What? I heard that," Susie screeched. "You can't kill me. Let me go, and I'll give you whatever you want."

Adam ignored her, and Donna laughed.

"We have lots of money stashed away. It's yours if you let me go." Susie's desperation was not a pretty thing to witness. She'd throw us all under the bus without hesitation.

I leaned over. "Archer, they plan to kill everyone. Do you

have a plan?" I took note of his missing eyelashes.

"Not yet. I knew I had to get to you." His eyes scanned the room. "Don't worry. I'll figure something out." He leaned over and kissed me lightly on my lips. "Beaches, by the way."

"Aw. Isn't that sweet. Even after all our efforts to keep you apart, the soul mate love did its magic," Cyneric said in his sweet-as-pie voice.

"Soul mate love?" Lucy asked.

"Archer and Sadie were destined to be together from the beginning. We didn't figure it out until Ann rejected him for Devon." Adam shrugged. "We changed our plans and used his DNA to make the clones."

Archer scowled. "That's why you knocked me out in my house that day. You didn't want me to interrupt Ian and Sadie's date."

"Smart guy." He scowled. "The more you and Sade were together, the better chance she'd notice when we made the switch. Ian was a convenient distraction."

Eve jumped off the chair and began to rub against Archer's leg. Lucy and Ann quietly cried. Both lost their loves in a matter of minutes. My heart ached for them.

Archer leaned over. "I'll get us out of this, I promise."

I pressed my lips together. Determination raced through my veins. I was not going to watch them die. I dug my mother's necklace from my back pocket. The clasp had worked as a key, but on the other side was a serrated edge. Could it work for cutting the rope? With sweaty hands, I began the tedious sawing motion, trying to keep my body as still as possible. Ten minutes and my hands were free. Now I needed to wait for the right moment.

Ann whispered to Archer, "Donna is Cyneric and Atarah is the cat."

His eyes grew large, and his gaze landed on the cat purring and rubbing against his leg. He kicked her away.

Adam picked up Eve. "Let's get the transfer done. Atarah, does this human meet your approval?"

Eve meowed and nodded her head. *Freaky.*

In the next second, Eve collapsed, and the girl on the couch sat upright with clear eyes. With a big stretch, she said, "Oh, it feels so good to be in a human body again." She smiled and wiggled her fingers. "And I can use my fingers again. Talk about tedious, using a paw to tap letters into an iPad. So annoying."

I'd heard about how the Jacks transferred, but had never seen one happen.

Her eyes locked on me. "Thanks for the kibble." Her laugh could only be described as evil. "And I'm going to miss our girl talks."

Heat and a pinpricking sensation ran through my arms and legs, ending at my face.

"Because of you, I know everything about the Readers. And I was happy to update the Jacks with your iPad." She snickered.

She may as well have shoved a stake through my heart. It would have felt less painful than this.

She ran in place for a few seconds. "It's good to have the valium out of my system." She smiled at Adam. "But I did enjoy it while it lasted."

"Valium?" Archer asked.

"We're always a step ahead of you. We figured out, well, a

little late, Ann could read me. How else could she get the jump on us to destroy the Jacks? If she caught one of my thoughts in Samara, they'd need to be happy, sunshine ones like all you boring Readers. Ugh. I'm so glad to be rid of you."

That's why she slept so much. It wasn't the new environment and her being in her carrier like I thought.

Atarah pranced around the living room. "Do I still look beautiful for you? Do you like this human form?"

Adam smiled. "I'd love you in any form."

Lucy made a gagging noise.

"It was genius how you threatened Eve when Sadie arrived at Samara. Sadie kept me with her around the clock. I have so much to tell you." Atarah stretched again.

Would this misery ever end?

"You are evil, Atarah. You'll never change," Archer spat.

She ignored him and spoke to Adam. "We'll wait for the Readers to return to Samara, then we'll detonate the bomb you planted. Tit for tat and all that." Her eyes narrowed when they rested on Ann. "You destroyed the Jacks, and now it's our turn to destroy the Readers. Now that we're rid of your strongest, Devon, the rest should be smooth as the skin on a newly formed clone. They are soft, aren't they Adam?" She chuckled.

Ann perked up. "Adam. There's something you should know. Atarah's right. I can read her. Once you've fulfilled this job, she plans to kill you. She doesn't want one single Reader left alive. You've done this for nothing, and she'll discard—"

"Enough of your lies! You're desperate, and Adam will never be fooled by you," Atarah screeched.

Adam paused before glancing at Atarah. "Our love is real. No one or nothing will ever tear us apart."

Brainwashed. Or just stupid?

Cyneric clapped his hands together. "Enough. I've had to tolerate a damn cat for two years." He turned to Atarah. "I liked it better when you couldn't speak. I'm running things now, as it should be. You sit down and keep your mouth shut."

While they were distracted, I reached under my chair, untied the ropes binding my feet, and grabbed the gun I'd fastened there earlier. Darn, my palms were sweaty. The gun held six bullets, more than enough. Cyneric, Adam, Atarah. I closed my eyes, visualizing the sequence of shots.

The back door flung open, and in walked Devon and...Archer?

Time to assess and make my move before the Jacks made theirs. All the information from the last fifteen minutes filtered through my brain. Only one chance, and I had to take it. Remembering the exact place to plant a bullet to kill a Jack, I stood up and went into laser focus mode. The training I'd received came back with such clarity, it made me wonder if there weren't other forces at work. First bullet, Cyneric. Second, Atarah. Third, Adam. The next was the clone sitting in the chair next to me. "Nice try," I said and fired the last shot.

EPILOGUE

Sadie

THE SMELL OF antiseptic burned my sinus passages. My body was unable to move. Was I drugged? I tried to turn over, but the tubes around my arms stopped me.

Where was I?

I couldn't open my eyes, but the beep-beep sound of the machines next to me gave me a clue. A hospital. What happened? My body felt completely numb. Had I been hurt? The last thing I remember...oh no. The shooting.

Did I get them all?

Hushed voices murmured next to me. I strained to hear.

"She's still in shock. We want to keep her sedated for a few more days." Doc's voice.

Was I at Samara?

"But, but she'll be okay, right?" Lucy's voice wobbled.

"I think so. You're going to have to give her small doses about what happened. Just a little at a time. I'm worried about a mental breakdown if we don't approach this right."

"Okay."

Oh no. Lucy was crying.

"When she first wakes, tell her everything will be okay," Doc instructed.

"What else?"

"Tell her she's not alone and that you'll be there for her."

She sniffed. "I will be there for her. As long as it takes."

"If she asks about Archer, try to change the subject. We want to make sure she's strong enough to hear the news."

"I don't want her to blame herself."

"If handled right, we might be able to help her through this. But it won't be like a normal loss, because Archer and Sadie were soul mates."

Were? Were!

"I hate Atarah! I'm so glad she killed her."

"Atarah was the most devious Jack in their race. When she was in cat form, she knew if she rubbed against Archer, it would make Sadie think he was the clone. Such evil."

"Poor Sadie. I would've done the same thing. She only had a second to make the call."

Noooo! I ripped at the tubes, trying to pull them out. I screamed and screamed, but only in my head. My mouth wouldn't move. I needed to throw up. I killed Archer? Sadness like I'd never known filled my body with heavy darkness. I would never forgive myself. I should've died with him so he wouldn't be alone. *Oh, Archer, what have I done?* There were tears, but I couldn't feel the wetness.

My bed shook and shook, sending vibrations throughout my body. Wait. Someone was shaking my shoulders. Why couldn't I open my eyes? Was I blind?

Someone yelled my name. "Sadie, Sadie." Why couldn't I see them? Was I in a coma?

"You're just having another dream. Wake up, Sadie. Wake up." Archer's voice?

More shaking. I cracked open an eye to see a tiny bit of light creeping through the shutters. Not totally blind. But what was going on?

"Sadie. Come back to me. I'm alive. Please wake up."

I groaned. My body was soaked in sweat, almost like I'd been swimming. Wait, water, lots of it, splashed against my face. I spluttered and coughed.

"That's it. It's almost over."

Arms went around me, and an overwhelming sense of peace flooded my body.

"Archer?" I managed to croak out.

"It's me. You had another night terror. I'm so sorry."

It was only a nightmare. My pulse beat like a hummingbird. I finally opened my eyes, and Archer's beautiful but concerned face looked back. "You're alive?"

"Very much so." He grinned.

"It was so real." I took the towel Archer offered me and wiped my face.

"Doc says the PTSD and short-term amnesia should work its way out eventually. You've struggled with these dreams for two months now, but everything else is good." He held me in his arms.

"I can only remember the dream right now."

"Again, normal. It'll come back. That's usually how it goes when you get the dreams."

I looked around the room. "I'm home. This isn't Samara. I guess Doc and Lucy aren't here?"

"Usually they aren't, but today you'll see them because of the party."

"What party?"

"We can wait until your memory returns, or I can tell you."

I sat up. "Tell me now!"

Archer chuckled. "Well, don't freak out, but we eloped last week."

"We did?" But I knew before asking, because my entire being was filled with euphoria. "It was a garden in Italy." My racing heart settled down a bit. "Did I ruin the honeymoon with my nightmares?" I cringed, waiting for the answer.

He leaned over to kiss me. "You didn't. We had the best honeymoon in the history of honeymoons." He smiled and smoothed some wet hair from my face. His kiss sent all sorts of sparks through me.

Eve jumped up onto the bed and began to rub against Archer. He leaned down and scratched behind her ears and accepted her lick on his cheek. "Whoa. Hang on a minute. You and Eve?"

He stifled a smile. "Once Atarah left, Eve and I became acquainted."

"Acquainted?" I pressed my lips together, trying to keep from laughing.

"Yes, well, you know. Cats can be selective, and I never measured up before now. I think Eve understands my goal in life is to protect you." He kissed my hand. "And love you." Another kiss on my cheek. "And to cherish you." A soft kiss on my lips.

My heart rate kicked up. "That makes sense." A memory flashed. "Oh, I just remembered. The clone mistakenly believed that just because you shared DNA that meant the soul mate match would work."

"Yep."

"But when he kissed me, I felt nothing. At the time, I thought it was because of the high-pressured situation. But it makes sense—because the soul mate bond isn't physical. It's a bond between our souls."

"You didn't feel it with him. But he definitely felt it toward you."

"What do you mean?"

"We had a short conversation at the Space Needle. He mentioned he was going to enjoy taking my place."

"How did you escape from him?"

"He didn't know we'd found the antidote for his poison darts. We assumed it would be his weapon of choice because they have metal detectors at the Needle. Anyway, he shot Devon, who really did go over the rail, but he was able to grab onto the vertical metal tubing in the center shaft. The clone tased me with a stun gun and thought he finished me off with the poison dart."

"I'm starting to remember."

"You're getting better. It usually takes you a few hours."

"How long does Doc think this will keep happening? That

was the worst, most convincing dream I've ever had."

"He doesn't know, but his guess is six months."

"How many months has it been?" I held my breath, waiting.

"Two with the dreams, four altogether."

My shoulders sagged. "I'm sorry."

"Why?" He took my hand.

"You have damaged goods for a wife." I smiled through my tears.

"Considering you saved Ann, Henry, Devon, Ian, Lucy, and me, I think we can let it go." He paused. "I guess I should add Susie, but I'm not sure whether that was a good thing."

I pushed his shoulder. "You're so bad."

"Also, your shots were so precise, the doctors were able to save Donna and the kidnapped girl, Becca. You are one hell of a sharpshooter."

"I guess all those centuries of training paid off."

"Thank you, by the way. For knowing the difference between me and the e clone."

I squeezed his hand. "I'd know your touch anywhere."

"We tried hard to ignore it." He chuckled.

"Did I tell you about...um, the, uh..."

"You mean your mission to kill the last Jack?"

"Yes." I held my breath and waited.

"Yeah. I know all about it. I thought your attitude was about the Jacks in general. That must have been hard for you."

"And confusing. I wanted to hate you, but every time we were together, I felt so drawn to you. It also didn't help matters that, when we touched, it was like a fireworks show." I laughed. "I guess someone should have clued us in about what happens when soul mates touch."

"Are you okay now? Or should I cancel the party?" Archer raised an eyebrow.

"No." I threw off the covers. "I want to celebrate our wedding. And I also want to celebrate the dream. I mean, that it was only a dream. But it seemed so real!"

"Doc says that's a big part of the problem. Your dreams are more vivid than most because of your Seer abilities."

Great.

"Does anyone else know about the dreams?" I bit my lip and waited.

"Oh yeah. Everyone." He stopped when he noticed my pained expression.

"It's okay. I'll deal."

He paused for a moment to make sure I was okay. "The first one you experienced was at Samara, and Doc really did have to put you under sedation because you didn't believe anything except for the dream."

"Well, that's embarrassing."

"Everyone loves you. You saved us all, remember?" He kissed my hand. "You were up and out of the chair, firing your pistol. Within a nanosecond, two Jacks, the betrayer, and the clone were dead."

"I'm glad."

"And after my dad viewed all the video files and was updated about all the events that took place, I actually received an apology about how he's treated me."

"Wow. It only took him a couple thousand years." I rolled my eyes.

"It will take some time, but we're working through it."

"I get it. I'm happy for you."

He hugged me. "I'll go clean up and meet you in the kitchen." He stopped. "Are you okay? I can sit longer if you'd like."

"No, I'm good. The fog has lifted. I remember almost everything. Thanks for jogging my memory."

"I'm here to serve." He bowed and kissed my hand.

"Oh, that feels good." I closed my eyes and let the warmth travel through my body.

"There's more where that came from." He winked.

"Do you think it will always be this way?"

"I know it will."

I smiled and let the happy glow continue to expand.

"And our children will need to save the world."

"Children. Almost forgot about that." I giggled.

A tap, tap, tap interrupted us. The door cracked open, and Lucy poked her head in. "You really need to get a lock on your door."

"No Jacks, remember?"

"Still."

She studied us still sitting on the bed. "Uh, did I break up more honeymoon activities?" She put her hands over her eyes.

"No. She had another nightmare." -

Lucy clutched her chest. "Oh no! The same one?"

"Unfortunately."

She came into the room to give me a hug.

"Lucy, you're okay, right? About everything?"

Her eyes softened. "Thanks for asking. The first few months were hell, but now I'm remembering all the little red flags. I guess I just didn't want to believe it."

I rubbed her arm. "I'm sorry about what happened."

"Thank you." Her eyes watered, but she smiled.

Another knock. "Okay, that's it. I'm getting out of bed. I'll meet you in the kitchen in five." I jumped off the bed and headed for the shower.

Five minutes later, I felt like a new woman. The fog lifted, and my memories of the past few months came back, all the love, support, and fun. I entered the kitchen just in time to see Ian and Lucy argue about how to frost the cake.

"Hey guys, I don't care how it's frosted."

Ian smiled, but his eyes still held the same sadness as the day I told him it would be only Archer for me. With all the confusion surrounding the clone attack and evacuation, he didn't know about the email I forwarded to all the Readers. He admitted trying to destroy the video files because he wanted another month to sway me, thinking I'd hold back my feelings for Archer if the uncertainty of the murder hung unresolved. He believed we were the soul mates in the vision. We both cried that day, but it was something neither of us could fix. Love, chemistry, connection have always been a mystery. I hoped he'd find someone soon.

Ann, Devon, and Henry were the next to arrive in a flurry of congrats, hugs, and kisses.

"Will Donna be able to make it?" Ann asked.

Donna had a full-time nurse taking care of her until she was able to live independently again. "Yes, Miss Aui will wheel her over in about fifteen minutes."

Eve jumped up on the counter. Something Atarah would never have done. Sometimes it felt strange to hug her knowing such evil had lived in her, but we were slowly getting to know each other again.

Lucy, in her usual fiery temper, turned her livid eyes on Ian. "Would you quit doing that? It's annoying."

"I didn't do anything. I'm innocent." He held up his hands and laughed.

"Every time we get close, it's like you have a mini stun gun or something." She rubbed her hand where he touched her.

Archer and I looked at each other with wide eyes. "Should we tell them?" I asked.

Archer shook his head. "No. It'll be fun to see how long it takes them to figure it out."

The immortal hid behind some bushes, watching the party taking place inside Sadie's house. Her beautiful laughter flowed out like a musical chime, soothing him to the depths of his soul. He closed his eyes and let the happy sound penetrate his heart.

A pang stopped him for a moment. He knew her happiness would continue without Archer. Because she'd never be without him.

He would kill the original Archer and become Archer in every way. She'd never know.

A quick switch.

The immortal smiled and relaxed. Somehow, Atarah kept her word and didn't tell anyone she could harvest four clones every year, not three. Eighteen months to go and four more would be born. He would search them out and kill them before they awakened. All clones were wired to have a natural yearning for Sadie. Archer's DNA was strong. The soul mate bond wasn't just emotional; it was physical too. The immortal would kill anyone who got close to his Sadie. Love surged through his heart. An obsessive love, but he didn't care. He would joyfully wallow in it all day.

Archer came out of the cottage and retrieved a bouquet from the back seat of his car. Another thing to remember. Daisies. Archer stopped and smiled at the flowers Sadie loved and called friendly.

Archer's deep love for Sadie would not deter him. He would make sure Sadie never knew he wasn't the original. He'd done his homework. Sadie would be much happier.

Archer turned toward him and blew something out of a straw. A sharp pain hit the immortal's neck. He pulled the dart out, but it was too late. The immortal fell to the ground and landed on his back, his life force seeping away.

Archer stood over him and said, "I love her more than you."

"No." The immortal struggled to breathe.

"Ann read Atarah's mind before Sadie killed her. We've been waiting for you. We knew there was one last clone we needed to deal with."

"I'm not the last." And the immortal closed his eyes and died.

THE END

ENJOYED THIS BOOK?

Would you leave a Review?

I highly appreciate the feedback I get from my readers. It helps others to make an informed decision before buying books.

If you enjoyed this book, please consider leaving a short review.

Visit www.mkharkins.com/want-a-free-book for a Free Book!

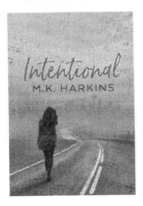

ACKNOWLEDGEMENTS

I've mentioned before that it takes a large village to write a book. This book needed a huge village (A lot of plot twists to keep track of!) I honestly couldn't have done it without the help of many special people.

My editor: Nancy Saling Thompson. You are a rock star! I made you work hard on this one. Thanks for talking me off the author bridge and always having an encouraging word. Life would be gray and white without you (or is it grey? 😊).

Iveta Cvrkal: I think you should get an award for Best Proof-reader on the Planet. Thanks for all your questions and challenging me to make things more understandable. My characters will never tap their fingers again—lol. (Don't hold me to that).

Sarah Hansen from Okay Creations—Wow. Your talent is amazing. Thank you for making my covers a work of art.

Thank you to all my Scribophile Critters! Deidre Huesmann, Claire O'Sullivan, Anya T. Catmus, Kristina Luckey, Anne Howes, Maggie Penn, and Lisa Born I always look forward to your insights.

Thanks to my team of super-star beta readers: Maari Hammond, Kimberly Black, Kathy Knuckles, Karen Kumprey, Kimberly Nelson, Jan Hinds, Serren Callister, Melesia Tully, Donna Feyen, Mari L. Yates, Jennifer Ford, Sherry Christenson, Patricia M Jackson, Jodee Arellano, Alicia Gioia, Tanya Wheeler, Mylissa Dagmar-Buysse, Francis Vanessa Valladares Duarte, Julianne Roberts,—and last but not least: Kathleen McGuire.

A special shout-out to my friend and personal assistant— Maari Hammond. This year has been rough for you—but you always keep a positive outlook and are selflessly supportive. You are that one-in-a-million person that is rare in this world. I treasure our friendship!

Julie Hartnett—You are a forever friend. It doesn't matter that you live an ocean away. You are a bright light of wonderfulness (I thought I made up a word but it's actually in the dictionary—so there you go).

Laurel Harkins—My Sista! You helped me more this year than you'll ever know. When I wanted to throw in the towel you said, "This is the best one yet!" I'm not sure if it's true, but thanks for always being there for an encouraging word.

To my family—All of you picked up the slack when I took off on my Author Adventure to Australia. And with no complaints! (I might have heard a little grumbling about no food—but that doesn't count). Thanks for being excited about each new book set free into the world. I couldn't do it without your support (Big Doran gets the most credit—for the record ☺).

BOOKS BY M.K. HARKINS

Intentional:

Intentional is a real page turner which got me more and more involved. It developed into an intense situation which developed into another and then exploded into a great climax!

~Amazon Reviewer

This book is a great read. It is very well written and I would recommend it to anyone who is interested in intense romance novels with a little bit of suspense in the process.

~My eBook Café

Have you ever read a book and once you are finished you want to seek out the highest mountain to shout to the world "READ THIS BOOK?".

~ Lola Kay

Unintentional:

I have to say in all honesty. . . . I LOVED this book!!!!! I actually liked it even more then Intentional. I thought this book flowed very well and I loved how she switched off the POV's during the chapters. I felt we got the full feeling of the story that way. This book is listed as a standalone and I truly believe it can be read as one. The author does a wonderful job of recapping the end of Intentional from Cade's POV , that you really don't miss anything from the first book.

~ Jennifer from Book Bitches Blog

This story is great. I love how the author gave me a love story with some mystery thrown into it. This is one of those books that you don't want to put down until you've finished it, because you have to know what happens next. So in this book you have a great story, awesome characters, excellent writing, and a happy reader at the end. I highly recommend this book.

~ Leigh Broxton

Breaking Braydon:

I was left in complete awe after finishing this unbelievably heart-felt book. M. K. Harkins has stolen my heart, and I honestly don't want it back. This story left me wanting so much more and yet feeling completely content and satisfied. Watching these amazing characters love and support each other was beyond description at times at how it made my heart swell with pride and admiration. What a magnificent journey I was given the privilege to watch and take part in, and I will forever remember the story that made me cry tears of joy and rapture.

~ Shadowplay (Amazon Reviewer)

I loved this book! It's hopeful and uplifting, emotional without being overwrought. And the author has made incredible, jaw-dropping strides in her craft. The writing is clean, the plot swift, the characters engaging, and the dialogue snappy and often quite funny. Even the secondary characters have heart and humor, and it's my great hope the author will spin-off a story or two for each of them.

If you enjoy inspiring, witty romance with an upbeat, playful vibe, Breaking Braydon is for you. It's the perfect way to spend the day, curled up with Braydon and Jain.

~ Story Girl

Taking Tiffany

This story has a lot of romance, adventure, mystery, intrigue, and surprises, one after the other. Just when you think you have it figured out it goes in a different way. It was a very entertaining read and I definitely recommend it. Of course, it has a HEA.

~ **Amazon Top 1000 Reviewer

This has quickly bumped up my favorite books list. I really loved it. Loved it so much, as soon as I finished, I went right back to the beginning to read it again!

I highly recommend. Lovable characters, surprising plot twists and smoldering chemistry all make Taking Tiffany a must read.

~ More Than A Review

Sweet with just enough mystery. I never would've guessed the outcome which was amazing. At the same time it was touching and adorable which made it the perfect romantic book. There's just enough romance and just enough mystery/suspense.

~ Amazon Reviewer

The Reader (The Immortal Series Book One)

"This story is incredibly original and really intense! Overall I would say that this is one of the books to watch, and I predict it will be huge!"

~ NetGalley Reviewer

"This is a fast-paced page turner that had me from the beginning. I read the book in one day as I could not put it down."

~ Amazon Reviewer

"The Reader is different, mysterious, & intense. A paranormal fantasy trip with secrets, suspense, romance, seers, immortals, hunters, much more! The characters are well developed & full of life. The plot is full of intrigue & twists."

~ Goodreads Reviewer

Famous by Default

This book held me from page one. Written so beautifully. Absolutely fell in love with the characters. Would make an amazing movie. Highly recommend. Can't wait to read more by this brilliant author.

~ Amazon Reviewer

I was overwhelmed with emotion so I can't write this review without being emotionally involved. I am not saying much of the story because I would not know where to start. Famous by Default was simply wonderful and real. It shows that struggling with Love and Life has no age. One of the best epilogues, I have ever read.

~ Goodread's Reviewer

This book had me intrigued from the first page. I fell in love with the characters and I just want more. This book had everything that I look for in a good book, love, loss and laughs. I can not wait for more from this author. I am hoping for the brothers stories..??

~ Amazon Reviewer

Coming Soon: Famous by Design

Add to your Goodreads TBR

www.goodreads.com/book/show/41062067-famous-by-design

CONTACT M.K. HARKINS

Want to chat?

Here's where to find M.K. Harkins

Email: mkharkins@hotmail.com

Facebook: www.facebook.com/marilyn.wellnitz

Website: www.mkharkins.com/

Twitter: @mk_harkins

Newsletter: www.eepurl.com/baBOrz

BookBub: www.bookbub.com/authors/m-k-harkins

Goodreads:
www.goodreads.com/author/show/7067079.M_K_Harkins

Instagram: www.instagram.com/mkharkins/

Made in the USA
San Bernardino, CA
16 August 2018